THE SOURCE

C.S LUIS

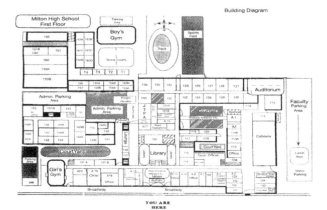

Building Diagram

Milton High School
First Floor

YOU ARE HERE

Milton High School
Second Floor

Building Diagram

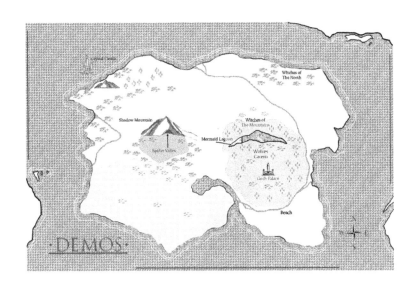

CONTENTS

Proem - Extraction   xiii

1. Belle's Ring   1
2. Arrival   10
3. A New Home   16
4. Presence   21
5. The Gift   25
6. Family History   30
7. The Balance   35
8. The Shadow in the Hall   38
9. High School Acquaintance   46
10. The Man in the Black Suit and Red Tie   65
11. The End is Always the Beginning   73
12. Michael McClellan   78
13. Goodbye   83
14. Milton High in Mourning   95
15. The Lecture   111
16. Lunch Group   114
17. Among Friends   127
18. Goth Girl   132
19. The Eerie Sound   141
20. Invited Guest   144
21. The Mysterious Quentin   171
22. The Morning After   184
23. The Absent   198
24. Troublemaker   200
25. At the Principal's Office   202
26. Denial   212
27. Memories   227

Dear Reader   233
You might also like   235

THE SOURCE

THE
MINDBENDER SERIES

1

C·S LUIS

PROEM - EXTRACTION

Glass prison cells lined the long white corridors, the lights of sensor mechanisms blinking on and off. In one such cell, a young woman with smooth skin untouched by the sunlight lay upon a bed. Strands of long black hair draped across the white linen pillow. Within her diamond-shaped face, delicate cheekbones rose above full, rosy lips.

She lay far too still, dressed in a white, long-sleeved shirt and pants. Only when she took a breath and the sheets shifted did she reveal any sign of being alive. A steel collar hugged her neck, tiny green lights along the outer edge flashing across the surface with her breathing pattern. This blinking also mimicked the pattern of similar lights in the corner of the room, near the entrance. When the green flashed to yellow, her body seemed to relax. Her once stiff muscles eased, allowing movement once again.

Her eyes opened.

"Hello?" the woman whispered, staring up at the white ceiling. She was alone, but something had awakened her. She looked around, now remembering where she was with an unagonizing certainty. Her dreams provided the only release from this reality.

The same day repeated itself—tests and challenges. She recalled a flash of her earlier days, sitting across from a man in white. Her sisters called them the Whitecoats. Some wore a black or blue uniform with strange red emblems on the side of the arm. Those were the guards, who brought her to the room for conducted tests.

The tests were always the same.

There was always a wall between them, the lower half solid and the upper half glass. The Whitecoat asked questions using only his mind and allowed her to read his thoughts. She thought it a boring game; she always answered correctly.

Sometimes, she was unstable; that was what they called it. His nose would bleed, a smile wrinkling her lip until a violent shock raced through her body. Then she dropped. That was what the collar did when they activated it. It had happened the day before, and she'd stayed in her quarters, still as a board and unable to move. Perhaps it was her punishment. Of course, they wanted control over those in containment.

She was, after all, a prisoner of the men in white coats. She was special, they said. She was among the few others who could talk to *them*—the creatures in the containers, those same beings she found in her dreams.

Had she heard a voice calling to her just before she opened her eyes, or was it all inside her head? She pulled the cotton sheet off her body, crawled to the side of the bed, swung her legs over the edge, and sat up.

'Maya.' This time, she was sure she heard it. A whisper somewhere, hidden behind or even traveling through the vents. No, it was in her head.

The small room she occupied had no windows, only the clear glass door revealing the outside hall—stark and sterilized.

She knew the corridor's dimensions by heart. She saw it in her dreams.

'*Maya.*' The voice was clearly in her head. Someone was trying to reach her.

'*Quinn?*'

'*Yes...*'

'*I hear you. Where are you?*'

❋

'*Who are you?*' she'd asked.

'*Someone who loves you. Do you not sense it?*'

The collar's shock set her upright. A needle pierced her skin, and his voice faded.

He found her mind during tests and experiments—her first indication he was real. The collar and their needles subdued both her skills and their link with each other. Control. He taught her the skill, the craft of their connection, and with time, she had mastered certain movements.

'*You're getting stronger,*' he'd told her with pride.

Their life unfolded in her mind, and a vast civilization flourished; she was part of that world. He stood beside her, holding her in his arms and observing the world with her.

"We once had a life together," he said. "We came from the stars. A lot was lost. Including loved ones." He turned to look at her. "But I found you again."

"What happened to our world?" She knew this was now what she saw before them—a once lively and beautiful planet, diminished, depleted resources and vast, cluttered landfills of waste. The air had thinned, becoming unbearable. Fires took the place of green fields, destroying the few remaining crops. Skies darkened, and storms increased. They stood watching it unfold.

"We took and took until there was nothing more to use. We

killed everything for power, and on the brink of finding a solution—our breakthrough—we created more chaos."

Crystals lit the corridors of a vessel traveling in the deep expanse of space, the corner line with a black tar stained the surface of the space's floor and hibernation chambers.

"They're beautiful," she said.

"They're deadly..." he whispered. "We destroyed our only home. The crystals only brought disease, and the tar came after." She found sadness in his voice, disappointment in his purple eyes.

When they were together, it seemed they existed alone in another plane; their connection had achieved a deeper bond not even the Whitecoats could detect or possibly understand. The world he had once known was now gone; she knew this because he did. His people's search for a new home had brought them to earth—and to her.

'I'm close. Closer than you think, my love... Come to me. It's time.' His words brought her back to this reality—a reality she hated.

She rose from the side of the bed, the dressings of a white linen uniform caressing her form. The red markings on her collar was identical to his. The bed's metal frame had been etched with single lines to record her time there. How many days had it been? How many years? She'd scratched eighteen lines in the metal before he found her, and then she'd stopped counting the days; she couldn't be sure how many more she'd spent within these walls.

'Come to me, Maya. Please,' he begged. 'I need you more than ever. Don't let them keep us apart any longer. I want you close. Come to me. Please...' She missed his arms around her and yearned for the comfort of his presence in this reality.

'I miss you too. I love you.' A surge of energy flooded her body, reaching out from an unknown place where he dwelled in the darkness, like a current racing from one end to the other until they were linked, mentally and spiritually. "The genetic disorder," the Whitecoats called it. For her, it was love.

'*How? I can't—*' She froze.

'*Yes, you can. Trust me,*' he said.

She pressed her face against the glass of the door, feeling the energy run through her fingertips. The lock above the door was electrically charged, the mechanism operating just like the collar around her neck. She reached out to touch the metal choker. Her fully charged fingers sent a shock through it, and it dropped with a clang at her feet.

'*Together we are stronger,*' he whispered. They had practiced the act repeatedly; several times, she'd taken the brunt of the powerful force, leaving her immobile for the rest of the day. They'd learned how to change the pattern. Then she'd discovered a brief moment when the collar was less active inside the cell.

'*Together we are stronger. They don't know the strength of our power.*'

The switch above blinked off, and the locked door popped open.

She stepped into the corridor, white ceilings and walls stretching in each direction. Rooms like hers lined the hallway.

'*Don't be afraid,*' he said. '*Maya, hurry. There's no time to waste...*'

She raced to one end of the corridor; above her, the air vent rattled. The screws slowly fell from their sockets onto the floor, each landing with a light thud in her open palm. The grate over the vent followed. Maya caught it quickly and placed it on the floor. Then she leaped to grasp the lip of the ventilation shaft, pulled herself up, and disappeared into the darkness.

"I'm coming," she whispered.

The vents composed a vast a labyrinth, made of so many twists and turns to open into other corridors where guards patrolled the halls. Maya despised those brutes.

She crawled forward, his voice leading the way. *'Don't be afraid. Once you are here, we will be together forever, and no one will separate us,'* he encouraged.

An image of a young man dressed in black leather attire flashed in her mind; he waited. He was there in her dreams and in her thoughts. His face was creamy white, locks of dark hair cut short and practical. His purple, almond-shaped eyes gazed back at her from some dark place.

Her uniform caught on a loose screw in the vent walls, ripping when she pulled it away. Distant voices caught her attention, carried up to her by a nearby vent. She leaned toward the grate for a closer look.

The room was large and white, filled with lab equipment. A large container held a figure, dressed in a scaly, leather uniform, sitting within it. She recognized the uniform. Quinn wore one just like it.

"Careful," a male voice warned. At the far side of the room, she caught the movement of a mechanical arm. She couldn't clearly see what was happening.

"The cells are splitting. It's working!" another man exclaimed from the other end of the room. "Congratulations, Dr. Nicholson. It appears the procedure was a success."

"I never doubted it," a third, much darker voice replied.

"Do you realize what you've created here, sir? We must notify The Company immediately..."

Their conversation filtered away as Maya lost interest and prepared to move on through the vent. She couldn't gauge the full scope of what had happened from her position in the ventilation shaft, no matter how closely she looked.

She stopped when a loud thump followed by the crackle of shattering glass rose from the room, and she glanced behind her to peer through the grate once more. A body lay on the floor below her, then she heard another loud crash. Sparks flew and smoke billowed in the room.

A stifled cry squeezed through her throat, but she covered it with her hand. Another figure now stood over the motionless body as flames rose, consuming and destroying everything inside the white walls.

The figure, barely visible, looked up at the vent. Maya felt sure he saw her, could feel him staring hard into her deep, dark eyes. For a moment, she couldn't move; her lip quivered. Then the man was gone.

Maya hurried through the vent. An alarm wailed and lights flashed from all directions. *"Warning! Alien life forms have been detected."* The mechanical sound of the computer's warning system echoed through the vents. *"Alien life forms have been detected in Sector 10. Warning! Possible contamination..."*

She reached the end of the vent and knocked open the grate before dropping down. A large, darkened space spread before her, the ceiling lamps above giving dim, ineffective light. In every direction, row upon row of containers held lifeless figures, floating in a liquid substance within the clear glass.

'*Maya,*' he called. She moved swiftly through the containers, which rattled when she passed them.

The alarms still sounded in every direction.

She hurried, sensing him closer than ever before. For a moment, she had to stop and drop to her knees, feeling suddenly weak. The containers shook and wobbled, cracks splintering in sections of glass. Steam and fluid spilled through the fissures, which snapped and sprayed more liquid through quickly widening cracks.

Maya whirled around to watch the other containers smoke and hiss. Then, one after the other exploded into countless pieces, filling the facility's room with an icy mist.

The voice on the intercom spoke again:

"Warning! All containers in Sector 12 have been breached. Alien life forms have been detected. Warning all personnel. Evacuation

protocol is in effect. All personnel, evacuation protocol is in effect. Warning! Alien life forms have been detected."

Beautiful, pale faces with matted locks of hair and dressed in dark leather uniforms emerged from behind her. Maya struggled to rise but couldn't lift herself, fear paralyzing her at the sight.

'Maya.' He emerged from the surrounding figures and extended his hand toward her. The others scattered away into the corridors.

"Maya," Quinn said aloud. "We've been kept apart for far too long, my love."

She reached for his hand, and he pulled her close.

"Alien life forms detected in Sector 10. All prisoners' cells have been breached."

"I've waited for this moment for far too long. To feel you in my arms, to have you by my side. My beloved Maya. They will pay for keeping us apart." He lifted her in his arms as the ceiling above them began to crumble.

"Burn it down! Destroy everything!" he shouted. The ceiling fell away, and through the gap, beings ascended into the sky. In their arms rested the women they'd rescued—prisoners like Maya—friends, sisters.

Quinn ascended with them while the building, her prison, crumbled and burned. The skies crowded with the angels of her dreams. Maya closed her eyes, clinging to Quinn's embrace as he lifted her into the heavens.

1

BELLE'S RING

MARCH, PRESENT DAY

The plane landed in Houston, Texas. Father said he and Mother would arrive later that day. I thought it was strange, that I would go alone. I didn't like it. But I couldn't question it. I'd learned at a very early age never to question my parents' ways.

"A car will be there to collect you," he'd said. He'd handed my luggage to the chauffeur, who placed it in the trunk. "Just wait outside."

Then the chauffeur opened the front passenger door to the black Range Rover, and my father ushered me toward it.

"You won't be there?" I'd asked. This was sudden. Why was I just hearing about this now? My father gave me a stern look. I knew better then to keep pressing him, but I was angry.

"I have business to attend to in the morning..."

"What sort of business?" I said. "Can't it wait? I thought we were going on a cruise. You said we were finally doing something together as a family."

"Don't argue with me. You know I have no choice in the matter. If I'm requested there, I have to be there."

"And what's Mother's excuse? She doesn't want to be alone with me?"

His brows furrowed. "If you're trying to start a fight with me, it isn't going to change my mind. You'll be fine... until we arrive. As I instructed, a vehicle will be there to collect you."

And that was that...

Now that I'd landed, I collected my bags from the baggage claim and made my way to the airport entrance. Outside, other travelers crowded the sidewalks, vehicles backed up in the lane to pick up friends and family.

I sat waiting, like my father instructed, until a Lincoln with tinted windows pulled to the curb. I wondered how pitiful I looked, sitting there waiting like an abandoned child. The door slowly opened, and for a moment I expected my father, even though he hated American cars.

A man in his thirties wearing a black suit and a pastel green tie stepped out. He was tall and slightly chubby. He didn't smile. The nest of his dark hair sat in disarray, and the dark circles beneath his eyes seemed to indicate he'd been up late. My first impression of him was that of a highly unprofessional and disorganized person. His suit was a little too big, the pant legs were far too loose around his calves and ankles, and his tie was an ugly color.

He knew who I was before I could introduce myself. "Miss Claudia Belle?" he asked as he approached.

Curiously, I looked up at his face, afraid of what he would reveal.

He dipped his head slightly; his eyes took on a deep sadness. I already knew long before he told me.

I answered, "Yes?"

He took a breath. "I'm Mr. West, a friend of your father's." The world continued around us without the slightest care.

For a long moment, I didn't say a word, afraid to see his thoughts plastered across his tired face. Tears pooled in the corners of my eyes, and a tiny gasp escaped me.

"He asked me to come." Mr. West paused like he also found it hard to talk. "I'm afraid I have some terrible news," he added, and I choked back a sob. "Your parents have been in an accident," he finally managed. A tear rolled down my cheek. I gazed at him, my eyes wide open. "I'm sorry."

Speechless, I sat there and cried, wiping at the tears breaking loose from my eyes. I didn't know what to say. I didn't believe it, but it was the truth. I knew it.

"Is that why you're here?" I asked, trying to stop myself from crying, but it was no use.

"I was instructed to take you to a friend," he said. He opened the door of the Lincoln. At any other time, I would not have believed a stranger. Of course, no one in their right mind would have just accepted anything so outrageous without certain proof, but I knew how to tell a person's truths from their lies. Mostly, I heard it in their thoughts..

I wanted to run from the truth, from him and everything real, but I just stood there. He held open the door of the Lincoln and gazed at me.

"I have something for you from your father. He instructed me to give it to you, if anything ever were to happen to him or your mother..."

I took a breath and climbed into the Lincoln. The chauffeur stepped out of the driver's seat and grabbed hold of my luggage. Mr. West closed the door behind me and climbed into the car. It was quiet for a moment before the chauffeur took his seat again and drove.

"Your father made this for you," Mr. West said. "He asked me to come, if anything ever happened. I'm an attorney."

"Are you my father's attorney?" I asked. He wasn't, I suddenly realized.

He took a moment. "I helped your father make the arrangements with my client."

"Arrangements?" But he didn't answer, busy pulling a device from his briefcase.

I already knew. Father had hired him to handle the paperwork for someone else. I stared at Mr. West, and one name rang clearly from his mind—Edwards. This Edwards was someone my father had trusted.

He took out an iPad. "He asked me to give you a message."

"What is it?" Mr. West angled the device toward me, and I realized it was a video. When I grabbed the iPad and pressed play, my father's face appeared on the screen.

"Claudia," he said, "if you're seeing this, then I'm afraid..." He paused. "You must listen very carefully. Listen to what Mr. West tells you. I can't fully explain everything, but with time, you will discover the truth on your own. Right now, you must go with Mr. West. I've secured a place for you with a person I trust. He will care for you now. All the arrangements have been made for your comfort and your safety. You must believe me, that I did all this to protect you. We love you. Never forget that. We love you."

"Nicholas, please let me..." my mother pleaded off camera. "I love you..." she said before breaking into sobs, unable to continue.

"Stay safe..." Those were my father's last words, and then the image was lost.

Mr. West pulled the iPad back and tucked it into his briefcase, sitting up silently. "That's the message. I received word of the accident early this morning. Again, I'm so sorry for your loss."

Early this morning, I thought. I had left the night before. He said a car would be there for me. I thought he meant a car with him and my mother inside it. Or perhaps he'd planned on sending a company vehicle. He said we were going on a family vacation. Then his job called, and things changed. It felt oddly staged.

"All final burial arrangements have been taken care of by your father's employer. The details are in these documents." Mr. West pulled a stack of papers from his briefcase. "Do you have any questions for me?"

"I don't understand. We were going on a cruise... and now..." The car exited the airport pick-up lane and turned onto the exit road that would take us out to the highway.

"Honey, did you hear what I said?" he asked.

"How did they die?" I asked.

Mr. West looked at me with wide, surprised eyes, hesitant to answer. "They were hit by a passing truck on their way to the airport..." As far as he believed it, that was what happened. It was all he knew. "It was a bad accident. Nothing anyone could have done." He returned to his documents.

"Where will the funeral be held?" I asked, looking down at my lap.

"There won't be one. Your father's employer gave specific instructions on the handling of your parents' remains. Their bodies will be cremated immediately. Your father signed off on this before he died."

I glared at him. I was their *daughter*. Didn't I have any say in this?

Mr. West's phone rang, and through the muffled speaker, I heard the name Edwards again. "Yes, she's with me now," he said. "I've just picked her up at the airport. I'll be dropping her off at your residence— No?" He frowned and blinked, unable to look at me. "That won't be a problem. The school is fine. No, I won't be coming in. I hope you understand. I have urgent business back at the office... Very well, then."

"I want you to do something for me..."

A memory crept into my mind. I'd been standing outside my school at the end of the day, and he'd come to pick me up himself in his own car. Normally, he sent one for me, or if he ever decided to join me himself, he hired a driver and traveled with his security.

"What's going on?" I joked, realizing he'd seen me looking around for his bodyguards. "Where your friends?" I got into the car and set my school bag on the floor between my feet.

"I gave them the day off," he replied, but I could tell he was hiding something.

I took a moment to look at him. His blond hair was always so well groomed, and that day he wore a dark grey suit and black tie. I couldn't recall ever seeing him in casual attire, even when we were alone at home. I often wondered how I could be his daughter and still look nothing like him.

"What's the occasion?" I asked. There had to be reason for his decision to get me himself; he'd never gone out of his way to lose the bodyguards on my account. I pushed back my long brown hair and pulled it into a ponytail, then let it fall back over my shoulders.

"I can't pick up my daughter from school?"

I made a face at him, noticing for the millionth time how light his skin was compared to my golden-brown tone. My mother was the same color.

Outside, other parents picked up their children and cars lined the side street, crowding the main road. Then he veered out of the pickup lane and drove forward, leaving it all behind.

"No, really. What's this all about?" I asked.

He tried to smile, but it looked more like a grimace of disappointment. I thought maybe it pained him that our meetings always indicated something bad. "I just want to talk to you. See how things are going in your life. We haven't talked—"

"We never talk, Dad."

"Exactly. And that's why... that's why we should."

I wished he would just tell me. I wanted to read his mind,

but breaking that rule made him angry. I wasn't supposed to do it with anyone, and I didn't dare try it with him.

We took the long ride home and stopped at the ice cream store. When he pulled up in the parking lot, I didn't know what to say. Was he dying? Were we going to have *the talk* along with a cone of vanilla ice cream?

"What are we doing?" I asked.

He turned off the engine and smiled. "We're getting ice cream." Then he opened the door and got out.

I didn't know what to think or what to make of it, and things seemed oddly normal until halfway through our after-school treat.

"I want you to do something for me..." he started. I knew it couldn't have lasted—both of us happy and me finally meeting all his expectations. "Claudia, if something ever happens to me and your mother, I want you to forget."

I narrowed my eyes at him. This was not the kind of conversation had with one's father over ice cream. "Dad, stop."

"No, listen. This is important, okay?"

I stared at his baby-blue eyes, unwavering in their deadly seriousness. We looked like an odd pair sitting there—him in his business suit, me in my school uniform, sitting in rigid silence with ice cream melting over our cones. People always gave us critical glances when we were out together. Dad ignored them with efficient detachment, but I was still learning —and I still worked on my control. Everything spun, pulled, and tugged at me, the voices of those around us growing louder, whispering their insecurities and suspicions. The minute he sensed I was losing it, he redirected me.

"Stop," he snapped, and something inside me returned to normalcy—like it had never happened.

"Okay."

"Things will happen that you can't stop," he continued. "Things you will not agree with, perhaps that you might think are not right. No matter what you feel, what you've lost... your things, your paintings... I want you to forget them. All of it. Including us."

I wrinkle a brow. "What? Why?" I looked up in disbelief, and he's just staring at me. No change, no emotion—I just had to do what he said.

"They're nothing but things."

"And you. And our memories. Are those just things?" I'd asked.

"Listen... Yes, but you don't need them. Not when we're in here." He tapped his chest. "All those things can be replaced. Your clothes, your paints. The important difference is that you never worry about them. We might lose what we have, but they're just things. Okay?"

"Okay." It didn't make sense to me, but I agreed, just to keep from inciting an argument.

"Let them have those things." He smiled and took a bite of vanilla. In that moment, I saw a peace in his eyes, but I still didn't understand.

Let them have those things?

"So, you don't have to worry about anything," Mr. West continued, pulling me back to the car and our impossible situation. "All the arrangements have been taken care of. There's nothing for you to be concerned about." He gave a sympathetic half-smile.

"Who is Dr. Edwards?" I asked. The name kept popping into his head, and I had to bring it up, though I'd absolutely expected his wide-eyed reaction of shock.

"Your father gave specific instructions that you should be brought to Dr. Edwards if anything happened to him and your mother," he said quickly. "Dr. Edwards is your grandfather." He stopped, waiting for my reaction, but I didn't have one.

I'd only known one man who was remotely close to grandfatherly, and Mr. Valentin was a rich man Father knew. Father brought me to see him a few times in his large, extravagant house. Apparently, the man had been like a parent to my own father, had raised him and given him the tools he needed to succeed. Father hated bringing me to see him; he always grew tense and irritable on the days we visited. But he always prepared me for the day. He told me to limit my power when I met with him. The man knew about our ability and it had made him rich.

"Never impress them," he'd said. "If they ask you a question with their mind, don't answer. The less you can do, the better." So that was what I'd done. No matter what they did to test me, I never answered.

2

ARRIVAL

THE LINCOLN CAME TO A STOPPED JUST OUTSIDE AN ABANDONED building. At least, it looked that way. At the side entrance, I caught a face or two peering through the door's small windows. I cringed. Where had he taken me?

I pulled out my earbuds; the faded crash of *Rammstein* playing on my iPod would have to wait as I looked at our new surroundings. The building was definitely old, with an exciting creepiness to its deserted appearance. It was characterized by semi-circular arches of medieval European design, things I only saw in cathedrals. A Romanesque exterior—thick, round arches, sturdy pillars, and decorative arcading—seemed to be the only thing I enjoyed about the building at first glance. My father had been a great fan of architecture and had taken every opportunity to teach me what he knew of different styles.

A blond-haired man, who from this distance looked like an actor whose name I couldn't remember—stepped through the front doors. With him was another very tall man with a greenish-gray suit and a thick mustache. They looked like a strange pair.

"This is it," Mr. West said.

I looked over at Mr. West, who didn't seem prepared to move though the driver was already opening his car door to get out.

"This is where you get out, my dear. I won't be coming with you. I'm needed at the office. Don't worry. Dr. Edwards is aware of your arrival." He looked out the window.

"What is this place?" I asked, finding my voice at last. The sounds of my favorite band had me wishing I could go back to the world of industrial metal and muffle the cries of reality.

"This is Milton High School," he said. I had a hard time believing my father had left me with a teacher. "Ah, and here he is now."

Two more men joined the others through the double doors. Both were older, one with a full head of white hair. As he stepped onto the top rise of the staircase, his large eyes met mine from beneath thick black brows. He wore a gentle, patient smile.

The other man with him looked even older; he also had white hair, but it was thinning, and he was significantly heavier. They both wore white dress shirts and ties.

The driver took my one bag from the trunk.

"What will happen to my parents' house?" I asked. "All our stuff? Will I be able to go back?" I wanted our picture albums, my paintings, all the things we'd shared.

"I'm afraid all that's been left to your father's employer. They will take care of those things. The house will be put up for sale, though I'm not sure about everything else..." He glanced at the paperwork in his folder. "I don't see anything on that here." Somehow, he didn't look concerned.

Father's words came back with glaring meaning. *'Let them have those things.'* Everything I had left behind was now gone. I couldn't take anything with me beyond what I'd packed for a nonexistent cruise.

Mr. West frowned, seeming genuinely concerned for my

emotional state. "I'm sorry, my dear. Those are all the details and instructions I was given. I'll check for any documentation of a storage unit. I might have missed that."

"Don't worry about it," I muttered. This was the way it had to be.

'Forget them. Forget us... we're in here. Let them have those things.' Father tapped his chest.

"I'll prepare an envelope for you and have it delivered to Dr. Edward's house within the following week."

"An envelope?"

"Yes, detailing information of the inheritance your parents have left for you." Mr. West looked at his watch. "I have to go. Again, my condolences for your loss." He pushed open the door for me and quite literally shoved me out. I grabbed my backpack and pushed the door open, though the driver had already grabbed it to help me.

Emerging from the car, I glanced at the four strange men staring down at me from the top of the steps. The driver placed my one suitcase near my feet, and the men walked down the stairs.

I put the iPod back into my backpack and took in my new reality. "This is a school?" I managed when the men finally stood in front of me. The parking lot had been filled with gravel, and a few pebbles slipped into my shoe as I slid my foot across the ground.

"It's an old building rich with history," the man with white hair and thick black brows said. I frowned at him, but I believed him. "I assure you, you'll never find any place quite like Milton." It made me wonder who he was trying to convince.

The two other men, the strange pair, stood behind him, looking kind of silly as they both grinned. The one wearing the greenish suit looked like an overgrown kid—very tall with a thick mustache, light brown hair in thick waves, and a light tan. His grey-green eyes flashed back at me, though he looked friendly enough. The man beside him wore a white, long-sleeve shirt rolled up to the elbows, his tie black, and blue eyes gazed at me beneath thinning, ghostly strands of blond hair and barely visible eyebrows.

"Welcome, Claudia," the older, heavier man said as he glanced curiously at me. I immediately wondered if he knew what I could do. "This knowledgeable individual," he added, gesturing toward the man with white hair and black eyebrows, "is Mr. Michael McClellan, our assistant principal." Mr. McClellan smiled and nodded.

"You must be him. Dr. Edwards," I interjected before he could introduce himself. He looked surprise for a mere second, but then his eyes softened, and he finally smiled too.

His companion's minds whirled with excitement, and I heard them. *It's her! That's his granddaughter. She's so beautiful. She's really here.* Dr. Edwards was more in control than they were, I could sense that. He had the gift. Like Father, like me. If he was my grandfather, there was no doubt our abilities had come from him. But he refrained from connecting with me. He wasn't stronger than me, but he was more in control of himself than I ever had been. Still, I knew even he was over-whelmed.

The uncertainty here scared me. I had so many questions, most of them centering around why Father had taken such measures to bring me here instead of leaving me with someone I knew.

I looked at the building behind the men, hesitating to believe this would be my new home. Would this be my new reality, too?

"Yes, I'm Dr. Edwards, principal of Milton High." His smile slowly widened. "I'm also your grandfather."

The other men stared at me, waiting for my reaction. I didn't think they expected the disapproval or doubt I couldn't hide. "My grandfather..."

"But you already knew that," Dr. Edwards replied, and I frowned. *'Didn't you?'*

'Yes,' I replied in my mind, and when his eyes narrowed, I realized he'd heard me just as I had heard him. "Why haven't I met you until now?" I asked aloud. My stomach lurched. I didn't know what else to say, confused by the apparent fact that it had taken their deaths to discover the truth.

"I'm sure your father had his reasons," Dr. Edwards replied. He gave a sympathetic frown, and our eyes met again. We shared the gift—the gift my father and I had shared. "I've been waiting a long time to meet you," he added. "Now, here you are."

"I'm sure you have a lot of questions for me." I blinked up at him and tried to look into his mind. It was easier than I'd expected to get a hold on him. I could feel the hazy trance within his mind at my touch, and he froze, unblinking. I found his conversation with father in his memories.

"I know you've been wanting to see her..." Father said. Dr. Edwards opened his mouth to speak, but Father silenced him with a cold glare. "And now, here is your chance. I want her to come live with you. I'll have my attorney make the necessary arrangements with yours Mr. West, correct?" Dr. Edwards nodded. "I need you to protect her," Father continued. "I can no longer keep her safe..."

I was gently shoved away, releasing the memory. Dr. Edwards had wrestled himself free. I let go, feeling him squirm like a bass tangled on a line.

Mr. McClellan touched Dr. Edwards gently on the arm. He blinked at me, and I wondered if he knew what I'd just done. "You should take Claudia home to get settled in, Neil. I'm sure she's tired from her long trip." The man's smile seemed a little forced.

"Yes, Michael. You're right."

"Don't worry. I know the drill," Michael added. "Besides, you two have a lot of catching up to do."

Dr. Edwards gazed at him and nodded. Behind them, the

two other men watched, still unintroduced. They gave me stupid grins instead, as if they were posing for a picture.

Dr. Edwards picked up my single suitcase. *'Claudia, come along. Let me take you home.'*

I brushed past him and headed toward the cars in the parking lot. "Don't do that," I uttered, loud enough so the other men could hear. Just because we'd connected didn't mean he could use that connection with me.

Dr. Edwards didn't say anything. When I approached his car, I knew he wasn't surprised that I knew which one was his. I stood by the passenger door to the Land Rover, and when he took out his keys, I unlocked the door myself. He only smiled— he knew how I'd done it—but I just climbed inside. I wasn't supposed to use my gift for anything, Father had said. But Father wasn't here anymore.

3

A NEW HOME

THE TRIP *HOME* WAS A QUIET ONE. I TRIED NOT TO START
conversation with him if I didn't have to; I think he got the
idea. Dr. Edwards lived in a modest, plain-looking, two-story
house. It seemed too big for him, but it was well put-
together.

The neighborhood felt hospitable and warm with the occasional white picket fence and colorful flowerbeds in the front
yards. Kids rode their bikes and tossed a ball out into the street.
There were joggers and people walking their dogs, and
everyone seemed to know each other. It was the kind of neighborhood where children had grown up together and lived in
the same houses for a long time.

Dr. Edwards looked out of place here—an old, white-haired
man living alone. When we pulled up to his house, I felt the
vibes of suspicion rolling off the couple next door as they got
out of their car.

There's that crazy old man again.

Oh, my. Who's that young girl with him?

They waved at me but seemed to regret making eye contact
when my grandfather looked in their direction. Dr. Edwards

waved back, but his neighbors darted inside and didn't look at us again.

Just don't attract attention to yourself...

He's so strange...

Dr. Edwards carried my bag, and I stumbled behind him into the house. I stood in the foyer, gazing at my new surroundings. The house was quite large inside. A staircase greeted us by the entrance, leading to the second floor with three bedrooms and a bathroom. The living room was located just off the foyer, and the dining room was near the kitchen on the other side of the house. I'd pulled this map from his mind, just as I'd known which car he drove, as if I'd been here before.

I followed him upstairs into one of the bedrooms. He entered first, and I waited in the hallway while he set my bag near the full-sized bed. This was smaller than my old room, and that thought alone made me miss home. I tried to conceal my emotions, not wanting to cry in front of him.

The furniture seemed as old as the buildings of Milton High. In the corner sat an antique dresser with a mirror. The bed had a simple mahogany frame and a blue comforter, on either side of which sat two bedside tables with antique lamps. I felt like I'd arrived at an old motel and took a breath.

"I hope this room isn't too small," Dr. Edwards said. "It's not much, but it's home."

"It's fine, I guess," I replied. Dr. Edwards glanced at me. He was trying hard to make me feel comfortable, I knew that. But I didn't want his understanding or his compassion. I wanted to be alone. My strange new life was beginning to sink in.

"I'm sorry," Dr. Edwards said.

I gazed up at him, moping in my own self-pity. I guess he could sense that—or was I that obvious? Most people said I had trouble showing my emotions but that I acted on them instead. "What did my father mean?" I rudely snapped. "What is he trying to protect me from?"

He knew what I meant but was still surprised by my question. The least he could do was be honest with me. "Today is not the right time to talk about that. You need time to mourn." Then he closed his mind to me. I tugged, and he pushed; it took everything he had, but he pushed back hard.

Dr. Edwards took a deep breath. "Claudia, your father was trying to protect you from... he didn't want what happened to him to happen to you. That's why he brought you to me."

"But we were supposed to go on a cruise... We were going to spend it as a family. Are you trying to say he lied, that he was planning to bring me here all along?"

"No, what I'm trying to say is that he only wanted to keep you safe..." It seemed he didn't know how else to express this, as was obvious from his having said that too many times already. "There's so much you need to know," he continued, "but I want you to understand that he was going to tell you when the time was right. He just didn't get that chance. None of this was supposed to happen. I was protecting him and you when I gave him up." He exhaled. "If anyone failed, it's me—"

"So, he planned everything, just to get me to stay with you?" I asked.

"Yes. We arranged it together." He frowned. "Your father merely wanted to prepare you for the worst. I never thought for one minute..." He paused, unable to push through his own mourning. "I never thought I would lose him all over again."

That surprised me. I didn't want to talk about it anymore.

My grandfather took a deep breath. I moved to the window. Outside, the wind blew swiftly; the evening seemed alive with movement. The sound of the wind had never bothered me, but now it did. I was angry, and it sounded angry with me. When father was angry, the skies would thunder and darken. When I was sad, it would rain. I thought this was the norm. Sometimes, the lights flickered and bulbs would blow out or sometimes pop.

"I got an email from him a few days before you were to fly in," my grandfather said. This surprised me. "He wanted to go on a cruise. All of us. That was what I had been waiting for. A chance to know your father. But I think he knew, deep down, that we would never get that chance..." A sigh escaped his pale mouth. "That's why he did all this... made arrangements in case the worst happened..."

I dropped onto the side of the bed. I didn't want to cry, so I forced the tears back. Outside, thunder roared.

'Don't cry. You're stronger than that, Claudia...' My father's voice broke through my thoughts. Was that what he'd really said?

'Stop it, Claudia! You have to learn to control your power. Haven't I made that clear to you? Do you want the bad people to take you away from us?'

"He talked about bad people coming to take me away..." I said. "I thought it was his way of getting me to eat my veggies when I was little." I laughed. Dr. Edwards smiled. "But they're real, aren't they?" He bit his lip and lowered his head. He didn't have to say anything; I knew it.

My grandfather gazed at me. "I won't let anything happen to you. Your father made a lot of arrangements to keep you safe. To hide any record of your existence and what you can do."

"How?"

He shrugged. "He knew people, I suppose..."

I held the tears back still, though now I was no one. I had no name, no real family. Not even on paper.

"You have a whole new identity. And you do have a family."

I didn't want to hear any more, and I think he knew that. I lowered my head, hands in my lap, and finally let the tears trace the sides of my cheeks. I wiped at them. Who was I?

'My granddaughter.'

I looked up at him, but Dr. Edwards didn't repeat it aloud. "You're not ready for school tomorrow," he said instead. "You should stay home. In fact, I don't think you should go anywhere. You need time to grieve."

"What difference does it make?" I whispered. I'd given up fighting. Lightning lit the sky, thunder followed like a growling hound, and it finally started to rain.

Unable to think of what to say, Dr. Edwards moved to the door. He looked back at me, took a deep breath, and slowly turned the knob. Before he walked out, he said, "I just want you to know that I'm very happy you're here. We will talk more... when you can. There is so much more you need to know about who we are..."

I glanced at him, perplexed by his words and unsure of what to say. I wanted to tell him something mean, but I didn't. He just left me in silence.

4

PRESENCE

I HEARD THE RAIN THROUGH MY WINDOW AND FELT SOMEONE sitting beside my bed. It felt like my father's presence, but my heart felt too heavy...

'*Claudia...*' It sounded like my father.

"Hello?" I whispered at the shadow, blinking and trying to adjust to the darkness. I sat up and reached for the light to find a man with blond hair and pastel-blue eyes glaring at me. A wicked smile curved his mouth, and his eyes seemed to pierce through my soul. I didn't recognize him, but I felt connected to him in some ways even more than to my own parents. He frightened me.

'*I found you at last. I found you... You are the source... you are the one I've been searching for. And I'm not letting you go...*' He reached for me, and I screamed.

I awoke, realizing I was alone in my bed. When I sat up, someone knocked on the door. I rubbed the sleep from my eyes, grateful it had only been a dream. Who was that stranger? Why did I know him? How? The feeling of somehow knowing him was too strong to ignore, but I wondered if it was even true. He'd worn a white suit—that much I recalled—with a blazing red tie and a black, silk shirt. I couldn't remember his face beyond the blond hair and blue eyes.

The knock came again, startling me.

"Claudia? Claudia, I'm going to work now." My grandfather's voice sounded shaky and nervous. "I'm going to school—to Milton. I understand if you would rather just stay home. I'm fine with that. I'm fine with you staying at home today or for as long as you need." Then he was quiet for a moment. I wasn't planning on answering. I figured he would get the hint. "I'm leaving my number, just in case," he added. "Use the landline if you don't have your own cell phone." I rolled my eyes. "Okay, I'm leaving now. There's plenty of food in the fridge if you get hungry." After more silence, I heard him walk down the stairs, open the door, and after a short pause, close it again. I was alone.

For the remainder of the week, every morning seemed to start the same way. Dr. Edwards left, and I stayed in my room. I never answered him when he knocked on my door, no matter what time of day it was. When he left, I finally left my room to ransack the fridge, grab what I needed, and head back upstairs to eat. I only came out again to put the dirty dishes in the sink, but always when he wasn't around.

At dinner, he left a tray with supper outside the bedroom while he cleaned the kitchen. Every time I opened the door to grab the tray, he'd run back up the stairs wanting to talk. But I closed the door behind me and said nothing.

He came to the bedroom door again every night before bed. I didn't know what he intended to do, but I only sensed kindness in his heart. Still, I didn't want to talk, and I couldn't bring myself to say anything. He stood in the hall and thought of what he could possibly say to me. I did read his thoughts; maybe he wanted me to. It felt almost like an invitation he thought might comfort me. There was something he wanted to share with me, but I shut him out before he could start.

I moved away from the door and pushed his thoughts away. Only when I heard him stumble and realized I must have pushed hard did I feel bad.

It rained the entire week, too, and the darkness didn't completely go away. Clouds never cleared the beautiful sky, yet something about this day was different; a little ray of sunshine now fell through the blinds, lighting up the room that was not familiar to me—the room that was just another room.

I grabbed my backpack; I'd spent the day drawing light sketches of my parents, not wanting to forget their faces. I wanted to make sure I always remembered them. Fearing now, as I had before I started, that I'd forgotten small details of my father's face, I turned back to look at the picture on the bedside table. I had placed that there the day I'd arrived, and it was the only picture I had of both of them.

My father's large blue eyes stared back at me from the picture. He was the image of perfection, with boldly blond locks. I often wondered why I hadn't gotten any of his beauty. I was more like my mother, whose dark eyes greeted me from behind the same frame. She had long, waist-length brown hair and bronze skin like mine. My father seemed so pale beside her, but he was so handsome, it didn't matter. I never realized how perfect they looked together. And now they were gone forever. I kept thinking I would see my father, that he would come through that door any moment and tell me he was sorry for frightening me.

But that was only wishful thinking; I would never see them

again. And the sooner I could come to terms with that, the sooner I could start to live.

I spent a few more minutes drawing, then rose from the bed and went to the window of the bedroom I had been so lucky to now call mine. There, I pulled open the blinds and looked outside. The day was bright and sunny; kids played across the street, others rode their bikes. It looked like a pleasant, normal day. The neighborhood was beautiful, heightened by the large, expensive luxury homes lining the street and the metal access gates requiring entry codes to open.

I stepped away from the window, feeling like a prisoner. But that was mainly my fault. Maybe it was time to get out of this prison and get to know my grandfather. I dreaded the idea of it, but I had no choice.

I took a breath, glanced at the picture of my parents, and opened the door into the hallway.

5

THE GIFT

HE WAS IN THE KITCHEN, HAVING WHAT IT SEEMED LIKE A LATE breakfast, when I came down stairs. I stepped into the doorway dressed in a pair of dark jeans and a flowery top and sweater, my long hair cascading down my back.

Dr. Edwards rose and smiled, and I thought of what to say to him. I must have looked like some kind of spoiled teenage girl. But I was embarrassed and uncomfortable for having acted the way I did. Maybe I should hear what he had to say. Maybe I should give him a chance to tell me what was boiling in his mind to reveal.

"Would you like some breakfast?" he asked. A dark cotton sweater covered his white shirt. The air conditioning seemed to be working really well, as both of us had needed extra layers. I pulled at the blue sweater over my own flowery blouse.

I gazed up at him and nodded slowly. Immediately, he grabbed eggs, bacon, and hash browns from the fridge.

"Would you like some eggs and bacon?" he asked politely, turning back with the egg carton already in hand.

"Bacon?" I had stopped eating any kind of red meat; my

mom thought it was cute, and my father thought I was going through a phase.

"Turkey bacon okay?" he asked. Had he read me? I nodded. He put the bacon aside on the counter, then grabbed a bowl to whip two eggs and continue making me breakfast.

I took a seat almost immediately on the opposite side of the table, and he took out the orange juice to pour me a glass before suddenly seeming to realize he hadn't asked if I wanted any.

When he did ask, I nodded, and he grabbed a glass from the upper cabinet. He poured it and placed it near my hand with such care that I tried to read him and found his mind wondering, searching discarded thoughts, lost threats. I was dazed and distracted by them, trying to dissect them as I pulled each thought from his mind. I lost myself in the moment, trying to connect without being noticed; I had tried that with my father, too. But he was far better in control of it.

I sensed my grandfather could easily lose himself in his own mind, but for some reason, he seemed to be in great control today. He thought the same, and that puzzled him. Then he gazed at me, and for a moment, we connected. Was I the reason we both thought? He knew I was reading him, which caught me off guard; I knew of no one else but my father and I who could do this. And now here was this man—my grandfather—trying to connect in the same way.

There was something different about entering this with him, and I knew he also sensed it. Was it because he was my grandfather? It felt just like the blond-haired man in my dream, though with Dr. Edwards, it felt even stronger. I couldn't quite explain it to myself, but that thought made me both happy and frightened.

He turned the bacon over, grabbed a plate off the shelf, and added the eggs to the second pan. I sensed him wondering what he could say to break the unusual silence gnawing at the both of us.

'*Claudia,*' I heard whispered in my mind. At first, I tried to ignore it. But I knew it was him trying to communicate. How many times had father scolded me and warned me? *Don't ever use your abilities in front of them. If they call out to you in thought, don't answer them.*

'*I used to talk to your grandmother this way.*'

I blinked up at Dr. Edwards; he wasn't going to let it be.

"Did you say something?" I asked instead.

He gazed right at me. '*Claudia...*'

I rose, pulling away from the table. "I'm not doing this with you."

"You don't have to be afraid," he said, regretting his attempt to invite conversation between us.

"I'm not afraid," I said, turning back to him. It was more than fear, but something had been drilled into me by my father never to disobey. I pushed against him, and the vibration of it moved him back.

He shook his head and put a hand on the counter to steady himself. '*Stronger than I thought...*' his mind whispered. Though he had the ability, just like my father and I, it still wasn't going to bring us closer, if that was what he expected.

"My father and I could do that," I said. "We used to have our own little conversations, just the two of us. It was the only time I was allowed to use it. He never wanted me to use it anywhere else. He said people would fear me, not understand." I met his gaze. Why did I think he needed an explanation? Even when I told myself not to, I started to tear up. "And now he's gone. I don't ever want to use it again."

"Claudia, you have a gift. A wonderful gift... your father did what he did to protect you."

"Protect me from what? All I keep hearing is he wanted to

protect me. From what?" I snapped. My grandfather was holding back again; he was afraid, and I wanted to know *what* he feared. He and Father seemed to have been terrified of the same thing. "Then he sends me away to live with you..." I lowered my head. "And the moment we're separated, he's dead."

"Do you think this is all your fault?" Dr. Edwards asked, surprised by my words.

Who else's fault could it be? Father had a saying, '*Together we're stronger, united we're bonded, the source of my strength is you.*' I always thought it was a silly phrase, but now it meant a lot. Now, I was beginning to wonder how much more of a meaning it could hold.

"If he hadn't sent me away, he would still be alive," I declared.

"You can't possibly believe that you're to blame for this. Your father wouldn't have wanted you to believe such nonsense." My grandfather turned suddenly to see he was burning the bacon. He took the pan off the burner, then tossed my finished eggs on a plate. "Sorry about that. I'll make some more." He threw the burned bacon into the trash, then started over.

"Don't bother," I said. I had lost my appetite.

"No, it's all right." He grabbed more bacon from the fridge and again added a few more slices onto the pan. The bacon began to sizzle under the cooking oil once more. The hash browns had been done along with the eggs and he also threw those on the plate. From what I could see on the kitchen counter, he'd already made some pancakes. One of these he added to my plate with a fork, then stared at the plate with wide eyes, as if he realized it looked like too much food as he set the plate down in front of me.

I reluctantly took a seat again. I was hungry, and that was the only reason I sat back down.

Then someone knocked on the door. I glanced at my grandfather, who returned my surprised, questioning gaze. He obviously hadn't been expecting anyone.

6

FAMILY HISTORY

I watched my grandfather make his way to the door. The food he had put in the pan was sizzling again. I stood up, went to the stove, and flipped the bacon with the fork he'd left out. It felt almost normal, though I was certain I would never feel normal again. Father was dead. Mother was dead. I was living with a stranger, although not an unkind one. I sighed, realizing I was being unfair to this man.

He returned with a large white envelope, which he sat on the edge of the breakfast table. I didn't turn around to look at him, but I could tell he was watching me. Maybe he was looking for a little bit of Father in me.

'*I know.*' I nearly spattered the bacon grease all over myself when I dropped the fork. I knew he could speak to me like Father could, but it made me uneasy every time. I leaned over to pick up the fork from the floor, muttering an apology.

"It's all right, Claudia. Here, I can finish that up."

He took a few steps towards me, and I retreated back to the table. The clinking of silverware and glass plates filled the silence between us, and he brought me the little plate of bacon added to the already substantial amount he'd put in front of me. I picked at it, my body telling me I was hungry, but my brain despairing of ever eating again in a world without my parents.

Grandfather slid the envelope towards me. "These documents are from Mr. West. Information about the inheritance you'll receive on your twenty-first birthday."

I stared at the white paper and all it entailed. This was blood money. I would rather have my parents. I frowned, realizing I was acting like a baby. I wasn't a baby, and then I felt it— grandfather reaching out to my mind, trying to figure out what I was thinking. I didn't know if he realized he was doing it, or even if he knew I would notice.

"Stop that," I said. He looked confused. "You're trying to read my mind. It won't work."

He blushed and looked away. "I'm sorry. I didn't mean to poke around. Most people, you know, don't realize when another person touches their mind."

I shrugged. I knew that perfectly well, and Father had told me not to do such things. It was dangerous; it would get us hurt. It had gotten him hurt. I gave myself a mental shake. I didn't know that for sure, I was just assuming. I picked up a piece of bacon and slowly chewed.

"There is a history in our family of this ability."

"Father told me," I lied. Of course he hadn't. He'd always refused to talk about it.

"I would expect that of him. He knew the dangers. That's why he sent you to me." This again. Grandfather was not going to let it go. "There are... things that hunt us." I tried to listen, thinking he might reveal something Father never had.

"Things?" I replied, sounding unbelieving even to myself.

"Yes," he said. "There is more to this world than meets the eye. Our power is very old and special to this world. There are... well, I suppose they are people in their own way. They seek us out from across the solar systems. They are drawn to us."

"Aliens?" I said. "Seriously?" Okay, now I didn't know what to believe, but I sensed *he* believed it.

"Yes and no." The corner of his mouth turned down. "I'm not explaining this very well."

I frowned at him. "No." I refused to mention the word 'crazy'.

"Did your father never say anything?"

"He told me to not show my ability, that there were people who would take me away from him..." And that was truth, ingrained in me from the young age of five. I recalled the scolding words of my handsome father yelling at me in front of my elementary school. I hid my memories from my grandfather, but he'd caught a glimpse of what I wanted to forget.

"Yes, there are those, too," he said. "Scientists. Others who would use us for their own agendas... for not-so-good things."

"This is crazy." Stop. The whole thing sounded absurd. He reached out and touched my hand, willing me to listen. My eyes widened when his skin touched mine. Behind his shoulder, I saw a dark, hulking figure, its face obscured by a deep hood. A skeletal hand poked from one dark sleeve, and an impossibly large scythe filled the kitchen. The head turned its searing white eyes. I yanked my hand back. The vision was gone. *The darkness* I'd seen there...

Grandfather stared at me with wide eyes. "What did you see?" he asked. He tried to reach out and touch me again.

"I didn't see anything." The words came out in a squeak. I definitely didn't want our contact to summon that horrible creature back into the otherwise normal kitchen. "I don't know *anything!*" I shouted, standing from the table. The vision hung in my mind. Father could sometimes sense such things as well; it must have been a vision of the future. I could do that sometimes, but only in slivers of moments that didn't make sense, like a puzzle I had to put together on my own.

Grandfather looked at me from the other end of the table,

his brow furrowed in concern. He looked so frail, and around the edges, it was obvious he was my father's father. "Claudia, it'll be okay. I will keep you safe."

Father used to say that to me too. "How?"

"Our abilities can give us warnings. Premonitions." He made us sound like we were fortunetellers or crystal-ball gazers. It was absurd.

"I don't believe in fairy tales."

"This isn't a fairy tale, Claudia. You know your ability is real." *'You know you can hear my thoughts, just as I can hear yours. When you let me.'*

I turned away, not wanting him to see my face. My hands shook. I was responsible for my parents' deaths; I didn't doubt it. And now I would hurt this man who had just come into my life. My grandfather.

"You're scaring me." He reached out to me again, but I moved farther out of his reach.

"Please, don't..." I whispered. "What if I hurt you too? I don't want to hurt you like I hurt them..."

He blinked at me, finally seeming to realize what I knew. "Claudia, this is none of your doing. You had nothing to do with this."

I gazed at him. "How can you be sure?"

He paused as if he didn't know what to say. "What did you see? Please, Claudia, I just want to prepare you for what may come. I want to tell you the things I know." He took a breath, considering his words, aware of my fear. "But I will wait until you are ready," he finally said. "Your parents' deaths were not your fault. Just remember you have *a gift*. You must learn to control it. I will show you how. When you're ready."

It was the second time he had said it, and I didn't believe it any more than the first time. If these premonitions he mentioned were real, I would have been warned. I would have been able to stop Father and Mother from sending me away. I

wouldn't be sitting across this table from this crazy relation I
didn't know I had.

I stood again. "I'm going to my room." He let me go.

When I got to the top of the stairs, I glanced back at him.
The shadow was there again, hanging over his head. I shivered
and tried to think of something else.

7

THE BALANCE

THE CAR CAME TO A STOP IN THE TEACHERS' PARKING LOT UNDER a sign that read *Dr. N. Edwards*. I sat in silence. I hadn't said a word all morning. I sensed my grandfather hoped that by the end of the day, we would be able to talk. There was more to discuss, more he wanted to share with me. I wanted to talk too, but I was afraid. He didn't believe I was responsible for what had happened to my parents, but I was sure it was my fault. Now, I feared I would hurt him in some strange way. I had seen something in that kitchen. And it had malice.

"Would you like to walk into the building together?" he suggested with a smile.

I wanted to, but I couldn't let myself get too close. "I want to... but I'm afraid," I confessed, sitting very still and staring at my lap.

"Claudia, there's no reason to be afraid."

"You don't understand." I wanted to tell him, but the terrifying memory of that shadow froze me into silence. Telling made things worse. I looked back up at him, the tears pooling in my eyes. "When I see something," I started, "when I see... these strange things... they become real." I'd often suspected that happened because I'd been seeing the future. The week before my parents died, I'd dreamed about coming home and not being able to find them—stepping into nothing more than an empty house. I didn't think there was anything wrong with them being gone. I had never told my father that; I'd never wanted to, hoping that by saying nothing, it wouldn't happen. Then I could write it off as just another bad dream. I grabbed my bookbag from the car floor.

"What did you see?" he asked again.

"I don't want to say."

He nodded, a surprising understanding in his eyes. Maybe the link between us was stronger then I wanted to admit. Did he really understand?

"Do you know where all your classes are?" he asked instead, turning off the car engine.

"I do..." Now, suddenly, I felt bad for what I'd told him when we'd first met. "I'm sorry about what I said... at the beginning." I felt like such a brat now. None of this was his fault.

"I know you're just trying to be nice to me..." He smiled. I felt the peace in his heart, a warmth that had come from me. Maybe I could come to understand him. I wanted to. "I'll be here when you're ready to talk," he added. "I can't imagine how hard it is being sent to live with someone you've never met."

"Can we try after school? To talk, I mean." I wanted to try to understand this man I knew carried nothing but kindness in his heart.

He nodded. "Sure. I really would like that."

We got out of the car and walked together up the steps and into the school's front entrance. We stopped right inside at the end of the hall, which was crowded with students. I swallowed hard, panic sinking in, and hoped this wouldn't provoke *the gift*, to use my grandfather's words.

A hand rested on my shoulder, and the chaos settled inside me, safety and calm easing over my anxiety. '*We have the power to ease other's fears. We connect... The strong help the young, the wise help the less knowledgeable, but sometimes it works the other way around. Just like you help me. This source balances all others and gives strength to the gifts of ours...*

'*Your strength, Claudia, gives me control over my power. And in return, our link provides you with guidance and helps you ease your own fears.*'

So we were feeding off one another.

'*In a way,*' he replied. '*Do you understand?*'

'*I think so,*' I said.

He let me go to walk off alone; he knew the routine. I turned to him. '*We'll talk more later...*'

'*I'd like that.*' He turned back toward me and smiled. "I'll see you at lunch?"

I nodded and walked into the crowded hall, leaving him by the door.

8

THE SHADOW IN THE HALL

I HURRIED THROUGH THE HALL. I WAS BEGINNING TO UNDERSTAND Dr. Edwards far more than I'd expected. I was afraid to tell him what I had seen in his kitchen; I was afraid saying it would make it come to pass. He knew now, without a doubt, I had seen something, but he obviously didn't know what.

Now, I found myself wanting to learn from him, especially the things my father had neglected to reveal to me. The idea of it terrified me, but at the same time, I was ready to learn who I was—what I could do. Reading minds and moving objects was a big part of it, as well as feeling emotions—sensing another's pain. I tried not to, but the connection was there, drawing me to the energy in other beings. Gifted people like my father and grandfather had an even stronger connection, a link to me and to each other, just like my grandfather had explained it.

Father was a little less complicated. He could read minds and move objects, and that was the extent of his gift. My father had a word for it—*mindsifter*. I often thought of the *Star Wars* movies when I heard that word, and he'd at first been irritated with me and the fact that I didn't take things seriously.

As I walked through the high school, eyes turned to watch

the new kid, even when I stepped through the side doors and passed the cafeteria entrance. They'd known who I was long before I stepped inside. One would think I was somewhat of a celebrity.

Was that a good thing? I was the principal's granddaughter. How strange—one minute, I was eating cereal at my family's breakfast table, and the next, I was riding to school on a busy day with a grandfather I'd only just met. Life was strange. I was alone. I'd always felt that way, alone even with my family. There had always been something missing in my life. I didn't know what, but a big piece of me felt lost. Though I still missed my parents fiercely, I couldn't decide if my life had ended with their deaths or if it had only just begun.

The hallway stretched ahead, crowds of students spreading to make a path for me, staring at me long after I passed them. I longed for solitude, a place to hide from all this—before I lost control. I couldn't stop it when I was angry or sad. I didn't feel like I'd be able to stop it now. But I didn't know this place; I had no idea where to go. It wasn't fair.

Then once again, my father's voice found its way into my mind, his image burned in my thoughts forever. He stood outside my bedroom door, telling me we were going to be moving.

"But I really like Trent, Father," I'd told him. "Why do we have to go?"

"Because you're my daughter, and I'm not giving them my only child. I've given everything already, and this is far too much. It ends here."

I didn't understand most of it, but I didn't have to, because I'd been so certain my father knew what was best for me.

"It's not fair," I'd protested, and he came to sit beside me on my bed.

"Life isn't fair, but you make the best of what you're given, sweetheart."

I knew the words by memory.

I raced up the stairwell, hoping to find somewhere private. I stumbled upon the girl's restroom around the corner on the second floor, where I ducked into the last empty stall and collapsed. I couldn't do anything but cry. Above me, the pipes rattled and groaned at the sound of my sobbing, and I thought they would burst.

"Stop!" I yelled, and the pipes settled instantly. Amidst the silence, the bell rang, penetrating my thoughts. I heard student voices in the halls, racing from one end to the other, doors and lockers slamming, tennis shoes sliding across waxy floors, and then finally, silence—save the sound of my own breath.

For a brief second, it remained that way. But then the bathroom door slowly crept open, and I heard an eerie whistling—a catchy and still creepy melody. Footsteps followed, echoing on the tiles of the bathroom floor. The whistling rose in tone, slowly fading, then started over again. Was that the theme song to *Sesame Street*?

I sat still, quietly listening and hoping whoever it was would leave quickly. The whistling continued near the sinks until I heard the faucet turning on and water splashing into the basin.

I peered through the cracks of the stall but couldn't see either who it was or where they stood. I heard a few more footsteps, then a figure came into clear view. A tall, slender, blond-haired man dressed in a black suit and red tie stood facing the sinks and mirrors. It seemed normal enough except for the simple fact that he was in the girl's restroom at a high school.

My palms grew sweaty, and I had to remind myself not to hold my breath.

In an incredibly robotic fashion, he tilted his head slightly and stared at his own reflection, as if he were looking at himself for the first time. His large, dark, dull eyes nearly flashed, and he curved slim lips into a crooked grimace. I could see the define cheekbone sink into the long and inner sides of his pale face.

Brushing a finger across his brows, the stranger grabbed a paper towel, wiped his hands, then straightened his tie. His reflection flickered slightly, distorting his image for only a moment. Beyond hollow eyes and a skull of porcelain, a row of teeth formed in a hooded head in the mirror—his reflection staring back at him.

I nearly fell against the stall door and choked back a scream. My heart pounded in my chest. Had I really just seen that?

The lights above me flickered again, then stopped. A single ceiling lamp went out completely. I glanced up at it, terrified.

Oh, you've got to be kidding me, I thought, glaring up at the lamp. If it didn't fear the darkness, the light had been my only protection.

The whistling continued. I froze, trying to take control of myself, and when the tune abruptly stopped, I pressed my face again to the crack in the stall. Our eyes met in the mirror, and I jerked back against the toilet. There was no question he'd seen me. Of course he had.

Feeling both brave and stupid, I peeked through the stall again only to find the bathroom empty—at least, what little I could see of it.

"Boo." A pair of dark blue eyes appeared on the other side of the slit in the stall door. I screamed and stumbled back again. A pipe burst above my head, and for a moment, I stood there, staring at the stall door and unable to move while the water sprinkled down on my head. But nothing happened, and when I finally shoved open the door and stepped out, there was no one there. I was completely alone again.

The light above the mirror flickered when I took a step forward. I stood now in the very spot where he had been. I didn't think I would ever forget his eyes and that clever, all-knowing grin.

The only reflection now staring back at me was my own. The light flickered again, and in the mirror, I saw him standing behind me in an open stall, fixing me with the same ill gaze. The lights went out completely, and I spun around to face him. My hands clutched the sink behind me as I pushed up against it. But he'd vanished again.

A small puddle had already formed inside the stall where I'd hidden, and the door swung open just a little more. The sound of the water spraying from the broken pipe kept me from going insane. I *felt* something staring at me from the darkness, quietly waiting.

Then the next bell rang. Startled, I snatched my backpack and rushed out into the hall.

I hurried toward a small, open balcony overlooking the first floor. Below me was the auditorium entrance, beside which was painted *Go Buffaloes* and a cartoon drawing of a buffalo puffing clouds of smoke from his nostrils.

There he was—the man in the black suit and red tie, standing against the railing. For some strange reason, I felt he was waiting for me. When his gaze met mine, it seemed to beckon me forward. A cold chill raced up the side of my arm as his vacant, dark blue eyes stared almost through me. Like a ghostly apparition, his lips parted slightly to whisper something I couldn't hear. Could no one else see this? He pointed a bony finger at me, and his eyes smiled and danced from that hollow, cold gaze.

'You... I've been looking for you.'

I backed away, falling into the paths of two other men coming down the hall. Terrified, I spun around, and for a moment, neither one of them said a word. The taller man, wearing a green sportscoat, managed a wave. He was a little hard to ignore as he towered in front of me.

His blond companion, the dead ringer for Ed Harris, smiled. "Finding your classes all right, Claudia? I'm sorry we didn't get the chance to introduce ourselves. I'm Mr. Claypool, and this is Mr. Vasquez. Are you all right?" Mr. Vasquez smiled warmly down at me.

I nodded, still trembling. I looked toward the railing, but the man in the black suit and red tie was gone. I tried to stop shaking, hoping they wouldn't ask any more questions; I didn't think I'd be able to say anything coherent.

I couldn't find any answer for *him,* though, and I wished I'd never had this vision. It was impossible now to shake the feeling that I wasn't supposed to have seen it at all. *'You... I've been looking for you...'* he'd said. What did that mean?

"Don't hesitate to ask us for help, okay?" Mr. Claypool said. Mr. Vasquez gave a goofy nod, his head bobbing. His lips seemed to disappear beneath his thick mustache.

They didn't even seem to notice my wet hair and clothes until a few students rushed up to tell them the girl's bathroom was flooding. Then they returned their gazes to me, looking me up and down, and I saw them putting the pieces together.

"Ah, Claudia. Would you happen to know anything about this?"

I managed a half-guilty smile, and all three of us glanced down at the trail of wet footprints coming from the restroom.

☀

Mr. Claypool and Mr. Vasquez ushered me into my grandfather's office. I looked around, losing myself in the awards and pictures on his wall. My grandfather stood by his desk, talking to Michael, and they both turned toward us when we entered.

"Hello again," Michael said. I only smiled at him before he seemed to dismiss himself and headed toward the door. "I'll talk to you later, Neil."

"Don't forget dinner at my house tonight. Mr. Claypool and Mr. Vasquez, you're both invited as well…" My grandfather frowned and squinted at me when he noticed my damp hair. Mr. Vasquez and Mr. Claypool both nodded a greeting to Michael as he passed us.

My grandfather's eyes flicked up to the men beside me, then back down to my head. "Why is your hair wet?"

"Sir, a pipe busted in the second-floor girl's restroom," Mr. Vasquez spat out, sounding as if he'd been waiting a long time to say it. I looked down at my shoes.

"Are you all right?" my grandfather asked me, ignoring Mr. Vasquez's sudden outburst.

His concern surprised me, and I wondered if he knew something—if I'd given something away. I looked up at him and nodded.

"What happened?" he asked, and his frown deepened. This uncannily accurate empathy was always odd to anyone who didn't know the gift as we did. But we knew. We always knew. He knew I had seen something.

"I don't know…" I said. "I saw something… I really don't know." I silently begged him not to ask again, still terrified of what would happen if I said it out loud.

"Sir, if I may," Mr. Claypool said. "Those pipes are pretty old. Best they burst now so we can ask for money in the budget to repair the rest."

My grandfather nodded; they didn't understand our inner pain. He knew the pipes were not an accident.

"I can take Claudia to the nurse's office," Mr. Claypool added. "Mrs. Jenkins always keeps a spare pair of clothes in her office for such an emergency."

"That's a good idea." My grandfather stepped toward me and put a hand on my shoulder. I gazed into his sad, under-standing eyes. "Are you sure you're okay?" he asked again. I nodded. He took a deep breath, then seemed to make a decision. "There's something I need to give you. Something we should talk about. Is that all right with you?"

I stared into his eyes, and his images flooded my mind. He held the crystal in his hand, which glowed red and sometimes blue—red for danger, blue for peace. The crystal cast emotion and warned of impending danger, like a strange, powerfully accurate mood ring. Any shadow, any presence, was quick to retreat from the crystal's light.

"Do you understand?" my grandfather said. He showed me that brief image again. I knew he wanted to give the crystal to me, but I also sensed that far more came with such a gesture than simply handing it to me.

"I think so," I said. And now I was far more curious. "It keeps you safe?" I asked.

He nodded. "And it does far more than that. I will teach you how to use it. After school, we'll talk more." He glanced again at Mr. Claypool standing behind me. "Please have Mrs. Wallace call the plumber," he said. "Tell her to use my credit card."

"Yes, sir," Mr. Claypool replied, turning to leave. Mr. Vasquez waited for him by the door.

My grandfather turned to me once more before I left. "If you need anything, I'm right here. No matter how small. You come see me, okay?"

I smiled, feeling the warmth of his heart spreading through my own. It seemed we both shared the connection for that brief moment. He was glowing. And I felt this was the happiest he'd ever been in his life.

9

HIGH SCHOOL ACQUAINTANCE

MRS. JENKINS CERTAINLY KEPT QUITE A BIT OF SPARE CLOTHES—
old garments from students who had left them behind in the
gym. She'd kept them in a donation box set up in the nurse's
office.

After towel-drying my hair, I went through the items, but
there was no way I was going to wear any of them. Some items
seemed older than the seventies.

The bell rang again when I left the nurse's office. Mr.
Vasquez and Mr. Claypool stood in the hall, and I tried to
ignore them. They'd really failed at not looking so obvious.

The second bell sounded just as I entered my history class
with Mr. Peterson, and I found a seat in the back. I hoped the
teacher didn't call on me to introduce myself, seeing as I was
the principal's granddaughter on her first day.

Mr. Peterson's glaring gaze never left me, even once I took
my seat. He was filled with resentment, not toward me but my
grandfather. *'Is she odd like her grandfather?'* I heard him think.
*'It's the lack of religion that's the problem. If I were in charge here, I'd
make some changes... We need prayer, we need religion in school...'*

His eyes drifted in the other direction, hushing the voices

beginning to disrupt the classroom. Then he took to the chalk-board and added an assignment.

A few students glanced over at me, whispering. A mutter of voices chattered inside my ears.

'I bet she gets special treatment...'

'Since when did Dr. Edwards have a granddaughter?'

"Hey, you're Claudia Belle, aren't you?" A girl sitting in front of me spun around to face me. Her bouncy, curly brown hair fell over her square, dark-framed glasses. Caught by surprise, I didn't answer right away. Her words had interrupted and strangely silenced the voices almost immediately, and I couldn't focus on anything else but her.

"I'm Tina Watkins." She offered a hand. I hesitated. Did people still shake hands? "I think that's so cool, you being related to the principal. I bet you can get away with a lot," Tina exclaimed with a grin. A sigh of relief escaped my mouth. This was a fact I hadn't considered. "So, how do you like Milton so far?"

I found Tina curiously odd—a little overzealous. She seemed far more interested in me than what the teacher was writing on the chalkboard. Mr. Peterson cleared his throat to get her to turn around, but she only faced him briefly, wrinkling her nose at him in reply.

He glanced away when their eyes met, which I thought was more than a little strange. Then he turned again and continued writing his instructions.

"It's interesting..." I said, finally answering her question. "Different..."

"You don't know the half of it." She giggled.

I tried to concentrate on the lesson, but it was hard when Tina wasn't the only other person not paying attention. A few girls on the other side of the class giggled, and I knew they were talking about me even before I glanced at them and they wrinkled their noses in my direction. Rachel Westcott—I caught her name in my thoughts. Ginger and Becky were the other two. They reminded me of a scene from *Mean Girls*.

Tina whirled back again to talk to me. "Don't let them bother you," she said.

"They're not," I replied, meeting her gaze. She smiled, her eyes flashed at me, and I dropped back in my seat, catching looks from the mean girls on the left and hearing their giggles. The lights above flickered. *Not here,* I pleaded, more giggles echoing from the side of the room. *Please don't.* Something popped above us, and Mr. Peterson stopped his lesson to turn and glance at the ceiling.

I exhaled. *Breathe...* Another pop sounded, then two more, and the light fixtures above Rachel and her friends sparked and completely went out, glass shattering down over their heads. I gasped, Rachel and her friends screamed and scattered away, and the other students scrambled to the edges of the classroom.

Tina laughed. When I turned forward again, she was the only other student still at her desk, flashing me a huge grin. Rachel glared at me, and I wondered if she really thought this was my fault.

The incident was accredited to faulty light fixtures. Most of the class period was spent watching the janitor remove both the light fixture and the mess of scattered glass. After a few more minutes of this, the bell rang above us.

I stepped out of the classroom with the rest of the students, Mr. Peterson now standing behind his desk and watching us leave. I only turned back when I noticed Tina slowly pass his desk and eyeball the man, slowly sweeping a finger along the edge of his desk. But it was the manner in which she did so that caught my attention; she used the sharp end of her fingernail to scratch the surface of the wood.

I hurried away. I had seen my share of students go rogue enough to know that she might be one of those. I thought the hall was too crowded with students for Tina to see me, but then she appeared at my side.

"Hey, what's your hurry?" she said, putting a hand on my arm to stop me, almost as if she knew quite fully I was trying desperately to escape her.

"I'm just getting to class," I muttered, feeling pressed to justify myself.

"Oh, don't feel bad," she said. "It's not like it was your fault." She didn't leave my side.

"What do you mean?" I glared at her. Tina grinned wide, and I doubted she realized how much that creepy smile implied she knew otherwise. "Right..." I said. "It's not." I didn't have time to explain why I was upset, if she'd even noticed it. But it seemed she didn't want an explanation at all. She was polite—strange, but polite nonetheless. And it wasn't like I had any friends anyways. Could I honestly afford to be picky?

"So, who do you have next?" Tina asked. I noticed Mr. Peterson staring back at us from the doorway of his classroom.

"What's his problem?" I asked. "He hasn't stopped staring at me since I walked through the door." Or, I wondered, was he troubled by Tina and now the fact that I'd made an unnatural alliance with her?

Tina laughed. "Oh, don't let him bother you. He's a religious fanatic. Probably thinks you're a demon or something and wants to exorcise you."

"What?" I uttered, staring back at Mr. Peterson. He'd now taken a step through his classroom door and grabbed at the golden crucifix around his neck.

"I'm just kidding. That man is way bitter," she said. "He thinks Dr. Edwards is the devil."

"What? Why?" I exclaimed.

Tina rolled her eyes. "He thinks everyone's the devil. Ever since Dr. Edwards made him take the crucifix off the wall, he's been like that."

"A crucifix? So I guess he still believes in prayer in school?" I asked.

"Something like that." Tina grinned. "I think he thinks he's like Jesus Christ reborn." She laughed again.

"Great," I whispered. "Like I need any more problems."

"Some teachers get so attached to their classrooms, you'd think they live there or something. And they think they can hang up all sorts of crap." Tina shook her head, then glared back at Mr. Peterson. This sent the teacher fleeing back into the safety of his classroom. Maybe he really was crazy.

"So..." Tina turned back toward me. "Who do you have next?" She smiled, revealing a set of straight white teeth.

I tried not to let her disturbingly zealous smile overwhelm me. I looked down at my schedule card and found math with Mr. Thompson and PE on the list next. I had already missed my first two classes—English and Science.

"We should memorize each other's schedules," she suggested with a full smile. It sounded a bit odd, but I figured there was no harm in it. I shrugged and showed her my card. "You have English with Mr. McClellan." Tina frowned. "Oh, bummer."

"Do you have him?" I asked, wondering why she seemed so disappointed. I had only met the man twice, and he seemed nice enough. He was a close friend of my grandfather's, that much I felt from the two of them, especially Mr. McClellan; he was far easier to read.

"Nah. I had him last year," Tina said. "Now I have the old hag Mrs. Whitman. God, I hate her class."

A few students passed us by, and she waved in a rather robotic way, as if she'd been programmed to do so. She seemed almost unreal in that moment—just as unreal as her smile, I realized. I wondered why she was so excited to talk to me. Could it be my status in this place as the principal's grand-daughter? Or was it something else? I wasn't much for conversation with others, always having worked better on my own. Sometimes, I thought the distance I kept was what attracted others to me in the first place.

"Hey! What lunch period do you have?" Tina asked. I didn't answer right away, so she looked down at my card. "You have B lunch like me. We can sit together." She said it without a hint of a question, like she either didn't think I'd say no or didn't care if I did. I smiled, nodding, unable to offer anything else. "Well, I got to get to class. I'll see you around. Don't be a stranger." Then she was swept away by the crowd of students moving in the other direction.

I moved through the crowd alone.

After math class with Mr. Thompson, I walked down the hall towards the cafeteria and spotted my grandfather talking to one of the teachers. He was so happy; I felt his heart soaring. Then I saw an image of myself appear in his mind. I wanted to go to him—he wanted to have lunch with me—but an uneasy feeling pushed me the other direction. Afraid to bring any other strange feelings or ghostly figures into his day, too, I decided I'd stay away until we could talk later that night. He had news to tell me, I knew. He would teach me who I was and what my father had failed to tell me about our power. And about the danger.

Mr. Thomas, the security guard, and another Hispanic man in the same uniform came my way down the hall. The second man seemed to be shadowing Mr. Thomas for training, and they both waved back at me as I passed them.

A few students behind me wandered out of the stairwell and into B-lunch, catching the guards' attention. I stood at the entrance of the crowded cafeteria for a few seconds, staring into a mass of faces, none of which I recognized. Finally, and reluctantly, I stepped into the lunch line.

I paid for my lunch and wandered around, trying to pretend I knew where I was going. I found a nice, empty corner of the cafeteria and sank into a book on my Kindle app.

Something moved in the corner of my eye, and I blinked, looking to my left. Tina stretched her arm in the air, waving it back and forth and looking right at me. I felt my face burning red and wanted to disappear. I had a feeling this girl would have stood on the table just to get my attention. She waved me over with smaller gestures now that she knew I'd seen her, and another huge smile surfaced on her tight, distant face, like she wasn't all there. With a sigh, I stood and made my way toward her, where she sat at a table with just a few friends, away from the rest of the student mass.

An exploration of her inner thoughts brought with it a wave of distorted sounds instead of clear ideas of what kind of person she was. A quick glare from her nearly knocked me over, frightening me enough to make me stop. But she smiled again just as quickly, as if nothing had happened, and tilted her head. Warily, I stepped up to the table.

Tina's friends immediately looked up as she introduced us. They all seemed friendly, except for one.

The kid named Sean looked like the class president. He had dark hair, framed glasses, and well-combed locks. His eyes shot up from behind the pages of his Chuck Palahniuk novel. He smiled, putting the book down; it seemed his attention could rarely be diverted from Mr. Palahniuk. He seemed out of place, an intellectual in a cafeteria filled with misfits, quite the opposite of Tina and the other two. He looked like an English gentleman in a sea of high-school idiots.

"Hello," he said with a musical voice, and I blushed.

Ruben, a skater, had been stuffing a piece of bread into his mouth when I stepped into the picture. He had shaggy golden hair and a delicately structured face; a surprising metal ring pierced his lip. He froze when I looked at him, swallowing the bread already in his mouth.

"That's gross," said a girl to my left, dressed in black lace and a corset. I couldn't tell if she was ready for a funeral or a heavy-metal concert. She rolled her eyes when Ruben directed his attention towards me and waved.

She didn't seem quite as friendly as the others. Darting her clear blue eyes toward me, she pushed back her black, shoulder-length hair, sizing me up at first glance with a sneer.

"Oh, look, it's Pocahontas... with daisies," she leered.

The insult wasn't a new one. I took a seat next to Tina, facing Alex and Ruben. "It was my mother's favorite flower," I admitted, feeling slightly childish both for having worn the daisy pendant around my neck and admitting my reason for it. The Goth girl just rolled her eyes in response.

Ruben and Sean seemed to silently absorb my every word, just like Tina had when I spoke to her in the hall. I wondered if they both knew my parents were deceased. Their rapt attention would make sense if they felt a little sympathetic towards me.

"I think it's lovely," Ruben said with a smile.

"Daisies have always been one of my favorite flowers," Tina proudly voiced.

"They're known to represent innocence and purity," Sean said, curving his lips into a wrinkling smile.

Alex furrowed her brow. "Innocence and purity?" She rolled her eyes at them. "Really?" Their long, uncomfortable silence stretched across the table.

"So, what do you guys do during lunch besides eat?" I asked, hoping to break the icy silence.

Alex glared at me, but the others seemed eager to answer my stupid question.

"Talk about other people." Alex grinned.

I managed an uneasy smirk and figured I had already been one of her victims.

"So, your grandfather is the principal, huh?" she asked.

Sean narrowed his brown eyes, seeming bothered by the sudden turn in conversation. Somehow, I sensed this hadn't been news to them. Who didn't know by now that I was related to Dr. Edwards?

I nodded, hoping to get off the topic, then grabbed my fork and picked at what looked like mashed potatoes.

"So, like, you can do whatever you want?" Alex added.

"I guess," I managed to say, distracted by what might have been meatloaf on my plate. I looked up and noticed the two assistant principals entering the cafeteria.

Alex looked back and saw them too. "Friends of yours? Looks like your bodyguards are here. And just in time," she added in a mockingly musical tone.

"Alex," Tina said firmly, her eyes darting toward the raven-haired Goth girl. She turned to me with a glance that said, *Ignore her.*

"They're not my bodyguards." I felt the need to say something, to clear that up, at least. I hoped Mr. Claypool and Mr. Vasquez wouldn't see me, but then they both looked my way and waved. I just about died, wanting to return the smile but dreading the consequences, especially when Alex almost sneered at me.

"You know them?" Alex said. Clearly, I did. Nevertheless, she made me rethink my answer. The other kids at the table all turned to stare at me. Was knowing school officials a big no-no for them?

"No. Not really," I said and lowered my head.

"How could she? This is her first day," Tina answered for me. She laughed, oddly reassuring the others. Alex gave her a peculiar stare. Tina seemed strange all around—I could agree with that—like she'd lost a few marbles, and I was glad I wasn't the only one who found her individuality strange.

"We make it a rule to stay away from authority figures when

we're skipping," Alex explained. "I don't trust them. Always trying to get me in trouble. Picking on me because I'm different. So, I'm Goth. My soul is dark." She grinned. "They just like giving out detention slips. Pick on the Goth girl."

The others didn't say much of anything. I noticed Sean had resumed reading his book, observing me from behind his framed glasses whenever he had a chance. I thought it odd that he still lost himself in the pages of a hardback book instead of an iPad, like most kids our age.

"They're wasting their time trying to get this place up to code," Alex added.

She seemed to be the only one talking and the only one who seemed remotely normal, even if she was also a little hostile. Sean was mostly busy with his book. Tina and Ruben silently observed the scene from the other end of the table. They seemed almost robotic in their own skin, looking at the world as if they didn't recognize it and had to be reminded how to act.

"I agree. There are far more important things to worry about," Sean said with a callous smirk from behind his book. I couldn't help but feel he was talking about something else, but then our eyes met, and he grinned.

"I think the school looks fine the way it is," Alex continued, glancing around the cafeteria. "It gives the place character. Far more character than some people here."

Sean slightly repositioned his glasses, narrowing his large eyes as he stared at me and apparently tried to ignore Alex's ranting.

Mr. Claypool and Mr. Vasquez walked up to the front of the cafeteria and stood there. I knew they were keeping an eye on me, even though the thought was ridiculous. But it made me feel safe. They kept glancing at our table, and I sensed they wanted to come by and say hello. But they resisted. I had already won them over, and I'd only smiled at them once.

"Are you guys skipping now?" I asked, not knowing what else to say.

Alex wrinkled her nose at me. "You're not going to tell on us, are you, Pocahontas?" She twisted the pentagram necklace hanging from her neck, furrowing her brow.

"*Alex*," Tina hissed in my defense.

"Just asking," Alex said with a grin, picking at her food. "What the hell is this?" She scowled and lifted a piece of something from her tray. "You should really get your grandfather to do something about the cafeteria food," she told me, then dropped her fork again in disgust.

"Don't listen to anything Alex says. She's just being... *funny*," Tina said, trying to laugh it off then shooting the Goth girl a glare. Despite everyone else acting annoyed by Alex's comments, for whatever reason, they remained seated like a group of mannequins. The only genuine person here seemed to be the girl insulting me.

"She's the only one skipping," Sean answered me. "And as for character, she has none. Literature builds character. Far more than the black lace she calls a wardrobe." He lifted his gaze from his book to smirk at her.

Alex flipped him off. "Fuck you. Everyone skips class. It's a requirement of being a teenager." Sean didn't respond, concentrating instead on his book. "Whatever. You're just trying to impress Pocahontas."

Sean blinked, his eyes darkening in a firm frown, but as soon as Alex dropped the argument, he seemed to do the same.

"Her name is Claudia," Tina corrected.

The table fell silent again; only the sound of other students in the cafeteria kept me from feeling the ugly discomfort of it.

"So, what's the deal with your grandfather, anyway?" Alex asked. It seemed to bring everyone to attention again; the others exchanged glances, then stared at me. I wasn't quite sure what she meant, and yet I knew exactly what she'd asked. Her mind blasted angry distrust and a little jealousy—it was pretty dark in there—but there was also something else I hadn't picked up before. Kindness.

'*Stop it,*' a voice whispered.

I glanced at each of the others at this table, but no one gave any indication they'd said anything. I always figured my snooping into someone else's mind was going to get me in trouble, but I shook it off.

"What do you mean?" I asked Alex. "I just met him a few days ago."

"No way!" Ruben yelled, surprising me with his first actual reaction. "You mean you've never met him until now?"

"My parents died..." I said. "That's why I'm here." I shrugged, and Alex blushed.

"How does that happen?" Ruben said. Sean shot him another glance, and it seemed to both calm and almost silence him.

"Perhaps the real question is why he waited so long to meet you?" Sean added, slowly leaning forward again, smiling, and for a second, I couldn't move. There was something about his eyes; the color swirled in golden sparkles. I must have been seeing things, but the way the specs danced in a mixture of bright blues and purples was mesmerizing.

"You know what I mean, Pocahontas," Alex said, smiling sheepishly back at me from the pallor of her face. Beneath it, I found two blue eyes staring at me, hidden by the powder of makeup. Why did I feel she hid something even darker? Or was it that she tried to hide herself from that darkness?

I caught a glimmer of shock on her face, and my stomach lurched. There was no way she had read my mind, right?

"Doesn't he strike you as being a little odd?" she continued, closely gauging my reaction. I didn't give her one, trying to remain as blank as I could. "Jessica from English class said she lives across the street from him. She said he's a very strange person. All the neighbors think so. They're scared of him. He makes strange things happen. Cats die, things go missing. Weird thunderstorms out of nowhere. Creepy, huh?"

I realized now she was trying to get to me, and I just stared at her.

"I hate to break it to you, Pocahontas, but you're related to a load of weirdness. Don't tell me you didn't know that." Then she smacked her lips.

"Strange?" I asked. She smiled. I knew what she meant, remembering the neighbors next door who looked away when my grandfather only tried to be friendly with them. Separated by the gift—that was my problem too. "Strange how?" I continued. "Because he keeps to himself? Maybe this Jessica in English is a total bitch and should mind her own business."

Sean let out a small laugh, which he concealed with the palm of his hand.

Alex looked at me with wide, surprised eyes, and above us, the cafeteria lights flickered. A light hush settled across the cafeteria, but when the flickering stopped, a mutter of disappointment rose around us.

I took a deep breath; I couldn't lose control here—not in front of them.

When I looked back down at Alex, she still seemed to be examining me, and we stared at each other.

"Well that was interesting..." She smiled.

"Not really," I said. "I heard it happens a lot... here."

"That's right," Tina intervened. "Wasn't it you who said this place is falling apart?" With a gleaming grin aimed at Alex, she stabbed her piece of meatloaf with her fork.

Sean put his book down and removed his glasses, the conversation having apparently sparked his interest.

But Tina had strangely frozen, staring wide-eyed at her tray as if her meatloaf wiggled in front of her eyes and tried to escape. She didn't move until Sean touched her hand, then she blinked and smiled as if nothing happened. I almost didn't notice any of it until a mechanical laugh burst out from her mouth. Only Alex and I stared at her in surprise.

"Okay..." Alex said, rolling her eyes at Tina's odd display.

Sean put on his glasses again. They made him look rather serious and observant. "I personally have no ill feelings towards Dr. Edwards, but I am curious as to why he was absent from your life for so long. That's the part that bothers me." I found myself unable to answer, and he shrugged, adding, "Well, I'm sure he had his reasons."

"Did he?" Tina asked. Alex wrinkled her nose, still frowning at the girl who'd acted so strangely just a few moments before.

Sean sat up, setting the book down to lean forward and rest his folded hands on the table. Now he stared at me with his apparently undivided attention, and it made me nauseous.

I forced my lips to move; his stare seemed to demand an explanation I couldn't give.

"How unfair to keep you away from me," Sean said, but when I blinked, he was once again staring at the pages of his open book.

"What did you say?" I asked.

He looked up at me with a smile. His eyes were very brown now, almost as lifeless as these other kids' expressions had seemed from the beginning. "I said it must have been harder for him to stay away," Sean answered, then fell back into the pages of his book.

"Why would somebody do that?" asked Ruben.

"I don't know," I answered, trying to forget what I wrote off as my mind playing tricks on me.

"Well, I don't think I could trust someone like that," Ruben said. "I mean, how can you? What's he hiding? And what does he want when it's taken him this long to show up in your life?

He was never there, then suddenly, *boom.* I'm your grandfather!"

"That sucks," Tina said. "Listen, if you ever need anyone to talk to, you can talk to me." She offered an oddly large smile, her eyes growing surprisingly wide.

"It's nothing like that..." I tried to say. It wasn't at all what they thought. My grandfather was the kindest person I'd ever met. And I wanted to get to know him, but I was afraid I had brought something dark with me into his life. As my gift grew, it seemed so did the darkness around me. I never told my father what I felt or what I had seen. Then again, I'd felt I didn't have to; part of the time, it seemed even he feared me—and was crueler to me because of it. It made me wonder what secrets of his own he'd hidden from me.

"Oh, it isn't?" Alex scoffed. "Ruben's right, and even Miss oddball here has the right idea..." Ruben and Tina both looked over at her with frowns of confusion. "He's a con artist after your money. He has all the right documents and said all the right things. I saw a special on it on MSNBC."

The others glanced over at her, bewildered and far more annoyed than anything else, until she burst into laughter and swallowed the gum she'd been chewing.

"I'm joking! Oh, come on... I'm just messing around. Dr. Edwards is odd, I'll give him that, but one thing he's not is in desperate need of money. I heard he's loaded. Maybe it's the other way around and *you're* trying to get *his* money," she said, pointing at me.

I wrinkled my nose at her, starting to feel as irritated by her as the others.

"You're not helping," Sean uttered.

"Well, if not, this might be the best thing that ever happened to you," Alex said, glancing at me. "Now you can get whatever you want from the old man. He owes you big time. You could probably even get a car out of the whole thing."

Sean's eyes again found me from behind his book; his tightly pressed lips made me think he was beginning to lose his patience, and I found that hard to imagine. He seemed so calm and composed, unlikely sent over the edge by someone like Alex. I wondered how they'd ever gotten along before I came into the picture.

"I just want to get to know him. He's all I have," I whispered. Sean's eyes softened in unexpected surprise at my words.

"What? Take advantage of the situation, sister!" Alex laughed.

"Well, what a surprise," Ruben told her, rolling his eyes.

"I understand how you feel," Tina said, nodding at me.

"How can you?" Alex asked.

Tina and Ruben frowned at Alex, and Tina stuck out her tongue at the other girl. Then they leaned toward each other, and Ruben whispered, "We need to walk her to class." They leaned even closer toward me. "Can we walk you to class?"

Sean lifted his eyes from the book. He listened, waiting perhaps to see what I would say.

"I guess," I said, feeling remarkably uneasy.

"We can accompany you to all your classes, if you'd like," Sean added. "We're somewhat of a unit now." A unit? The others happily agreed. "After all, we're all friends now."

"You don't have to," I replied. "Really."

"But that's what friends do," Tina said.

"They help each other," Ruben offered.

"We can hang out after school. You must say yes, Claudia," Tina pleaded. "We can go to the mall, if you like. We can do anything you'd like to do."

This felt like the oddest interaction I'd ever had. "Well... I'll have to ask my grandfather," I softly offered. They didn't seem terribly disappointed, merely accepting that answer as if they'd expected it. But they were more robotic in their understanding than what I'd expected.

"Of course. I'm sure he won't mind," Ruben said. He stared at nothing in particular and grinned.

"We can ask him for you, if you'd like," Tina offered.

"No, I think I can handle that." I glanced at Alex to see her grinning at me in amusement.

"Here, take my number," Tina said. "If you need anything, call us. It doesn't matter what time."

"Your parents don't get mad if people call late?"

She laughed like I'd just told a really funny joke. "No, of course not. Don't be ridiculous. Call us, really, any time you like."

"You're suddenly the popular one, Pocahontas." Alex smiled, coming to sit right beside me. "*Creepy*, isn't it?" she whispered. I glared at the two assistant principals on the other side of the cafeteria. "Look at the gruesome twosome up there. You think we can't see them constantly looking over here?" Alex said.

"Sorry. I think I'm the reason they're here," I admitted. "My grandfather has them watching over me."

"He has, has he? Well, you don't have to apologize," Tina said, her smile stiff.

"What? Oh, great," Alex exclaimed. "They're gonna find out for sure that I'm skipping. Thanks a lot, Pocahontas."

"I should go." I stood from the table, but Tina stopped me.

"You should!" Alex shouted.

"Don't be ridiculous," Tina added, pulling me down as I tried to get up. "Stay!" Her oddly tight grip on my arm and her strained smile made me freeze.

"Really, guys?" Alex snarled, glaring at them all.

Tina, Ruben, and Sean offered no apology or explanation at all, beaming still from where they sat and turning to face her. Angrily, Alex rose only to drop back to her seat when she noticed the assistant principals finally approaching our table.

"Great. Here they come," she whispered, trying to hide her

face behind her hand. "If they see me, I'll get another week of detention. Why did you bring her here, Tina? She's gonna get me in trouble."

"Perhaps you should have stayed put," Sean said without glancing away from his book. Alex made a face and offered him her middle finger. "How mature," he whispered without looking up from his reading.

I stood, and even after Tina called out to me, I moved towards Mr. Vasquez and Mr. Claypool. I couldn't let Alex get in trouble because of me. The two administrators greeted me with smiles.

"She saved your ass," I heard Tina tell Alex behind me.

"Don't expect me to thank her, your highness," Alex grumbled.

"Perhaps you should," Ruben said.

"I like her," Sean added.

"Me too," Ruben agreed.

"Oh, fuck you guys!" Alex yelled, leaving the table as I led the assistant principals out of the cafeteria at the other end.

I stopped in the hallway with Mr. Claypool and Mr. Vasquez just as I noticed Alex stepping through the other set of the cafeteria doors down the hall. "Can you guys show me to my next class?" I asked them, directing their attention in the opposite direction as Alex ducked into the stairwell nearby and disappeared.

The assistant principals had been more than happy to offer their help. I had never seen any administrators like these two, but now I was stuck with them—*the gruesome twosome,* Alex had called them.

As we walked, Mr. Vasquez wouldn't stop talking about faculty get-togethers and dinners at the old man's house. Mr. Claypool, although kind and sweet, was a bit of a nerd, lecturing me on grades and schoolwork. I thought of what Alex had said about them. They seemed fairly nice to me.

"Wait until Christmas," Mr. Vasquez said. "We have faculty parties and then Thanksgiving dinners for the whole staff."

"But you know that's not what life's all about, my dear," Mr. Claypool interrupted, glaring at Mr. Vasquez. "Good grades and studying hard are always more important than parties." Mr. Vasquez agreed with a nod almost immediately.

They stopped at the end of the hallway. I noticed the entrance to the gym—where my next PE class was—but I didn't just want to dart away. Luckily for me, I was saved by the bell, and even as the men kept talking, I broke away.

"That's me. Thanks for the help," I said and rushed toward the doors.

10

THE MAN IN THE BLACK SUIT AND RED TIE

UNFORTUNATELY, PE WAS REQUIRED FOR EVERY STUDENT, BUT since I didn't have any real athletic skills, I figured I'd just sit on the bleachers to pass the time. And maybe the teachers would be sympathetic to that and the fact that Dr. Edwards was my grandfather.

But when I arrived, the gym was empty. I glanced at my schedule card to double check; yes, I had gym this period. So where was everybody? I took only a few steps into the quiet, empty gym before a hand came down on my shoulder, startling me. I spun around to meet the round blue eyes of the gym teacher, who just stared rudely.

"You're late," she said, waving for me to hand over my schedule card.

That didn't make sense; the bell just rang, making me fairly early, if anything. The gym teacher looked over my schedule card, then handed it back to me. "I was at the principal's office," I said, but the woman, dressed in a blue and white shirt two sizes too small and tight blue shorts, obviously didn't care for excuses.

"Go to the locker room with the rest of the girls," she

snapped. I tried to smile, even when she didn't in return, and slowly walked towards the locker room door.

"Oh, and Miss Belle," she called after me. When I turned, she placed her hands on her hips, looking intimidating and still very gawky—taller and bigger than most women. "Let this be the last time you're late to my class. Understood?"

There was obviously no sense in arguing with her. I nodded and hurried to the locker room, feeling her eyes on me until I finally ducked inside.

The girls' locker room was a mess of lockers and benches, showers and individual bathroom stalls. The room was covered in a grey, checkered tile stained with years of teenage sweat and adolescent hardship. The walls were filthy and covered in pen and pencil markings, as were the bathroom stalls, inside and out. The lighting inside was poor; bulbs were loose, some were missing, and a few had gone out and not yet been replaced. Only some of them now worked, and even those flickered. It seemed more like a dungeon than a high school.

The other girls were all getting dressed; some already knew the routine and had quickly changed into their gym uniforms. When I found an empty bench beside the lockers, a few girls merely glanced in my direction; no one smiled at me or made eye contact, and if they did, it was followed by roll of the eyes or a grimace of dislike.

But I was accustomed to the stares of others.

I opened an empty locker and pulled out my gym uniform from inside of my school bag. A few girls looked in my direction while I changed, and I didn't need to be able to read minds to feel what they were thinking. I sat there tying my shoes and pulling back my hair, hearing their giggling whispers behind their hands and feeling their glares. My face grew hot, and the few working lights flickered even more intensely. The pipes rattled, and I told myself to calm down and ignore their judgements, stuffing everything into the open locker.

The coach's whistle startled us all, and everyone scattered out of the locker room toward the basketball court. I closed the locker and made to follow them until I heard footsteps across the tiled floor to my right. I glanced around the locker room and caught sight of a dark-suited man walking towards the back.

At that moment, I had no doubt what I saw. I stepped farther back into the locker room, curiosity pulling at me, and glimpsed the edge of a dark suit disappearing behind a swinging door.

I hurried towards the metal door, its glass window reflecting light on water from the other side. Only briefly did I look back to be sure everyone else had left the locker room; I was alone. It wasn't hard to picture the gym teacher's face, hear her voice and that whistle going off again in my head. I should have headed to the gym with the rest of them, but I didn't.

Quickly and silently, I pulled open the door and walked into the pool area. The pool sat only a few feet from the entrance, dark and still. The black water rippled as if a breeze had blown through the room. The scant light was dim, and those few bulbs hardly lit the large, grey room. Some had broken, and shattered glass lay scattered beside the pool, dangerously close to the dark water. I felt a cold breeze touch the back of my neck—almost like a hand, but that was ridiculous. Nevertheless, the thought made me shiver.

I stepped closer to the edge, trying to see the bottom of the pool, but that was surprisingly difficult. There was no visible bottom from where I stood, and I cringed. When I took another step, the water seemed to grow even deeper and darker. In an attempt to make light of my discomfort, I stuck my tongue out at my own hazy reflection, wondering how anyone could swim in that very murky water. It looked disgusting.

"I wonder how long they've gone without cleaning this dump?" I whispered.

I glanced around again, feeling a little better when I did not find the man in the black suit and red tie. Where had he gone? I was the only one here, and there were no other doors besides the one I'd entered. I turned to head back to the locker room, and the building groaned around me, the floors rumbling.

A bucket clanged to the ground and rolled out into the dim lighting; I nearly squeaked in surprise. I slowly backed away, and in the shadows, I caught a glimpse of an unnatural, shadowy figure standing there amidst the darkness, looking at me.

My sudden panic made it impossible to move.

"Hello?" I croaked, realizing how stupid that was given how many times I'd scolded hapless victims in horror films for doing the same thing.

Really? Just run!

The water in the pool stirred; a mass of bubbles gathered, emerging on the surface. Finally, I turned to leave, but the shadow appeared directly in front of me. A scream escaped my mouth, the figure lunged, and I stumbled backwards into the cold water.

Then everything went black.

☀

My body trembled, and a shudder raced up my back and shoulders, raising the hair on my arms. I opened my eyes. Another current vibrated through my body, this time into my hands, and I'd never experienced a sensation quite like it.

Then I sat up, finding myself lying on the cold wet floor, inches from the dark pool. My reflection mocked me from its edge. I pulled away. It was too quiet here; too dreadfully quiet. When I realized I hadn't heard the bell ring in what felt like a really long time, I wondered what exactly had happened.

An eerie ringing echoed all around me, and while I couldn't

place its source, I had the feeling it was meant to warn me of something.

I rose, unable to look away from the dark water of the pool, and a strange dread consumed me. I stumbled away from the ledge and fought to breathe; there was something in there.

The world around me bent, then expanded. The tile floor cracked in front of me. Piece by piece, the tiles fell away into nothing below, finally stopping inches from my feet. I turned the other direction and tried again to head toward the door, but the floor crumbled away again around me. Someone—or something—didn't want me to leave. Swallowing, I glanced once more at the edge of the pool, where some unknown thing called to me.

Unseen hands rippled through the surface of the water, massive bubbles gathering at the center. Time seemed to slow their forming, and I backed away until there was nowhere else to go. Pinned against the back wall, I witnessed a figure slowly emerge from the dark pool.

Locks of blond hair fell neatly from his head. His closed eyes opened, arms extended as he slowly rose before me from the water. He hovered briefly in the air, our eyes met, and a smile curved his lips.

I shivered. It was the man in the black suit.

The figure slowly drifted away from the pool and lowered his arms as he came to stand only a few feet in front of me. Nothing about him seemed natural—a pasty, plastic doll. "You?" I breathed.

He moved toward me, then froze, turning slightly as a bright light streaked between us and engulfed him. It knocked him across the room and through the far wall, which collapsed with a thunderous roar.

I just stared for a moment, unable to process what had happened, until phantom hands reached from the wall to grasp at me. I darted away, screaming. The ghostly hands shriveled back like dried weeds and disappeared.

All around me, the room began to collapse; part of the ceiling crashed down, blocking my path. The water stirred again, and once more, something rose from its depths. It seemed impossible, but I had a feeling the man would return from there, and the thought terrified me.

In a panic, I tried to scramble over the fallen ceiling, desperately searching for an escape. With a splash, another ghostly figure leaped from the dark waters to land on the stained floor in front of me. He gazed down at me, and I shriveled back, too frightened to move. His radiant purple eyes drew me to him, staring deep into my soul.

'*Don't be afraid.*' His lips never moved.

Confusion and fear ran through me, but I was absorbed by his stare and couldn't move. Our gazes remained locked by an unknown force, and through the swirling purple eyes of his, a current connected us—an overwhelming energy flowing from him to me and back again. He was here to protect me.

'*Hurry. He draws near. He will not give up. Take my hand.*' I gazed at him, perplexed. '*Yes,*' his voice hissed in my mind. '*Hurry.*' He extended his hand and smiled.

I slowly reached for his outstretched hand, and he carefully drew me toward him until our bodies pressed together, our faces just inches apart. An overwhelming sense of safety flooded through me, and I felt myself blushing in his arms, absurdly unable to think of anything in these tense circumstances but how much I wanted to kiss him. I tried to speak but could not form any words I understood.

"Who are you?" I finally managed.

The man smiled, his eyes sparkling like rare gems. "You know me..." he whispered.

"I do?"

The words had barely left my mouth before a dark figure

emerged behind us. The man with the violet eyes shoved me away and turned to face the newcomer, who moved impossibly quickly to grip my protector by the throat and lift him off the ground. The neatly tailored black suit and red tie were the only things visible in the darkness.

My rescuer clutched at the hands around his neck, fighting to escape.

"Stop!" I cried. "Leave him alone." I grabbed a nearby chunk of fallen ceiling and tossed it at the dark figure. A growl escaped its unseen lips, and I cowered away again. The dark figure's mouth opened and grew wide, his hold hardened tightening on my still-struggling rescuer. Billowing appendages like tentacles emerged from the wide opening of his mouth. I panicked when they reached toward my rescuer's face.

"Stop. No!" I yelled again, hoping for a distraction.

At once, my rescuer raised his open palm toward the dark figure, and the sickening, waving appendages slowly pulled back into the gaping hole. The figure's mouth shrank to a normal-looking line upon his face. He turned his head and suddenly released the stranger who had come to save me.

My rescuer dropped to the floor and onto his knees, gripping his own hand. Had he been hurt? I didn't understand what had happened but soon found the dark figure's gaze upon me once more. Then it stepped slowly backwards and faded into the darkness.

The new stranger rose and approached me, where he knelt again at my side; a sweet concern consumed his strangely pale, diamond-shaped face. His strong jaw and dark, matted locks contrasted even more with such a pallid complexion. I found myself drawn powerfully to him once again. What was happening? Who was he? Why did I feel so connected to him? His large, strange purple eyes regarded me with curiosity. I felt like he needed me.

Then he smiled, as if I'd spoken these questions out loud.

His concerned frown softened, gentling into a surprising innocence, like a beast tamed by the guidance of the richest nectar.

He reached out his hand—something I sensed he had
longed to do. Then he leaned forward, drawing closer until he
nearly fell upon me, pressing his lips against my own without
warning. Startled, I made no attempt to pull away, and his hand
aggressively pressed the back of my head towards his soft,
gentle mouth. I collapsed into the warmth of his delicate kiss,
breathing in a deep taste of him.

Under his spell, an image of my grandfather entered my
mind. He sank deeper into the darkness of the pool, trying to
reach out but sinking all the faster for how desperately he
fought. I tried to grasp a hold of him, but I couldn't quite touch
his outstretched hand.

Our fingers came close briefly before he slipped from my
grasp. Then a hand grabbed my arm and pulled me out of the
darkness in which I was losing my grandfather. He sank until I
no longer saw him—until the darkness consumed him.

As the stranger holding me pushed me back, I opened my
eyes and stared deep into his, trying to enter his mind. But I
only found a mixture of images I couldn't make sense of,
feeling suddenly dizzy. The nausea overwhelmed me, a rising
pressure building in my stomach, and I choked. An unexpected
surge of water poured from my mouth. The new stranger
watched in passive patience as I fought the urge again, but my
stomach lurched, making me gag.

Instead of vomiting again, I collapsed to the floor, coughing
violently until another rush of water left my body and spilled
across the floor. Then I thought I understood; I had drowned.
And this beautiful protector with the purple eyes had brought
me back.

11

THE END IS ALWAYS THE BEGINNING

WHEN I AWOKE, I LAY ON AN UNCOMFORTABLE COT, THE SPRINGS digging into my upper back. I looked around and realized I was in the nurse's office. Mr. McClellan, the man I had briefly met the day I'd met my grandfather, sat beside the bed. Mr. Claypool and Mr. Vasquez stood nearby. All three watched me, eyes wide with worry and concern, and only moved when they realized I was awake.

Their presence made me uncomfortable, but I could only think of the stranger who had come to my rescue. How had I gotten here? What had I really seen? And if it had been real, where was he now?

Doubts stirred in me; could it have all been a dream? I didn't want that to be the truth. In fact, I wanted to run back to the pool and see for myself, but as soon as I tried to move, Mr. McClellan stopped me with a gentle hand on my shoulder.

"Lie still," he said.

I wanted to argue but, still dizzy, I dropped back onto the uncomfortable cot. My stomach swirled like I'd eaten bad fish. "What happened?" I asked. "How did I get here?"

"You don't remember?" Mr. McClellan asked. I barely

blinked up at any of them. "The students in your P.E. class found you passed out in the locker room."

I immediately sat up again, remembering the stranger's eyes looking at me from that pale face, the struggle with the menacing shadow that had been the man in the black suit all along, emerging from the depths of the pool before my rescuer had come between us.

He had saved me from something horrible—that much I knew—but what puzzled me was how I knew this to be completely true. Somehow, I realized, I knew because *he* knew. Because my rescuer understood these things, and that puzzled me even more. I had been drawn to him without thinking, without any understanding of my need for him, urging me to go to him—like a hunger I couldn't satisfy.

I looked back at all three men and realized my grandfather hadn't come. It made sense that he would be explaining my actions to the P.E. teacher right now, giving her the grieving news of my loss and using it as an excuse for how I acted. If he wanted to talk, I was prepared; I couldn't avoid it any longer. And I only had more questions for him now.

"Passed out?" I asked, still unable to grasp the timeline they'd presented. "That's not right. I was in the pool area. I know I shouldn't have, but..." I hesitated, debating whether or not I actually wanted to tell them what I'd seen. "Where's my grandfather? I need to speak to him."

Mr. McClellan slowly lowered his head.

"Claudia, honey," Mr. Claypool whispered, stepping toward the side of the cot. Mr. McClellan put a hand out to stop him.

"What?" I glared at them. "*What*? Tell me!" They didn't have to say anything for me to read the pain behind their dark frowns, the wariness of saying it out loud that made them look anywhere but at me. I didn't want to believe it, but I felt it. And when I peeked into their minds, I saw it there, too.

"I'm so sorry, Claudia," Mr. McClellan said. "Your grandfather has... passed away."

My stomach lurched. "What?"

"He suffered a heart attack four hours ago. The paramedics tried to revive him, but he was already gone. There was nothing they could do. I'm sorry. I'm so sorry."

I scrambled from the cot and raced out the door. I heard them rush behind me as I ran out into the hallway, finding it quite empty. Unnerved by the silence, I rushed through the gym and straight into the girl's locker room, stumbling through the maze of lockers and writing-covered walls. The assistant principals clumsily stumbled behind me, calling my name, but their voices made me more determined to prove to myself what I'd seen.

I froze at the back of the locker room, trembling and fearing what I would find on the other side. But instead of the swinging door I'd entered the last time, only a solid wall greeted me now. I must have taken a wrong turn, so I doubled back but found lockers instead and no door to the pool area. I stopped only when the three men were standing right in front of me, catching their breaths.

"Where is it?" I asked. They glanced at one another. "The pool! Where is it? That's where I saw him."

I couldn't make sense of anything else, because I couldn't remember what had happened after my rescuer had kissed me.

The administrators stared at me as if I had gone mad. "Claudia, what are you talking about?" Mr. McClellan replied.

"The pool in the girl's locker room. That's where I saw him. A man in a black suit and red tie. It has to be him! He did this. He's responsible. He's... *he's Death!*"

They exchanged glances again, warily eying me as if something had crawled from my ears.

"You don't believe me?" I snapped. "I'm not crazy! Where is

it? It was here. I saw it!" I yelled so loudly, the lights flickered overhead.

"Claudia, honey, there is no pool. Milton has never had a pool," Mr. McClellan calmly said.

"That's not true. You're lying. I saw it here. It was right there! There was a door and a glass window. And right behind it was a pool, a large dark pool, and that's where he went. I saw him!"

"Saw who?" Mr. McClellan asked. The wrinkles on his face softened. He was tall but also gentle, a soft-spoken man with widened, droopy, clear blue eyes. His hair was completely white, yet his eyebrows remained dark.

"A man in a black suit and red tie," I replied, fighting to calm myself again. "I saw him going into the locker room. I saw him before in the girl's restroom, too. He's after me. I know it. He's the one who did this!" The panic in my voice was real; I hadn't realized until I heard my own terror just how crazy it all sounded.

In that moment, I recalled the image of the hooded skull that had appeared on the restroom mirror the first time I saw the man in the black suit. That vision alone startled me so much, I couldn't speak until my rescuer's face resurfaced in my mind.

Mr. McClellan remained silent, glancing again at Mr. Claypool and Mr. Vasquez as if asking for their support. I knew they thought I was crazy. But the more I thought about it and tried to remember, the more I knew I hadn't dreamed it.

I moved to leave. "My grandfather would know what to do. He'd believe me!" I yelled.

Mr. McClellan grabbed my shoulders and turned me to face him. "Claudia, did you not hear me? He's gone. Neil is gone." He spoke gently enough, but I could only glare into his deep blue eyes in disbelief.

Then I dropped to my knees without meaning to; Mr.

McClellan caught me and gently eased me to the floor with me in his arms.

I couldn't make sense of it, and when I cried, I wasn't sure who the tears were for. But something inside me had broken free, something I couldn't control. I sobbed, recalling my rescuer's beautiful face, his sweet scent, and the masculine warmth and protective arms holding me in those few moments. I longed for them now.

We were connected in some strange, beautiful way I couldn't understand. I loved the idea. The more I thought about it, the more I wanted to know him.—And the more I wanted to understand it, the more I cried.

I wrapped my arms around Mr. McClellan, weeping, ashamed of the weakness I was showing. I hadn't been given the chance to cry for my parents. Now, I just couldn't stop. Everything I had felt after hearing of their deaths exploded from within me. I wanted to believe I was strong. But the honest truth was I felt helpless, a victim of my own endless emotions.

Mr. Claypool and Mr. Vasquez huddled around us. Somehow, I knew in that moment that it would always be like this.

12

MICHAEL MCCLELLAN

MICHAEL ARRIVED AT THE OFFICE BUILDING EARLY; THE secretary wasn't at her desk when he entered the attorney's office, but he noticed Mr. West's door ajar. He heard the man's voice coming from inside the office, so he approached, knocked, and entered, catching Mr. West by surprise.

The attorney was on a phone call, and as quickly as he caught sight of Michael, he dismissed the other party on the line and immediately hung up. Michael considered it a sign of respect, feeling warmth and assurance when Mr. West rose from behind his desk and stepped around it to greet him. Then he walked Michael toward one of the chair's meant for clients and visitors.

"Ah, Michael McClellan. Very nice to finally meet you in person." He shook Michael's hand firmly.

"I'm sorry. I hope that wasn't an important call. I got here early, and I didn't see your secretary," Michael politely said.

"No, no. Come right in. Have a seat. I have the paperwork all ready for you."

Michael took a seat in front of the attorney's desk as Mr. West made his way back to his own comfortable office chair.

"It's unfortunate we have to meet under such dreadful circumstances," Mr. West said, "but it's best we get this out of the way. Neil would have wanted it this way."

Michael agreed, though Mr. West's words sounded slightly arrogant and almost rehearsed, like an adult talking to a little boy who had just fallen off his bike, reassuring him everything was for his own good. He recalled it had been Mr. West who had delivered the horrible news to Claudia about her parents' deaths and her going to live with Dr. Edwards.

"By the way, how is Claudia?" Mr. West asked, leaning forward.

"She's doing better. She had a nasty gash on the back of the head. Must have been from the fall," Michael softly said, recalling the events of that day. They had only noticed it after they'd returned to the nurse's office. The pillow she had been lying on was spotted with blood. It hadn't been bad, but it was bad enough to concern him.

After the news of Neil's death had spread to reach the staff earlier that day, the school had let out early; it had been so quiet. The silence sometimes frightened him when he was working alone, and that day had been no different. The building was especially eerie after what had happened and even more disturbing now that Claudia had insisted she'd seen something.

But how was she supposed to act after such news of her grandfather's death? She seemed to have anticipated it already. He hadn't known himself until the paramedics were called, and he'd never had a need for a radio before, but Neil had handed him one that very morning.

Could Neil Edwards have perhaps sensed the imminent danger? His friend's gift had a knack for providing insights into certain otherwise unknowable things. Michael wondered if Claudia possessed the same power. Perhaps that would explain how she'd been aware of her grandfather's death before he'd told her, even if her mind had created an alternative reality to explain it all.

"It's no surprise she fainted when she heard the news. I can't imagine anything else."

"Perhaps," Michael said; a long sigh left his lips.

"And the man she claims she saw?" Mr. West asked.

"The nurse said she bumped her head pretty hard on the floor. She must have thought she saw somebody," Michael answered, scooting forward on his chair.

"Do you believe her?" Mr. West appeared foolishly concerned.

Michael found it hardly convincing. "I don't know what to believe. I just know I have a very young girl who's lost her grandfather, and I'm not sure where to begin."

"The mind can play tricks on oneself, especially after a dramatic episode." The attorney chuckled softly. "But I'm no expert on the ways of the human mind. What I can help you with is the legal part of this whole dilemma." Mr. West pulled a few documents from a folder, turned them around, and set them on the desk so Michael could read them. "Before he died, Neil asked me to revise his will, leaving you with custody of his granddaughter and guardianship of his assets to be distributed for her care until she turns eighteen."

"What do you need from me?" Michael asked.

"Nothing. The paperwork has been drawn up already. All I need is a signature proving you received it," Mr. West said, handing Michael a pen and pointing to the areas where Michael's signature was required.

Michael signed a few spots and initialed the rest. When he was finished, Mr. West grabbed the pen from his hand.

"Great. I'll have my secretary get you a copy and send it via email. There is one more thing," he said as he gathered the documents from the table and placed them back into the folder.

"What's that?" Michael asked.

"It's nothing major. Just a side note."

Michael glared at him. He hadn't known Mr. West for very long; he had been Neil's attorney for many years, and Michael had no reason not to trust him. But Mr. West's arrogance sometimes disturbed him.

"In the event that a next of kin is found, there may be reasons to contest the will."

"What? She doesn't have any next of kin. Her parents are dead. As far as I know, Neil was her only living relative."

"Then you have nothing to worry about. It was just a minor note that had to be mentioned," the attorney said with a smile as he returned the folder to his briefcase.

"Regarding Neil's property..." Michael began.

"It's all in the paperwork my secretary will email you. Read through it carefully, and if you have questions then, call me. Now, if there's nothing else, I have another appointment."

Michael nodded, stood, and stumbled toward the door. He figured he could move into Neil's house—a much better space than his tiny, one-bedroom apartment, which was no place for a growing teenage girl.

The attorney's words echoed in his mind. He couldn't understand why Neil would have added such a note to his will. Had he already had his doubts about being Claudia's only remaining living relative? Perhaps his friend had simply neglected to warn Michael of such a possibility.

The more he thought about it, the more he doubted his longtime friend would have believed anyone related to Claudia was still alive. But it was in the will, so the doubt lingered. After all, Neil *had* revised the will. And just what would anyone contest in her present living conditions? Who would Claudia live with? Wouldn't that be her choice? She was seventeen, and he thought that quite old enough to make this kind of decision for herself. Forcing her to wait another year really wouldn't do anything.

Michael glanced back. He meant to ask such a question, but Mr. West was already on another call, and as their eyes met again and Michael opened his mouth to speak, Mr. West motioned him out the door.

With that, Michael walked out.

Outside the office door, he took a deep breath and made his way through the lobby, out of the building, and towards the parking lot. The only remaining issue to resolve was the question of who they would place as Milton's new principal. He'd been appointed the acting principal—a dream he'd hoped one day would become a reality—but he'd already gotten word from the district that a more suitable replacement was on his way.

Michael wondered who had taken the difficult task of replacing such a great man. Whoever it was could not hold a candle to Dr. Edwards. The entire staff and faculty waited on pins and needles, literally worried sick as they wondered who would be brought in to manage a school that was already coming apart wall by wall—and now one faculty member at a time. Who could possibly meet that responsibility?

13

GOODBYE

THE FUNERAL FELL ON A WEEKEND, HELD AT A CHURCH IN THE Museum District. He was buried on a bright and sunny Saturday in the last week of March. I couldn't help but wonder why it had to be such a beautiful day for something like this.

Everyone was there—faculty, school staff, friends, students, and a lot of people I didn't know. Then Mr. McClellan took the podium. I watched him from my place between Mr. Vasquez and Mr. Claypool. He cleared his throat; it was already difficult for him, and he hadn't even opened his mouth yet. The paper he held shook in his hands. He looked down, then back up at the large, silent, crowded church and the many faces staring back at him and the podium. He then found me, met my gaze, and smiled. I hoped my presence gave him the strength to begin.

"What can I say about Neil that hasn't already been said?" Michael began with a shaking voice. He stopped and took a deep breath. "Neil was a man who loved life. He was a man who put everyone else's needs before his own. He was a kind and good friend. Those of you who knew him knew of his kindness, his warmth, his generosity, and his great devotion to help those less fortunate. He gave and never asked for anything in return, even though he was hurting inside and hiding a great amount of his own pain. But he never let that change him, never let it stop him from being who he was to all of us. We shared in his happiness and kindness. Even in his wondrous joy when his granddaughter came to live with him. I don't think I have ever seen him as happy as he was the day he heard that news. It had always given him purpose to know that, out there, there was still a part of him in the world. Claudia," he said, glancing at me once again, "you were the best part of his life, even though he only knew you for a short portion of it. You were his everything." A few murmurs filled the church.

The eulogy was beautiful, emotionally overwhelming, and draining as I sat there. I couldn't help but weep, filled with guilt as his words echoed around us. Why had I turned my grandfather away? Why hadn't I listened to him when he tried to talk to me? Why did I have to be so stubborn? Again, I blame my father for that trait.

The ceremony ended with a drive to the burial at the cemetery. A few more now joined those from the church; close friends and family lingered around the casket surrounded by flowers and funeral wreaths.

I sat by Mr. McClellan as the priest read from a black book and said a few words. Tears were shed. I wanted it to end.

Mr. McClellan put a hand on my shoulder when the casket was lowered into the ground, and then I lost myself. I grabbed a hold of Mr. McClellan and held onto him as if he were the only thing keeping me alive too. I was alone again, left first by my parents and now my grandfather.

Mr. McClellan returned me to my grandfather's house afterward. The ride home was quiet, even as we walked up the steps to my grandfather's humble porch. Even when we stood in front of the open front door and I thought Mr. McClellan would say something, I didn't give him a chance. Instead, rushed up the stairs, partly expecting him to come after me. He didn't. I caught a glance of him rooted at the bottom of the staircase, looking up after me, before I slammed the bedroom door.

I collapsed on the bed and looked around at the antique furniture. How I'd hated the style when I'd first come to live with him. And now, I couldn't help but remember everything I'd ever said or thought about him and his home. I didn't want anything to change. Anger made me stand again and grab at the posters I'd hung on my wall to rip them down. I took the jewelry box from the dresser, then shoved it into the drawer of the nightstand. Somehow, that just didn't feel right, so I pulled it out again and placed it on the table where it belonged.

I sat on the bed again and opened the nightstand drawer to take out the picture of my parents and me. This was the last picture we ever took together and the last of them I'd ever have with me. Remembering that fact on top of the realization that I'd just buried my grandfather—my only living family—I stared at the picture of when I had family and sobbed.

I must have fallen asleep. When I woke up, the posters scattered across the floor and the jarring picture of my parents made it seem like someone else had been in my room and trashed it instead of me. I sat up on the bed and stared at the walls.

The house felt eerily silent. I wondered then if Mr. McClellan had left me alone and what, if anything, would happen to my grandfather's house now. I hadn't given it much thought, but it concerned me. Would I even have a say in what happened next to what had become my home? If Grandfather had left it to me, I wanted to stay. I'd do anything I could to make that happen.

When I finally stood, I walked toward my bedroom door and listened. I heard the tiny murmur of a man's voice coming from downstairs; Mr. McClellan must have stayed. Slowly, I opened my bedroom door and noticed the door to my grandfather's room was ajar. Without looking inside, I walked down the hall, closed his bedroom door, and headed down the stairs.

Mr. McClellan stood in the kitchen, talking on the phone about some kind of arrangements for a moving truck. It hit me that this meant I was moving—again—but I couldn't just pick up and leave the only ties I had left to any kind of family. Not now.

When he hung up, I rushed into the kitchen. "I won't let you sell my grandfather's house," I told him. He raised his eyebrows, looking surprised to see me. "This is all I have left of him. You can't sell it!" My voice trembled with anger.

He shook his head. The pots hanging above the kitchen counter rattled for a minute, then a few dropped from their hooks and clattered across the kitchen. Mr. McClellan stepped toward me and grabbed me by the shoulders. "Claudia!" he yelled. "Listen." I gazed up at him, the furious tears already racing down my cheeks. I bit my lip so hard, I tasted blood. "Listen to me. I'm not selling your grandfather's house."

For a minute, I didn't know what he'd said. But when it sank in, the anger eased in me, and I studied him through my own tear-blurred vision.

"I would never do that," he added. "Neil left this place for you. This house is yours. It's what he wanted."

"Then why did you call for a moving truck? Why are we moving? Why are we leaving?"

He frowned in hesitation, and I realized I had it backwards. "You're moving in. Into my grandfather's house. With me." It came out as almost a whisper.

He nodded. "I thought it would be easier that way. This is your home, and it's the right thing to do. You're only a minor for a little bit longer. I figured I'd pack some things, stay here with you as a guardian, and keep the rest of my stuff in storage until I decide what to do next..." An awkward silence hung between us, then he let go of my shoulders and walked out of the kitchen into the foyer. Taking his keys from the table by the door, he turned back to me and added, "The movers should be at my apartment in a few minutes."

"Can I just stay here while you're out? I'd rather not go anywhere."

He opened his mouth, paused, and apparently held back from any objection. I saw a need in him to please, to be accepted by me by any means necessary. Mr. McClellan just nodded instead and opened the door. "I won't be gone long. Keep the door locked." I think he tried to be firm, but he only reminded me of a gentle bunny. "I have my phone on me. If you need me, please call." Then he stepped out and left me alone.

I almost regretted staying behind when I took a moment to look around my grandfather's old, empty house. In that moment, it just felt too big. So I ran up the stairs and into my room, dropping onto the bed once again. I just wanted this to end. I wanted to think of something else, but the pain inside me wouldn't allow it. The guilt, if nothing else, was eating me alive.

The guilt came from me knowing I should have listened to him the first time. It rose from not having nearly enough time with him and spending most of it sulking alone in my room. Now the only person who understood me was gone forever.

I was exhausted, but when I closed my eyes and tried to think of something else, the tears still wouldn't stop. But even when I finally slipped off to sleep, I dreamed of my grandfather.

He stood there in his office, smiling one moment, then falling to the floor, grabbing at his heart. As his body lay on the ground, a crystal rolled from within his limp fingers and out onto the ground. It just rested there until a pale, bony hand reached down and plucked the crystal from the floor. The man in the black suit and red tie straightened over my grandfather and clutched his prize.

"Grandfather!" The word slipped through my lips, and the man in the black suit whipped around to face me.

He pointed a thin finger at me, just like the first time we'd met. "You. I've been searching for you," he said. "You're the answer. *Come to me.*"

He lunged at me across the floor, and I screamed.

Then I shot up in bed and realized it for the awful dream it was. I couldn't make sense of it, and I didn't want to, anyways. Muffled voices rose up from outside, and I went to the window to look down at the front yard. Men in overalls lifted boxes out of a large truck and carried them toward the house, disappearing under me as they stepped through the front door.

Mr. McClellan stood beside the truck, telling the men where to put his things. Of course, he didn't look up at my window to see me gazing down at them. Still so tired, I climbed back up onto my bed and rolled to the side to stare at the picture of my parents and me.

Things were going to change—again. Nothing had ever been normal for me, even when my parents were alive. But at least I had something in common with my father, and I still always felt safe. Now, I had no idea what my future looked like, even though I did actually trust Mr. McClellan. My grandfather had trusted him enough to leave me in his care, and I didn't doubt Mr. McClellan was a kindhearted man.

We must have said only two words the first two days he was there. I spent most of my time in my room. I could tell he didn't want to bother me, and sometimes he left my dinner on the hallway table outside my door. Only after the fourth day did I actually decide to come downstairs and join him. He was loading the dishwasher when he turned to see me standing by the kitchen table.

"Claudia." He offered a nervous smile. "Are you hungry?

Can... can I get you something?" The dishes in his hands clanked together before he remembered what he'd been doing.

"No, I'm fine," I muttered.

He put the plates into the dishwasher and closed it, leaving a few dishes untouched in the sink. Then he approached the table as I took a seat. "I can get you something. I'm sorry. I forgot what time it was." He put a hand to his head for a minute, then looked back up at me. "I hope this is all right." I just stared at him and his sad eyes. "I mean me being here. It's what your grandfather wanted. I don't know what he was thinking when he chose me." A smile spread over his lips, then he looked back at me, and the smile faded. "Not that I don't want to be here, you understand," he added. "But me? Well, I don't know what I'm doing." He gripped the back of the chair in front of him. "And I don't want you to feel like I'm forcing you into this. If it's not what you want, I'm sure something else could be arranged." He took a deep breath, his eyes drooping, and glanced at the table. "If this isn't what you want." Slowly, he sank into the chair.

"If my grandfather wanted you to be my guardian, Mr. McClellan," I said gently, "then I want it too."

He nodded with a weak smile and said, "Okay. Okay." After a few seconds, he pushed the chair back from the table and stood. "I made enchiladas," he added, sounding quite proud of it.

That made me smile. "You cook?"

"Yeah." He grinned but looked away in embarrassment. "Your grandfather never complained. He was one of my biggest fans." He chuckled, and I realized right then how much he must have missed my grandfather, too. Then he blinked, seemed to remember who he was talking to, and went back to the sink. "Would you like some?" he asked without turning.

"Sure."

He moved quickly, seeming to really know his way around

my grandfather's kitchen. When he set the plate down in front of me, there were tears in his eyes, and he didn't meet my gaze. "They're really good. But I'm not just saying that because…" He drifted off, gave a small smile, and went to wipe down the stove.

He stumbled a little as he bumped into the countertop's corners, hitting his head on the top of the cabinet when he reached for the cleaner under the sink. Watching him, I realized I didn't actually know him at all. I didn't know any of the people in my new life, but now, I found that was something I wanted to do. I'd been too self-absorbed in my own tragedy, I hadn't given anyone a chance.

"You guys were good friends?" We were both aware that I already knew they were close, but I was starting conversation.

"Yes," he said, turning toward me from the stove. "We were very good friends," he said, finally looking up at me. Then he frowned.

"I'm sorry," I said. "I didn't mean to make this painful."

His teary eyes widened with guilt. "Oh, no," he said. "Don't be." Then he returned to the table and sat again.

I put down my fork, my lips quivering. "He wanted to talk to me," I told him, "and I should have listened the first time. I treated him so badly when we met. I'm sorry," I whispered, trying to swallow my grief. But the tears came anyways.

"You couldn't have known," Mr. McClellan said.

"I wish we'd had more time. He wanted to tell me something, and he was so excited about it. I should have listened. I should have—" I couldn't hold back the tears any longer.

Mr. McClellan pulled his chair closer to mine and leaned toward me. "How could you have known? You can't blame yourself."

"I can't help feeling like it was really important. Now it's too late."

"Claudia, you can't feel this way. He wouldn't have wanted

you to feel this way." Mr. McClellan moved his chair so it nearly touched mine, then brushed the hair away from my face.

I dropped my forehead against his chest and let out a long sigh. But it wasn't enough; the tears came again, and I wept, gripping Mr. McClellan tightly. When I finally calmed down, I whispered, "He was all I had, and now he's gone."

Mr. McClellan embraced me fully for a short, tight hug, then pulled me away from him and tucked my hair behind my ear. "You have me," he said. "I made a promise to your grandfather that I would protect you no matter what, and I intend to keep it." I nodded, sniffed, and wiped my eyes. "Now," he said, clearing his throat, "enough of that Mister stuff, okay?" He swallowed audibly, released me, and smiled as he furiously blinked his own tears from his eyes. "We don't have to talk about it anymore. Not if you don't want to."

"Michael," I whispered, unsure of what his promise to my grandfather really entailed. His words rang with uncertainty. "Protect me from what?"

He blinked at me, as if the question startled him, and sat back in his chair. It took him a moment to gather his thoughts, and I got the feeling he'd never told anyone else what he was about to share with me.

"Your grandfather tried to face certain fears of his, but he just couldn't battle them. You know, he lost his mother when he was very young." I shook my head. My grandfather had hidden that kind of sorrow very well.

"Afterward, Neil found himself wandering the streets alone, not knowing who he was or what had happened. Little by little," he said, lifting a crystal from his pocket, "it eventually came back to him. This crystal was the only thing he had in his possession, and it helped him remember what had happened."

"What?"

He held his open palm toward me in invitation, and I gingerly picked up the crystal. It looked like a normal piece of glass, but when I touched it, the sensation was electrifying. It felt like the thing was drawing from me, connecting and linking to me in some strange way. I dropped the crystal into his palm again and pulled my hand back.

Michael didn't respond to my surprise. "A creature abducted his mother," he answered with a frown. It seemed he didn't know exactly what, only that he repeated to me now the things my grandfather had told him. "When all his memories returned, he tried to go back for her."

"Where was she?"

"The thing that took his mother could travel through certain doorways into our world and back." He glanced down at the crystal. "This stone also serves as a doorway into another world." After turning the crystal over in his hand, he returned it to his pocket.

The whole story had taken on a rather Sci-Fi kind of feel, but I wanted to believe it. I sensed Michael trusted my grandfather enough to believe it, too.

"Needless to say," he continued, "your grandfather never gave up hope that one day he would find the right key to open this doorway again. But it didn't stop him from having a life. Getting married. Having children." He tried to smile, but it only looked painful now. "He wanted to tell you all this... before. But of course..."

I had to hear more now. This story made me feel more connected to my grandfather then I had in those few short days we'd spent together—the loneliness he must have felt, isolated in this world without his mother.

"Your grandfather always thought he couldn't have children. That relieved him, because he was afraid to bring someone with the same gift into this world." I leaned toward him, eyes wide. "When your grandmother was unexpectedly pregnant with your father, Neil's old fear returned. But before your father was born, I watched that fear give way to accepting he would be a father. It was actually the happiest I'd ever seen him. It brought him a new hope that maybe things would be different." He paused to let out a heavy sigh.

"What happened?" I prompted. Maybe I'd find out why my grandfather and my father hadn't spoken in years—find out what had separated them.

"Martha, your grandmother, died giving birth. Your grandfather was never the same after that." I looked down at the table, where Michael had put both his hands, and I took his hand for a quick, gentle squeeze. He gazed up at me and smiled. "After that, your grandfather grew far more fearful and distant. A strong paranoia took ahold of him in a way I'd never seen. He thought he was being watched, followed. That something evil stalked him."

I blinked. I wanted to say, 'He wasn't paranoid,' but I didn't.

"He felt he had only one option when it came to his son. He truly thought it was the right thing to do when he gave your father up for adoption. Neil said it was to protect your father from the evil he feared was coming for him."

"What?" I said a little more harshly than I meant it. "That doesn't make any sense. That can't be the reason why."

"I'm sorry, my dear. That's all your grandfather ever said. He loved that boy with all his heart, and I never understood either how he could make such a drastic decision. I tried to talk him out of it, but he was determined it was the only way to protect his son."

Something had to have really spooked my grandfather. He and I were the same; could he have seen something like I had the day he died? While definitely not what I'd expected, the rift between him and my father made just a little more sense now, too. But my grandfather must have known something else and not told Michael.

"I'm sorry if I frightened you," Michael added. "I just felt... well, that this is something your grandfather would have told you himself. Now that he's gone... I felt you deserved to know the truth about the man."

"Thank you." I nodded. "Thank you for telling me." This couldn't have been an easy story for him to tell.

"I wish there was more I could tell you about him, but that's all he ever told me about his past. He was quite a lonely person. He missed his family. When you came into his life, you brought that same magic back with you. He was his old self again, if just for a little while. You give him hope..."

14

MILTON HIGH IN MOURNING

Bright and early Monday morning, Michael's black Honda SUV pulled up into the empty space in the teacher's parking lot. He turned off the engine, and I just sat there, looking straight ahead. Neither of us spoke for a while, but then he turned toward me just a little.

I had missed a week of school after my grandfather's funeral, and now I wondered if I was even ready to face the countless whispers and sympathetic stares of so many strangers.

"You don't have to do this now," Michael said very softly. I looked at him; he was genuinely worried about me. And right now, I knew he would do and say anything if it helped me at all.

"I know, but things aren't going to change." I smiled back. "I have to come to terms with that."

"Claudia—"

"I'm all right, okay?" I stared back at him, forcing that smile to stay on my lips.

He nodded with a frown, then said, "But if for any reason you feel—"

"Michael." I put a hand on his shoulder to get him to stop.

He looked down at my hand, then smiled. "Very well," he whispered and took a deep breath. "I'm still assisting with principal duties, so if you ever need me, chances are I'll be in the main office. Ms. Witherson is our new English teacher. I moved you into her class. I hope that's okay. The other English teachers have way too many students…"

"It's okay," I said again. "I can take care of my classes. Please stop worrying."

"Sorry. All of this is so new to me too." He glanced out the windshield at Milton's entrance set in the stone building. The school buses started up in the parking lot, pulling out one at a time in a long yellow line to start picking up the students. "I don't want to fail you," he said, turning toward me again.

"You're not." I appreciated all the attention he gave me—the concern in great abundance—but it was also a little too much. I couldn't blame the kindhearted man with only the best intentions, so I just tried to reassure him instead.

"I'll have a radio on me, just in case," he said, looking both tired and overwhelmed. He shifted uneasily, holding his shaking hands, at one point forgetting to turn off the car and grab his keys. His nerves had gotten to him, but I didn't know if it was from taking over as principal or from caring for me—or both. Michael had earned the right to assist as replacement until the new principal showed up in the next few days. He'd done a great job so far, but I was still a little tender about anything regarding my grandfather; I didn't know if I could even enter his office without breaking down. I didn't want to find out.

We got out of the car and made our way across the gravel parking lot and into the building. Michael held the door for me, and once we stepped into the hall, the place seemed like a totally different building—darker and colder, like the life had been sucked right out of it. I liked to think my grandfather's absence had a bit part to play in that.

At the end of the hall was the main office on the left and the library on the right. Through the windows in the library doors, I felt the abundance of literature calling to me despite the darkness there and the locked doors.

Michael unlocked the office, then turned to me before he opened the door. "I know we're here really early. I just have a lot of work to do." He frowned and tried to smile, but it only made him look a little nauseous.

"I know," I said. "Don't worry about me."

"It's kind of my job now," he said. "To worry. I know you don't want to wait in here," he said, nodding toward the main office and where my grandfather used to spend his days. Then he reached into his pocket and took out a pair of keys. "Ms. Witherson won't be in for another few minutes," he said, handing me the keyring, "but I'm sure she won't mind if you sit in the classroom and wait for her. It's a master key." I took the keys and nodded. "Room 205. Do you need help finding it?"

"Nope," I said. Apparently, I didn't hide my irritation as well as I'd hoped.

Michael rubbed the back of his neck and said, "Sorry. I know. You'll be fine. I'll just be in here."

I nodded and walked away before he opened the door and I accidentally glanced inside the main office. Across from the library was the dark stairwell in the corner leading up to the second floor. As I climbed it, the sun was just beginning to come up now, filling the empty hallways with new life. I moved down the eerily empty hall toward 205, then saw the door propped wide open and the light on inside.

Apparently, she was already here.

For a minute, I thought about going back downstairs and telling Michael she'd gotten to school before us, but I didn't want to bother right away; he needed some time alone. If Ms. Witherson let me stay, I might as well use the extra time here this morning to make up all the work I'd missed before and after my grandfather's funeral.

When I stopped in front of the open door, I found her writing an assignment on the chalkboard. She stopped, glanced at me, and an instant blast of dislike shot from her mind straight into mine.

She was a slender, brown-haired woman, probably in her thirties, dressed in a tacky pastel-pink blouse and black slacks. She'd never been married and was still slightly bitter because of it, having watched all her other friends get married while she stayed a bridesmaid.

God, I hated being able to see all that inside her head just from a glance, but she was apparently one of those people who were *so* easy to read. It was more of a challenge *not* to look at what was there.

She stopped writing and directed her attention toward me, her mind nearly screaming that she wanted to make the best first impression with me for the sole reason of getting ahead among the faculty.

"Ms. Witherson?" I called anyways, stepping into the class.

"Yes." She forced a smile, tossed her head back and spoke in a musically lilting voice. "You must be Claudia Belle. Michael has told me so much about you."

I knew instantly she was lying. The vibrations of a person's voice and how much their tone varied in range always revealed a lot to me about what they really meant. More than anything, though, her innermost thoughts were as clear as day.

'*Spoiled little rich girl.*'

Why did she hate me? It really was this simple for her; I was a child of privilege and had inherited everything from my parents when they died. And then from my grandfather. The fact that I'd only gained such a fortune by losing the only people I loved had never even crossed her mind.

"Michael said it would be all right if I waited in here until class starts," I said. "I honestly didn't think anyone was here yet. I don't think he did, either."

Her eyes grew wide and incredibly round, then she laughed softly—a very fake, childless laugh, phony as the smile she flashed me. "Of course, there would be someone here. I take my work very seriously. You make sure you tell him that."

"Sure. Since you're here, though, I don't want to bother you." Really, I didn't want to have to listen to her think about all the reasons she hated me. "Would it be all right if I spend some time making up my work?" I asked.

"Of course!" she answered immediately with a blinding smile.

"In the library?"

Her thoughts bombarded me like she'd shot them out of a gun. *'What's wrong with my classroom? Is it not up to your expectations, rich girl? Why is everyone so worried about you? At least I don't have to keep looking at that perfect little face.'*

"Oh," she said sweetly, but her nostrils flared. "Sure."

I nodded and turned to leave, feeling the hair on my arms rise under her mental assault.

"Miss Belle," she called. I stopped halfway out the door and turned around slowly. She stepped around her desk to approach me. "I'm so sorry to hear about your parents and your grandfather. Dr. Edwards was the kindest and most generous man I've ever known. I can't imagine what you're going through. If you ever need a friend or just someone to talk to, I'd like you to consider coming to me. Remember that, okay?"

For a minute, I thought I might have been wrong about her. But then whatever wall she'd put up around her thoughts to make such a convincingly genuine offer burst like a damn. *'Your grandfather was nothing but a crazy old man. I say good riddance.'*

I angrily rushed through the doorway and into the hall, where the lights flickered in response. Furious, I pictured her large metal bookcase and swiped my hand across the open air in front of me. From inside Ms. Witherson's classroom came a loud crash, a scream, then muttered cursing. I smirked. Maybe she needed a better shelf; then she wouldn't have so many books to pick up when it fell.

My enjoyment didn't last very long, though, when I realized I'd never destroyed someone's things on purpose like that before. Why now? As I walked down the stairs and came up on the library entrance, the guilt just grew even stronger. Sure, it was just a stupid shelf, but I'd sent it to the ground out of anger. Hell, I couldn't even control myself most of the time, but I'd executed my intention with that bookshelf perfectly. I couldn't help but think it had more to do with how angry I'd been at her than anything else.

Daddy would be so pleased.

No he wouldn't; he'd be scolding me right now, just like the countless other times he'd reprimanded me for losing control.

'Claudia, you know better,' he would have told me. 'What were you thinking?'

Great. I'd been spending so much time alone, now I was hallucinating my father dealing out punishment in the middle of the school hallway.

He wagged a finger at me. 'Claudia, you know better.'

After using Michael's master key to unlock the library, I turned on the lights, grabbed a chair, and buried myself in a textbook.

I nearly dozed off a few times, bored by the schoolwork until I couldn't keep my eyes open. My mind wandered into another realm just to keep me from thinking about what I'd done. But who was I kidding? This would never be something I could just lock away and forget.

Being back in this school was harder than I'd expected, and I found myself thinking about the first time I saw the man in the black suit in the bathroom. I'd never know if it was real, but it had been real enough that day to seriously scare me. What if he was the same creature that had taken my grandfather?

As if to keep me from reliving the horrors of that day and the dark, abandoned pool that didn't actually exist, the strong, confident face of the handsome rescuer flashed into my mind. I tried to ignore it; he probably didn't exist, either. But the memory of him looking at me with so much relief and the feeling of his arms wrapped around me kept popping up in my head like someone was trying to send me a message. But how ridiculous was that? Did I really want to believe in him so badly?

Still, I couldn't forget what I'd felt when he appeared by my side—some deeper, intriguing thing that made me feel more connected to him than to anyone else. Maybe I was going crazy, but the feeling of having known him from somewhere was as real as the book in my hands.

I closed the book and gave up on the report I had to submit in two days. Just one of the perks of having an assistant principal as my guardian—I never got to skip homework assignments.

When I looked up through the library windows, the door to the main office was propped wide open. Men I'd never seen before carried out boxes and furniture. One of them set a box down in the hallway, its contents nearly overflowing from the open top, and turned to help another mover with a heavy-looking desk. His foot knocked against the box when they passed, and a picture toppled from the top of the pile and to the floor. The glass frame shattered, but the movers didn't stop with the cumbersome desk between them.

I couldn't help myself; I stood and left the library, watching the box like something might jump out of it. When I got close enough, I bent over and picked up the shattered picture frame, overwhelmed by anger and sadness.

Then my mind filled with images all at once, each of them

fighting to be seen; I had no control. I saw my grandfather drop his crystal—the same Crystal Michael had showed me. The man in the black suit bent down to pluck the crystal from the floor. Then he smiled, his eyes flashing a bright gold before they filled with darkness.

'I've come so far... and now I've found you. My source.'

The light in his eyes grew, then cleared to reveal a world falling apart, the skies on fire, and all around, the earth collapsed beneath its people trying to flee. The man in the black suit was there too, but he looked different—normal.

The destroyed world fell away, replaced by a glass tank. The man in the black suit was imprisoned inside, fighting to escape. A group of men in lab coats examined him from every angle, studying his struggles as he submerged in a thick liquid. Another black, tar-like mixture poured into the tank, entered his lungs as he fought for one last breath, and then the man in the black suit stopped moving.

Then his eyes shot open, and *it* smiled back at me—not him but a darkness that pooled in his eyes and consumed him.

I blinked and gasped, my heartbeat pounding in my head. Then I dropped the frame back onto the pile in the box and headed into the main office.

Those images hadn't come from the man in the black suit; I knew it in my bones. This was a warning from my grandfather, meant to be shown when I touched the picture frame—about the man and the darkness.

Mr. Claypool and Mr. Vasquez disappeared into my grandfather's office at the back of the main office. I stood there and stared at that open door, wondering what my grandfather had actually tried to tell me. Or was this another premonition—something like the awful shadowed figure I'd seen beside him in his kitchen? Father had told me once that the gift of seeing future events was also mine, just like I saw things that had already happened—if I chose to use that gift. The difficulty now was in telling them apart.

When Mrs. Wallace saw me, she frowned and leaned forward in her chair. "Claudia. Is everything okay?"

"He was trying to warn me," I muttered.

"I'm sorry?"

I blinked, realizing I was staring right at her and had actually said that out loud. "I'm fine," I whispered. She smiled politely, but she had to think I was mad.

Another mover stepped out of my grandfather's office, wheeling a dolly stacked with several boxes. My eyes danced back toward the open door, and Mrs. Wallace asked, "What can I help you with?"

"What's going on?" I moved forward, and when she moved as if she were about to stand, I stopped.

"They're clearing a few things out of the office for the new principal," she said, her voice barely above a whisper.

When I turned slowly to look at her, her eyes met mine with nothing but distress and genuine concern. "New principal?" I knew this was coming, that someone had to take my grandfather's place at the school, but I still felt dazed—like I wasn't even here. The images kept flashing in my head. I had to see more, to find the answers my grandfather had tried to give me before he ... was taken from me.

I could see Mr. Claypool and Mr. Vasquez from where I stood, their backs turned toward me.

"Yes," Mrs. Wallace replied and gave a slow, gentle nod.

The suited administrators emptied the bookshelves and packed my grandfather's books into a box, then gathered the last pictures from his desk and stuck them in another box beside the door.

An image of large space filled with glass tanks invaded my thoughts—the same as the glass container holding the man in black in that first unwanted image. Where were these visions coming from? I felt some other presence strengthen—some force invaded me, and I connected with it whether I wanted to or not. But I had no idea what it was or where it came from.

"Where are they taking my grandfather's things?"

It hit me that I'd find an answer there, among the items that had surrounded him for so many years.

My face burned as an inexplicable rage and urgency gathered inside me, like I'd been set on fire. I wanted to find out before I lost the connection. My grandfather would have wanted that from me, at least. If these messages were coming from him, there had to be an answer in his things.

The pens and pencils on Mrs. Wallace's desk rattled where they lay, then the desk itself trembled. A few pens rolled on their own and hit the floor before I could stop it.

Mrs. Wallace grabbed at the desk, unable to stop it from dancing. "We're not getting rid of anything. It's all going to your grandfather's house," she said.

Her desk settled as I moved away toward my grandfather's office, and I took a deep breath. What did he want to show me?

As soon as I stepped inside, Mr. Claypool and Mr. Vasquez turned and smiled in greeting until they realized something was bothering me. I went straight to the boxes and picked up another framed photograph—of me. My grandfather had framed an old picture of me a week before the accident.

I recognized the picture, but I had no idea how he'd gotten it. Still, the fact that he'd taken the time to frame it and put it in his office made my heart ache.

Above us, the lights flickered repeatedly, and I heard Mrs. Wallace's desk rattling again. The poor woman was apparently doing a good job of keeping it steady; no one else in the office seemed to notice.

"Claudia?" Mr. Claypool called, slowly looking up at the lights.

"Something's coming..." I whispered. The words sounded

far away, and it took me a second to realize I had no idea why I'd said it.

"Something?" Mr. Claypool asked. I turned to look at them, feeling my eyes grow wide. "Claudia, my dear, are you all right?"

Then I felt it, like a white-hot knife poking into my head, and the words tumbled out of me again. "Something's here."

A few of the lights blinked out; one or two others flickered. Mr. Vasquez pointed, but Mr. Claypool didn't seem to notice. My grandfather's old desk almost jumped, echoed by the thump of Mrs. Wallace's outside; she was now sitting on top of it, looking slightly ridiculous.

"Mr. Claypool!" she squeaked.

But Mr. Claypool only stared at me, and I found myself opening up to the thing trying to reach me.

Hello?

'It's you again,' came a man's voice. *'Where are you?'*

How can I hear you?

'I don't know. This shouldn't be...' The voice grew distorted, then disappeared entirely. *Who was he?*

"Claudia?" Mr. Claypool grabbed my shoulder. "Claudia, wake up!" He looked up at the lights above us, then the quivering desks. Did he know? Had he always known these things happened because of me and that I couldn't control it?

He shook me a little, and I blinked to see him staring straight into my eyes. His mouth opened, but nothing came out, and I felt it rolling off him in waves that he didn't know what to do. "What did you see?" he finally asked. "What's here?"

I frowned at him, too confused myself to answer. Then he released me, and when I took another deep breath, the lights blinked on and the desks fell still. I stepped back, absently lifting a framed picture of my grandfather from the nearest box. "I miss him," I said, though I knew that wasn't really an answer.

Mr. Claypool nodded, looking shaken and confused. Then he lowered his voice. "What happened Claudia?"

"I... don't know." I stared at the picture of my grandfather, and then the voice hit me again full-force.

'*Hello?*' It came with an echo, and then a pair of eyes flashed at me from the face of a tall, brawny young man with golden-blond locks. He stood a fair distance away, dressed in faded jeans, a silk patterned shirt of pastel blue with the sleeves rolled up, and a gray vest. He tilted his head, examining me with those eyes, and he felt so... close.

"Hello?" I couldn't help but ask it; now we were the only ones in an empty hallway. He frowned in confusion, and when he stepped toward me, a powerful surge of energy vibrated between our bodies. I felt it coursing through him, too, the electrifying current racing through me. Then I realized it was coming from him, and he gasped. The energy surrounded both of us, drawing us toward each other like to magnets; the closer he came, the more powerful it grew, and his eyes flashed a bright, brilliant gold.

"Who are you?" he asked, then bit down on his bottom lip as the force shoving us together hummed through and around him. His eyes filled with agony, and he struggled against the power drawing us closer. But the next surge between us weakened him even more, and his shoulders slumped in defeat; it seemed the more he tried to fight it, the more he couldn't help but give in.

Then he stopped struggling, and the energy shoved him forward until he stood right in front of me. I stepped back and found myself pinned against the lockers, staring up at him. His cologne—citrus, peppermint, and spearmint—engulfed me.

This was real. The energy of us together this close was overwhelming, pulsing through our forms, my heartbeat pounding in my ears. His eyes lit up, flashes of gold dancing in the center of his pupils.

"You're real?" he gasped in delight. "I feel like I've known you my whole life." He drew closer, now just inches from my lips. The warmth of his breath against my cheek sent chills up my spine.

I blinked and reached up to touch his cheek. He exhaled at my caress, almost as if in pain. I felt the same thing here with him as I did the night my grandfather was taken; this man would protect me no matter what the cost, even if I didn't understand the danger.

"Who *are* you?" he asked, but I couldn't give him an answer. I didn't even know.

Without warning, I felt a tug against my heart, against him —something pulling us apart and trying to separate us. I couldn't stop it. The wall behind me collapsed, and I stumbled backward into it, almost as if I'd been sucked through to the other side. He reached for me and managed to grab my arm, but the pull was too great. My arm ripped from his grasp, and he ran after me through the shattered wall. Whatever force had a hold of me pulled me further away from him and wouldn't let go, taking me farther and farther into a nothingness I didn't understand.

"I'll come for you," I heard him calling out. "I'll find you. I promise!"

"Claudia?" The sound of Michael's voice made me blink. Then I realized another man stood behind him, also staring at me with more than a little concern.

I couldn't believe it. The man from my vision was here, now, in my grandfather's old office, staring at me with those green eyes beneath golden-brown hair. The flecks of gold exploded around his pupils even here. I swallowed; while the electrifying current between us wasn't nearly as strong as it had been in my vision, I definitely still felt it now. He was real. I felt myself blushing when his mouth curved up into a small, confused smile.

Hello? I figured I'd try speaking with him this way; we'd done it before.

'*I didn't think you were real,*' he replied, and my heart fluttered to realize we could actually communicate this way, standing right in front of each other. '*Why do I keep dreaming about you?*'

I don't know. That was the only way I knew how to answer. *I thought I was the only one.* A warm blush rose up my cheeks, and I watched him watching me.

Then he glanced down at his wristwatch, which wasn't really a watch at all, I realized, when I caught a glimpse of his frustration at the fact that it didn't seem to be working the way he wanted.

'*You... happy,*' he thought. '*I can feel it.*'

I smiled. *You're like me?*

'*No.*' He looked up to lock his gaze onto mine again, his eyes revealing what the rest of him tried to hide. I saw flashes of pain there, and images of people—others, just like me—being captured, tortured, experimented on, delivered to people in white coats. Instantly, I remembered what my grandfather had said about scientists selling us to the highest bidders.

'*You're not like the others...*' he added. '*I don't understand why I feel so...*'

I reacted to his sudden intensity and mentally pushed him away, needing just a little bit more space. Apparently, it did nothing to discourage him, only fueling his curiosity and his desire for more.

"Claudia," Michael asked again, interrupting the moment. "Is everything okay? Did you need anything, honey?"

I stared at him, and then another man stepped into the office to join Michael, the blond young man with the green eyes, and me.

"And who is this lovely young lady?" the stranger asked. He wore a dark blue, pinstriped suit and a striped grey tie. He looked Hispanic, his skin a darker tone and blond highlights in his dark brown hair. His thoughts and emotions were a blank canvas, nothing but a few wrinkles in his brow to show he was curious about me.

"Dr. Müller," Michael said, "this is the late Dr. Edward's granddaughter. Claudia Belle." I fidgeted, trying to give the newcomer enough of my attention to not be rude while still consumed by the sparking pull between the green-eyed man and me. The lights flickered again above us.

"How do you do, Miss Belle?"

A distortion of sound came from him, echoing, buzzing and making it hard to hear anything else. It grew louder, like someone kept changing the stations on a small radio. I caught him glancing at his watch and jiggling it on his wrist when Michael wasn't looking.

'Your assignment is to engage with Mr. Michael McClellan and the staff. As the new principal of Milton, you will assist John in this aspect of the job. Find out if they know anything.'

'Yes, Dr. Nicholson.'

'John will do the rest, as he always does...'

I didn't see faces, just heard the voices of this memory, a little flash of Dr. Müller's profile when he interacted with someone I couldn't see. And that was all I could get out of him.

Then I looked up again and saw the green-eyed boy still staring at me. I frowned. *Go away.*

"I'm so sorry for your loss," Dr. Müller said.

'No,' The boy who apparently went by John would not let me turn him away. *'I want to talk to you. You make me... I feel so much stronger.'*

I blinked in disbelief. He stepped forward anyway, and I wondered if he was going to get as close as he had in my vision.

But he stopped, the centers of his eyes still dancing with that golden hue.

"Hi," he started. "I mean... hello. I mean... I'm John." He blinked and frowned, clearly confused and unable to say out loud what he wanted.

I know, I thought. *John Slater*. I wasn't sure if he'd heard me; he looked disconnected and embarrassed.

"Ah, excuse my nephew, Miss Belle. He's not feeling a hundred percent. I think he's catching something going around..."

John glanced at Dr. Müller and frowned. "I'm fine." He said it just a little louder than necessary. Then he looked back at me, his unwavering intensity making me uneasy.

'I want to talk to you,' he told me. *'I won't hurt you. I just want to... explain.'*

I pushed at him again, not hard but enough to get him to move—at least, it would have made anyone else turn away. John didn't. The adults continued the conversation around us, and no one seemed to notice our own secret conversation.

The only thing I could think about was that both my father and my grandfather had warned me about people who would try to use me—people like this Dr. Müller, maybe.

'No,' John repeated, almost as if he knew I just wanted to get out of the office as quickly as possible. He wasn't going to get out of my way.

A row of lights flickered again in the ceiling, then popped and shattered. Glass rained down on all of our heads, and I made my move, shoving past John and out of the office. I thought I heard him coming after me, so I ran to the nearest stairwell and hurried up to the second floor. Halfway down the empty hallway, I stopped and turned around, only to find that I was alone.

15

THE LECTURE

A FEW MINUTES LATER, MICHAEL, MR. VASQUEZ, MR. CLAYPOOL, and I sat in Michael's office on the second floor at the back end of the school. It was almost a little nook, though much bigger than the offices given to Mr. Claypool and Mr. Vasquez. From where I sat on a ledge by the small glass window, I could see the entire library below us.

Michael sat behind his desk, his suit jacket hung over the back of his desk chair. This time, I knew without a doubt that all three of them knew the truth about my grandfather—about me. They'd spent years together before I came to Texas and Milton High School. How could they not have known?

"What happened?" Michael asked. I wanted to pretend I had no idea what he was talking about, but I couldn't anymore. "Milton has its faults and needs a lot of upgrades," he continued, "but we know those lights didn't shatter on their own."

"I'm sorry," I whispered, unable to look up at him.

"What happened? Did something upset you? I know you're still mourning, Claudia, and that's perfectly normal. I want to help in any way I can."

"I don't know." I wasn't sure what to tell them, or even if I should say anything at all. More than anything, the last few weeks were enough to frighten me into silence, especially now with our new principal and his strange nephew, if that was who they even were.

"You said you saw something," Mr. Claypool prompted. Michael looked up at him and raised his brows. "That something was coming."

"Did you have a vision?" Michael asked, which surprised me even though I'd expected something like that. "Your grandfather had visions, but most of the time, they were random things. Disconnected. Not easily clear to him. A feeling or a single image, harder to interpret. Is that what you saw?"

I nodded, thinking that was the best option. I didn't want to reveal the truth about John, or the things I'd felt connecting us and drawing us toward each other. I didn't want to frighten Michael or the other administrators, especially because I had no idea what was going on.

"I *am* sorry about the lights. I'll help pay for them."

"There's no need for that, Claudia. I just want you to exercise a little more control over your... abilities. We're running out of light bulbs." Michael barely managed to contain his smirk.

"Not to mention excuses," Mr. Vasquez added, which was more than I'd heard him say in weeks.

"Do you think the vision provoked your power?" Michael asked.

I shrugged, though of course I knew exactly what had made the lights shatter. "I'm not sure," I muttered instead.

Michael took a breath and leaned back into his chair, frowning down at his neatly organized desk. "Well, just like your grandfather. You have to be careful. Learn to control it." He finally looked back up at me.

"Did they say anything about it?" I asked, referring to John and Dr. Müller.

"As far as they know," Mr. Claypool replied, not missing a

beat, "it was nothing but the failing lightbulbs for which Milton is so popular."

"I'm sorry I caused so much trouble..." I said.

"Don't be. About the visions, though," Michael said. "Should I be worried about you, Claudia? Maybe you should go home. Take the day to just rest." Mr. Claypool and Mr. Vasquez both nodded in agreement.

"I'm all right. I just... got a little overwhelmed. Please don't send me home. I'll be okay."

"Are you sure?" He leaned forward over his desk, trying to smile beneath the genuine concern in his eyes. Mr. Claypool and Mr. Vasquez copied him almost exactly, and I suddenly felt like I had three new father figures, all ready to do what it took to make sure I had what I needed. "I can take you home," Michael offered.

"I'm fine." Somehow, I managed to smile back at all of them.

"All right, then," he said. I got up to leave, and as I opened the door, Michael added, "Try not to pop any more lightbulbs, please."

He smirked, and I couldn't hide my own slightly embarrassed smile.

16

LUNCH GROUP

I WANTED TO DISAPPEAR, TO BE LEFT ALONE. STUDENTS AND EVEN a few teachers had filled my locker almost completely with letters of condolences they'd slipped through the little vent. I tried not to let it annoy me; people were just trying to be nice. But it was only a constant reminder of what I'd lost.

My morning classes went by so incredibly slowly, and I found myself completely unable to focus on anything my teachers said. Instead, I kept seeing John's green eyes, heard him telling me he wanted to talk to me, that I made him stronger. I couldn't deny what I felt around him, but I had no idea who he was, and the truth was obviously not what Dr. Müller had said.

During lunch, I stepped into the cafeteria and glared at the nameless faces of other students who eyed me with concern. Some of them tried to hide their annoyance, but I heard their thoughts; they assumed I was just trying to milk their pity for all it was worth.

I didn't see anyone I recognized and considered fleeing to

the library. But I was starving, so I reluctantly stepped into the lunch line and waited. Then I saw Tina at the far end of the cafeteria, sitting with the others in their normal spots. Once I got my lunch, I made my way to their table with my tray and sat down without a word. They didn't even try to bring up my grandfather, though they'd left notes in my locker, too. Honestly, though, I was glad they didn't bring it up; I just wanted things to go back to normal, or as normal as they could be, now.

"I heard the rug in the new principal's office got ripped almost in half and they have to get him a new one," Alex said. "Serves him right for swooping in like that after your grandfather."

I looked at her blankly for a minute, then smiled. At least she was trying. Then a chuckle escaped me, and the rest of the group seemed to realized it was safe to relax around me.

"Sucks about what happened," Alex mumbled, smacking the gum in her mouth. "Sorry."

"Thanks," I whispered. She smiled.

But what could be said? I wasn't sure myself what people thought best to tell those who had lost loved ones. Still, I was grateful for her attempts to connect with me, especially after we didn't have the best introduction.

"Are you all right?" Tina asked. Ruben and Sean gazed back at me too.

I nodded. "It was harder in the beginning. Thank you, guys, for the cards and notes and stuff... I really appreciate it." I tried as hard as I could not to get all teary-eyed in front of them.

"Well, we're here for you. If you feel like talking about it," Ruben offered.

"Thanks." I caught Sean staring at me. He smiled, and I dropped my gaze, certain I was blushing now, too.

We caught up with school gossip and talked about Alex's run-in with Thomas the security guard and the house party coming up the following weekend. For some reason, talk of a party made me think of my handsome rescuer from the pool and the gorgeous face that still kept me awake at night. What had happened to him?

Alex stood and walked out into the hallway toward the Coke machines. When she disappeared, my mind dove into that hole again, and I couldn't stop thinking the strangeness of my life these days—stranger than normal. Nothing made sense —that day at the pool; the man in the black suit and red tie; and now John and his uncle, the new principal.

I wanted to tell Michael what I'd seen. John must have known I would want to, and I wondered if that was why he'd tried to stop me from leaving. If everything I'd seen in his mind were true, was he really sent here to watch *me*? But then why did I feel he would protect me with his life?

I thought again about my rescuer and the evil lurking in the pool that of course hadn't existed. My rescuer scared and intrigued me at the same time, and I had no explanation for it. And I couldn't help but wonder what connection existed between him and the dark shadow in the pool that had tried to scare him away. The worst part about it all was that I had a feeling that I knew them both in some way and just couldn't remember.

"You're so quiet. You sure you're okay?" Tina's voice brought me out of my deepening thoughts. I glanced at her. It had always been hard for me to pretend I was normal, and having lost both my parents and grandfather in the same month made it even worse.

"I'm fine," I said. "I just have a lot of things on my mind, I guess."

She smiled and put her hand on my shoulder. "Don't worry. It's going to be all right." I wished I could believe her.

Ruben and Sean locked their eyes on me at the exact same time and smiled together. It was more than a little spooky.

"Yes, everything is going to be all right," Ruben said. Sean nodded.

"He's been looking," Tina said.

Maybe I'd missed part of their conversation while I went off into my own world. "He who?" They smiled but didn't answer. "What's he looking for?"

"He's looking for you, silly. He's found you. Praise him. He's found you."

"Yes, praise him," Ruben and Sean repeated.

"*What*?" I whispered.

Tina reached up and cupped my cheek. "When the time comes, he will reveal himself to you. That time approaches quickly."

I blinked, frowning, then had the strangest feeling that all three of my friends at the table knew something about what I'd just been through. If they hadn't been acting so weird, I probably wouldn't have said anything. But I took the leap. "Tell me," I whispered. "Please. Who is he?"

Tina simply smiled. "He rejoices at your longing for him." She leaned closer and whispered, "But he said be patient. Be patient, *my pet*."

My head started spinning, along with the entire cafeteria. I closed my eyes, my head throbbing, and then it all stopped. The voices and the loud noisy chatter in the cafeteria came back to me before I opened my eyes and blinked. Tina and the others were talking about the party the following weekend.

"What did you say?" I asked Tina.

"When?" she asked, taking a bite of her lunch.

I grabbed hold of her shoulders and turned her to face me. "Tell me! I have to know who he is!"

'*Be patient, my pet...*'

It was *his* voice, rolling through my head.

Sean and Ruben stared back at me, like two lifeless dolls,

and I let go of Tina. Then all three of them seemed to jump right back into their conversation like nothing had happened.

Alex returned and took a seat beside me. "Hey, want one?" she asked and put the soda on the table. I stared at the Coke can and closed my mouth when I felt it hanging open. "Sorry about being such a bitch the first time we met," she added. "Calling you Pocahontas and all. But the hair, you know. And, well, I'm sorry. I have issues, but doesn't everyone, right?" She laughed, cracking her own Coke open to take a long drink. "You okay?"

I looked up at her, as if just noticing she'd come back. "Yeah."

"So, we're cool?"

I nodded. "Yeah, we're cool. But the Pocahontas thing... it was clever."

She laughed. "Well, it kind of fits you. Now, if we can only find a guy cute enough to fit the image of John Smith..."

"Great," I uttered.

She smiled. "Are you going to the party this weekend?"

I glanced back at her, feeling like my answer had to be yes. I still couldn't think straight. From behind dark-blue eyes covered with dark eye shadow and mascara, Alex smiled at me. She twisted the pentagram necklace around her long pale finger, pulling at it. A tiny crystal sparkled from beneath the lace wrapped around her slender wrist. She nervously tucked it back in, dropping her hand under the table before I could ask about it. It looked almost like the one Michael had shown me.

"I like your charm," I managed to say, but she either didn't hear me or decided to ignore me.

"So, are you going?"

"Yeah," I said with a nod. "I think I am."

"Awesome. You have to let me do your makeup. Red lipstick with dark-purple eye shadow would be best for your eye color and complexion."

I frowned at her.

"Relax. I promise I'll keep it natural. It's hard work looking the way I do, but it's mine, and you can't have it." She laughed again.

I couldn't help but smile a little, and Alex fell into the group conversation with the others about the party. I listened to them make plans for the night, and apparently, I was going now, whether I wanted to or not. Surprisingly, Alex volunteered to pick me up. She was the only other senior with a car in our group.

She didn't have many friends; her parents were divorced. She lived with an alcoholic mother. Her father called every other week and rarely visited. Alex was easier to read than the others, because she didn't care and carried her feelings on the outside with her personal style.

I felt like an idiot examining and looking at the others, trying to see what I had seen in Alex—trying to read them too. But for some reason, I couldn't. When they all looked at me at once and glared, I darted my eyes away and tried to seem focused on something else. The only thing I could pick up when I searched them was just a bunch of useless noise.

Then strange sensation hit me like a wave of unbalanced energy unhinged, trying to connect to a receiver. Tina, Ruben, and Sean stared at me again, almost as if they'd felt the same thing. But that was absurd, wasn't it? Then they all looked past me toward something at the far end of the cafeteria.

I glanced at Alex, but she was busy watching something on her phone. She seemed completely oblivious, at least as far as the odd burst of energy I'd felt and how strangely the others were acting at the table. Then I turned to see what had caught everyone else's attention.

John Müller entered the other end of the cafeteria. Immediately, I ducked my head to hide myself behind my friends.

Nobody seemed to notice my reaction, no matter how ridiculous I felt.

"Hey, looky-looky at who just walked in," Alex said. Great. Now she'd noticed too. "Who's the new guy?" She looked back at me and saw me crouching over the table. "Do you know him?"

I blinked at her, feeling guilty as hell. "No."

"You *do* know him. Oh, do tell, Pocahontas. Please."

"He's the new principal's nephew," I said quickly.

A wide smile spread over her full, red lips. "Aw, seriously? Wow, he's hot. Like a chiseled god." She bit her lip and stared at him with wide eyes.

Chiseled god? Only Alex would pull out such a ridiculous term.

"Claudia, you bitch. Why didn't you mention him before?"

"I didn't think it was important..." I muttered, looking up at her from my ridiculous position where I'd tried to bury my face in my arms on the table.

"You serious?" She wrinkled her nose. "So then why are you hiding?"

"Hiding?" I joked, rising a bit. "I'm not hiding."

She tilted her head. "You like him?" Her grin widened.

"No—what? No." I felt like an idiot. Of course I didn't like *him*. John was bad, bad news for someone like me. It was the other way around. If anything, he wouldn't leave *me* alone.

"You *do*." Alex threw her head back and laughed.

"He's not so special," Tina said. "Looks like trouble, if you ask me."

"I think you might need to get your eyes checked," Alex told her. "He's gorgeous."

I fidgeted nervously and rolled my eyes, and Alex laughed again. The others didn't say anything else, but they glared at Alex, as if her behavior only annoyed them.

I looked away, hoping John wouldn't find me. I felt so stupid for avoiding him, but what I'd seen in his mind was a little terrifying. I didn't think I was supposed to have seen any of the images in his head—or for that fact who he was and that his strange watch had somehow failed him. And he seemed just as confused by me as I was by him. I never picked up anything from him that he was here to hurt me, just that he wanted to talk, like he'd said. Either way, I had no intention of giving him that opportunity, despite the fact that neither of us could deny that *something* drew us toward each other. Until I figured out why—if I ever could—I wanted to stay away from him. But when I glanced across the cafeteria again and saw him, my cheeks burned.

"You're blushing," Alex said in a teasing, singsong voice.

"I am not."

Did I really want to believe he hadn't stepped into the cafeteria to find me? Of course, he had; my name kept popping up in his mind as he scanned the tables crowded with other students. Then he turned toward me, and his eyes flickered over our table. Shit. I jerked back down again to hide behind my friends, pressing my forehead into my arms and hoping he hadn't seen me. He'd sensed me. Of course he had; he's a hunter. That was what I'd seen in his mind, but I had no idea what that meant. If I could control my power, I would have been able to avoid him. Instead, I was apparently summoning him. Now that was an odd thought.

"Looks like he's looking for somebody," Alex teased and squinted at me. Heat rushed to my face again.

"You look very nice in that shade of red, Claudia."

"Ha, ha, very funny," I said.

John walked to the very front of the cafeteria and stood where the assistant principals normally did. He definitely looked like he was on a mission, still scanning the crowded, noisy room. I felt his frustration; he sensed me clearly, but he couldn't figure out why he couldn't see me. He obviously hadn't thought I'd try to hide from him.

The panic of emotions I knew he'd picked up on made him anxious. Any emotion seemed to do that to him, as if they were hot and cold on his skin instead. I didn't dare sit up to look at him again, but I could still picture him perfectly. Those eyes never left my mind—the way they sparkled and lit with that magical gold in the center. What made them do that? He had to know what his own eyes looked like.

"He can be your John Smith," Alex said.

"What?" I gasped, and she giggled.

"Pocahontas, and he's John Smith."

Okay, now I was starting to regret complimenting her on the wittiness of that nickname.

"Well, you're Hispanic, and he's sort of peaches-and-cream American. John Smith and Pocahontas." She just wouldn't let it go.

"She was Native American," I corrected.

"What's the difference?" I looked up at her from my arms on the table and widened my eyes in disbelief. "He's white, and you're a nicely bronzed Mexican babe." Okay, it was starting to sound slightly racist at this point, but Alex was getting a real kick out of the whole thing.

"He's not at all right for her," Tina said. "He's too arrogant. Besides, Claudia's uncomfortable."

Yeah, I had to agree with Tina on the arrogant part.

"Uncomfortable?" Alex asked. "She's not *uncomfortable*. Can't you tell she's in love?"

I was *what*? I wrinkled my nose at her. Seriously?

"She doesn't know it yet." Alex smirked and nudged her elbow into my side. "You guys would look great together... So, what's his name?"

I blinked at her, frustrated by her continuous smile, like we were in on a joke no one else was getting. "Chris—John Müller."

"Ah! John!" she said with an exhale. "Dreamy Johnny. I wouldn't mind a few minutes with him..." The others spun their heads toward her in disapproval.

"You're disgusting," Tina uttered.

"Excuse me for being sexually active. I guess we know who the virgin here is," Alex said, raising her eyebrows with a sarcastic little shake of her head. She took out her compact and reapplied her red lipstick, powdered her face with more white makeup, then put the compact away in her black shoulder bag. "I'm only stating the obvious, right, Claudia?"

I didn't say anything, watching the others' eyes burning holes into her.

"Oh, come on. I'm kidding," she told me. "You guys need to chillax. You're so uptight."

Mrs. Whitman stepped toward John from where the teachers watched over the cafeteria, maybe wondering if he was lost. He seemed to be very popular; almost every other girl here had her eyes on him, too. He looked like he belonged in a Beverly Hills high school instead of ours.

"What is she doing?" Alex scolded, regarding Mrs. Whitman. The teacher was actually flirting with John now, and I had to look away. I felt John's impatience radiating from him, colored with irritation. He wanted to get away from her and find me, but the woman wouldn't stop talking.

"He's too young for you..." Alex said. I nudged her arm. "What? He is... I swear, she has no shame. I tell you what, that woman's gonna get herself into a lot of legal problems if she keeps this up at a high school."

The entire topic was now more humiliating that I could handle, but I still didn't want to get up and let John see me.

Finally, he broke free from Mrs. Whitman and walked through the cafeteria again—right toward our table.

"I dare you to talk to him, Pocahontas," Alex taunted. I knew that if I didn't, she'd do it for me.

"Why would she want to talk to him?" Sean asked, glancing at me.

"Oh, are you jealous?" Alex retorted with a smirk.

"What are you talking about?" He looked instantly uncomfortable.

"Like we can't see the way you look at Claudia. Are you afraid a real man will get her first?"

I blushed. Sean lowered his glasses, his eyes met mine, and he opened his mouth to speak. But he didn't get a chance.

"Do you ever shut up?" Tina roared, rising from her seat.

"Oh, he needs you to defend him, too?" Alex laughed.

Finally, I pushed myself up from the table. "I have to go." I had to get out of this ridiculous conversation before things got really nasty, and I didn't want to be the center of attention like *that*. As I headed through the cafeteria, I realized I didn't see John at all.

"Hey! Pocahontas, I'm sorry," Alex called after me. "Please don't leave. I'm just messing around."

The only thing I could think about was that John had seemed to disappear. When I reached the cafeteria doors into the hallway, I turned around to find Alex sitting alone now at the table. Her eyes grew wide and darted past me, then I knew *he* was standing behind me.

"Claudia Belle..." John's voice sent chills down my spine.

Instead of turning to look at him, I just dashed out into the hallway.

"Claudia, stop. I really have to talk to you." It sounded like a command—powerful, frightening.

What was he going to do, run after me?

I rushed away into the hall and raced into the stairwell. When I glanced back, I couldn't believe he was right there on my heels. I leaped up the steps, and the minute I reached the second floor, a hand wrapped around my arm, pulled me back, and spun me around. My back hit the lockers, and John leaned in close. I challenged his gaze, his warm breath brushing my face as he absorbed me with those eyes. Then he leaned closer, his breath heavy, ignoring everything else but me.

I trembled and exhaled slowly, the curious energy between us exploding with a force I didn't understand. It made those gold hues in the center of his eyes expand so much, his eyes almost glowed.

He seemed completely unable to pull away. I could feel his powerlessness, possessed by my presence, and nothing I could do or say would stop him. Not even the fear I knew he felt rising in me at this closeness. His lips came just a breath away from mine, and he repeated so slowly, "I need to speak with you..." With his next breath, his eyes had lost their green color completely, consumed by the gold that had flared up in them.

I had a feeling something irreversible was about to happen. "Stop," I begged, trying to jerk my arm out of his crushing grip. "Let me go."

Somehow, he snapped out of it and looked up to see me staring at him with wide eyes. The gold shrank again, returning his irises to that unnatural green. Then the force drawing him to me surged between our beings, as if it wouldn't let him pull away. He frowned just a little, and I knew he'd realized his mistake. John's regret surged over me; he hadn't wanted to frighten me at all.

"I'm sorry..." he muttered, then pressed his lips against mine.

He took in a sharp breath, his lips warm and inviting. I blinked, taken completely by surprise, then reacted. In a second, I pulled every inch of strength from my mind to push hard against his. John flew backwards, slammed against the row of lockers on the other side of the hallway, then dropped to the floor.

I gasped, not having expected any of this to happen. Hoping I hadn't hurt him, I took a few steps forward to see if he was all right, despite the fact that my gut told me to flee. Then I knelt beside him and slowly reached out to touch his shoulder. John moved a little with a groan, startling me so much that I fell backward off my knees and scooted away from him across the floor. John's groans stopped, and he rolled over to look at me.

"That was just self-defense," I said—not exactly an apology, but I didn't feel like I owed him one. He lifted his head, and that dancing gold glittered in his eyes again. The current between us pulsed and tightened, drawing us closer. John reached toward me, and I couldn't help it now—I did the same.

When our fingers touched, the hallway disappeared around us, replaced by images I'd never seen before. John stood guard as a huge, looming shadow drifted over us both. His eyes glowed again in the gold now, and I stood behind him, my arms wrapped around his waist, giving him strength. From the shadow standing in front of us, huge, coiling tendrils of darkness reached out to strike. John grabbed them both with a speed and strength I couldn't see but definitely felt through his body. He snapped these violent tendrils in half, but they only grew again to attack us...

I pulled my hand away from his, severing the connection to that odd vision, and John blinked at me. "I'm sorry..." I said, then stood and stumbled down the hall as the class bell rang over my head.

17

AMONG FRIENDS

I HEADED TOWARD MY LOCKER IN THE CROWDED HALLWAYS, MY heart still pounding with excitement and a little fear after what had just happened.

I didn't notice Alex at all until she caught up to me and fell in right beside me. "Hey," she whispered.

"Hey." There was a brief silence between us as we moved through the students swarming between classes. I'd left things kind of tense at the lunch table before trying to run away from John; Tina had been pissed at Alex, the rest of our group had just left Alex alone there in the cafeteria. "Did you talk to Tina again after lunch?"

"Nope." Alex just tugged on the strap of her backpack. "You?"

"Not yet." I wasn't sure I wanted to, but I felt like it was something I was supposed to do. "So, what are you gonna do?"

"About what?" She laughed. "Do you think it matters? I seriously could care less what they say or that they're not talking to me. Fuck them!"

"So, you're not going to the party?"

She looked at me and grinned. "Are you kidding me? Of course I'm going. Who else is going to give you a ride?"

I smiled back. "I can already see the look on Tina's face."

"Me too."

I veered out of the student traffic and stopped by my locker for my next class' textbook. A boy stepped up to open the locker next to mine, and I just glanced at him. It was the first time I'd seen the blond-haired guy at Milton, and now that I had, I couldn't stop staring at his beautiful blue eyes.

He seemed to notice me watching him, and he smiled down at me. A camera dangled from a strap over his shoulder, and he quickly grabbed it. "Photography," he said, glancing down at his camera before retrieving a small black bag from his locker and slipping a camera lens into it. "I'm taking photography." He blinked, darted his gaze all over, then looked shyly up at me again with an embarrassed smile.

I tried smiling back but felt myself blushing again and hid behind my locker's open door. His thoughts swirled around me; he was incredibly shy but really wanted to talk to me.

God, he was cute. I bit down on my lip as he grinned again. "I'm Jimmy," he said.

My cheeks were burning. "Oh. I'm—"

"Claudia," he answered for me. I gaze and had to look down again, embarrassed by being taken so off guard. Of course he knew who I was. I was the principal's granddaughter. Who didn't know me?

"Hi, Jimmy," Alex said, stepping between us. "Can you excuse us? Thanks…" Jimmy and I both tried to meet each other's gaze again over Alex's shoulder. She slammed my locker closed and grabbed my arm, leading me away from the cutest guy I'd seen in a while.

"See ya," Jimmy said slowly as we left him behind.

"So are you gonna tell me what happened with Johnny Boy, or what?" Alex asked. She was aching for details—I felt it—and at the same time ignoring the very fact she'd probably just ruined my chances of getting to know a very interesting guy.

I didn't know what to tell her—or even if I should.

"I saw him run after you," she added. "It sure looked like you guys already know each other."

"You saw that?" I asked. Butterflies erupted in my stomach.

"Yeah, and like half the cafeteria. Most of the girls can't take their eyes off him." I rolled my eyes and sighed. "So?" Alex grinned and inched closer. "Did he kiss you?"

I blushed almost immediately. She slapped the side of my arm, and I cringed.

"No fuckin' way! Claudia, what did I tell you? He's totally hot for you!"

She had no idea what had really happened, but I wasn't about to correct her. What I couldn't stop wondering about was the eerie vision I'd seen when John and I had touched—him fighting the shadows and apparently protecting me. That only made it more confusing.

"So, come on," Alex pleaded. "What did he say? Did he ask you to prom? I've never had a friend I could nominate for prom queen, so... yeah?"

"What?" I said stupidly, walking down the hallway toward Ms. Witherson's classroom. Then I caught sight of Tina, Sean, and Ruben across the hall.

Tina waved me toward them, and the guys joined in. I shook my head and pointed to my next class, and they passed us without stopping. Their inviting smiles all twisted into disapproving frowns when they saw me walking with Alex instead.

"You could have gone," Alex said, still hurrying to stay by my side.

"Seriously?" I asked. "I didn't want to. They're really... odd."

Alex laughed. "Yeah. Especially Tina. They're never gonna talk to me again, and I couldn't care less. I get if you don't want to keep hanging out with me either, since they're still your friends."

"You're my friend too," I said as we reached the far staircase on the second floor and stopped near the window overlooking the library.

"Okay, so you never told me what dreamy Johnny said to you," Alex reminded me. I kept moving around the corner to my next class, and we stopped just outside the door. "Well?" She jabbed her elbow into my side.

I didn't want to tell her the truth. What could I really say that wouldn't exactly make this a lie? "I don't know what he wants," I said. "It's weird..."

"He did kiss you, right?" Apparently, that was the only thing that had her interest. I nodded. Alex grinned and danced around like it had happened to her. "He's gonna ask you out. Wait, did he?" I blinked at her and shook my head. "First kiss?" I shrugged—yes it was—and Alex winked. "You're gonna go out with him when he does, right?"

"Does what?"

She rolled her eyes. "Seriously? When he asks you out. You're gonna say yes, right?"

"I didn't really think about it," I said. Alex just tilted her head like she wanted to say she knew I was lying. "I know what you're gonna say," I added. "But I'm serious. I'm not expecting him to do anything, and I'm not gonna read too much into this—"

"*Too much*? He chased after you to kiss you. That boy's in love."

I shrugged. "Maybe. I don't know."

Alex just raised her eyebrows and laughed, and I felt ridiculous for not having come up with a better excuse for why he'd literally chased me down the halls.

Above us, the bell rang again, and I saw Ms. Witherson looking at me.

"Hey, I can start picking you up for school, if you want," Alex offered. "Make it a thing."

I smiled. That wasn't really the most important thing on my mind, but I didn't want to say no. "Sure, why not? You should go. You're gonna be late to class."

"Class?" Alex scoffed. "I've got more important things to do. See ya." She waved, darting away in the other direction before I stepped into my next class.

18

GOTH GIRL

THE LAST BELL RANG BEFORE SHE MADE IT TO THE END OF THE hall, which were now deserted except for Alex. She heard footsteps approaching and guessed it was the patrols; they always made their trips around this time of the day. Thomas had a new recruit by the name of Sam, who didn't seem to know what he was doing.

But then, she thought the same of Thomas. How many times had it been now that she'd gotten caught? Last time, Thomas had sent her to Mr. Claypool's office, who'd then written her up for skipping. She had to be careful, now; two or more slips would bring her parents in for a meeting with the principal, and she couldn't afford to let that happen. The old lady she lived with had been more than generous in covering for her the last two times Mr. Claypool had threatened to call her parents.

Alex remembered sitting in front of his desk, his face a mass of lines and wrinkles and disappointment. He had on a white shirt and black tie. Something about a man in a tie made her squirm, especially a good-looking man like Mr. Claypool, who had a soft spot for his students. He always wanted to give her a chance, no matter how many times he'd seen her in his office. That day, though, it looked like he'd been slowly regretting it.

His blue eyes found hers. She'd smiled her best back at him; she'd often gotten away with almost anything by using that smile. Ed Harris, as she'd come to nickname Mr. Claypool, was a softie.

"As much as I enjoy these little meetings of ours, I have to say, this is really getting to be a bad habit. What is it, the third time this week?" Mr. Claypool asked, sitting back in his chair with a new stack of detention slips. Alex cringed, biting down on her lip.

"No, you can't count the other time," she said, "because I wasn't skipping. I was late, and Mr. Thomas always has it out for me. I tried to explain to him that I was going to the bathroom because..." She leaned a little closer. "Well... I had girl issues. You know..."

Mr. Claypool tried to clear his throat and blinked down at the slips. "Yes, I know. You mentioned that. But that doesn't excuse you for every other absence."

Alex lowered her head. "I guess not. But Mr. Claypool, I'm really trying. It's just hard to concentrate with all that's happened." She looked up and gave him her best doe-eyed-apology face. She was good at that. Or was it just that this man was a sucker for it?

"Oh, would you like me to talk to your mom? We can all have a sit-down and discuss this." He moved to pick up the phone.

"Can I just come talk to you? All I really need is someone to talk to. And you're a good listener, Mr. Claypool." She smiled as he moved his hand away from the phone. He was a total sucker for the old damsel-in-distress routine.

"Well, I guess that wouldn't hurt. But you must promise not to skip again. I know having to cope with your parents' divorce is hard, but you're strong, Alex, and with time, you'll be able to get past this. I know you will. And I want to see you graduate and succeed."

She had mentioned her parents' divorce a couple times; she'd thought it would have been worn out by now, but it was still working. Men were so easy to manipulate, especially these assistant principals. The easy part was pretending about the whole divorce and looking like a girl who didn't know her place in the world. But Alex had never been *that* girl.

Now, she turned the corner in the hallway, and when the coast was clear, she raced across to the lockers near the stairwell. At first, she'd forgotten the combination; those things were so annoying. But she finally managed to open the lock and the locker, then reached far into the back. The only thing she needed was the small black pouch she withdrew before closing the locker and locking it again.

At the end of the hall, she heard footsteps again.

Damn Thomas and Sam.

They were heading back; she was sure of it. If she got caught this time, it was back to Mr. Claypool's office. Or worse —Dr. Müller's.

Alex hurried away, dashing into the dark stairwell. She thought she was safe until she heard the footsteps hurrying behind her even up the stairs.

"Shit." Moving up the steps, she nearly lost her footing but managed to reach the second floor before her pursuers caught up. She raced down the hall, only to realize her error too late— the bathroom was in the other direction.

But now Thomas was at the top of the stairs. Alex just kept going toward the balcony area leading into the ROTC classes and tennis courts. No one was outside—at least, not near the balcony. She glanced at the time on her phone.

The ROTC students were back in class now too, and the tennis courts were empty. Alex could definitely escape via the other side of the building. Just before she reached the school's side entrance there, Thomas rounded the corner, so she doubled back and ducked around the closest corner just in time.

Except for now, Mr. Thomas' trainee was heading in her direction. If they found her, they'd give her more trouble than she needed. Then they'd try to call her parents, and that would not go well with the old lady who was letting Alex live with her.

The bracelet on her wrist glowed a light blue.

"I know. I know," she muttered.

Sam's steps got closer, and she was sure Mr. Thomas would appear at the other entrance and spot her any moment.

Then the final bell of the school day rang. Students poured out of the classes into the hallway. If Mr. Thomas wanted to get to her, he'd have to push his way through the hordes. Alex joined the wave of students, walking behind a huge jock and his buddies; the guy must have been well over six feet. It surprised her that he didn't yet have any facial hair.

Mr. Thomas finally came rushing in from the other end. The crowd swallowed Alex and moved her away from her pursuers. The new trainee scanned the milling heads, but as far as Alex knew, neither he nor Mr. Thomas knew exactly who they'd been chasing in the first place.

Alex came down the stairwell near the cafeteria; from there, it was a straight shot past the parked line of yellow buses into the parking lot, where her beat-up mustang waited. She took a deep breath and whispered, "Let's never do that again."

Before heading home, she stopped at the grocery store for some bread, milk, turkey, and cheese. Of course, she didn't have any intention of paying for any of it, instead stuffing the items into her backpack. This particular small store didn't have cameras, and no one ever paid her any attention. But she always bought something small—even just a pack of gum—so they wouldn't grow suspicious.

Alex couldn't pay for her groceries even if she wanted to;

she needed the last thirty dollars for gas. She made it out the
front doors again without anyone stopping her, but the store
owner had his eyes on her. With a wave, she hurried back to
her car.

Her house was at the end of a dead-end street; it was a
modest home, older but in decent condition. When she'd first
come to live here, the yard had been all but a junkpile, cluttered
with the old woman's decades worth of stuff. Alex had done
everything she could to make the place more homey. Beyond
that, she had to earn her keep.

When Alex opened the door, she found June planted on the
couch with a cup of English Breakfast tea. The old woman was
almost always there, watching her soaps and talk shows.

"Oh, dear. When did you get in?" June asked when Alex
stopped just outside the living room.

Alex sat beside her and put a hand over hers. "Are you
hungry?" she asked. "I brought us some sandwiches." The old
woman smiled with sad eyes, looking completely lost. She
seemed to forget who Alex was more often now. And sometimes, Alex found her staring at things, trying to remember
how to use them or who the people in the pictures were that
cluttered her coffee tables and mantle.

"That's why I love you so much, Jesse." June put a cold,
wrinkled hand to Alex's cheek. "You've always been so caring."

Jesse was long dead; a single photo of a woman sat on the
cluttered mantle a step away from them. The old woman hadn't
stopped referring to Alex as Jesse. The photo was just as old as
the rest of the house, and Jesse was most likely June's daughter.
She had no other family, and no one else who cared—no
friends to visit and no relatives to care for her.

A single old friend had died a year earlier, and if not for
Alex, June would have ended up in a home, where the old were
always abandoned by their own. With the little social security

coming in, the woman had barely managed to make ends meet. Alex tried her best to make the checks last for both of them, stealing when she could and skipping school to check on June as much as possible. They took care of each other. Most of the time, she skipped class to make it to her part-time job at Hot Topic for the extra money, which was also where she got most of her makeup.

"I'll make you something to eat. Would you like some more tea?"

The old woman smiled warmly but didn't say anything. Alex walked into the kitchen, pulled out a plate and knife, and emptied her backpack on the counter.

"A young man came to the house today," June said over the TV in the living room.

"Oh?" Alex responded, busying herself with the sandwiches. Had the old woman had one of her dreams again? Sometimes, she was confused by what she saw on the TV. Or maybe a salesman had stopped by. Did people still go door to door these days?

"He asked for Maya, but I told him he had the wrong house. Only my Jesse lives here with me."

Alex froze, dropping the knife on the counter. She poked her head around the corner into the living room.

"Then he made me some tea. We chatted a bit about Roman history, and he just went on his way. He was so polite, Jesse. Such a strange man, though. Those eyes..."

Slowly, Alex stepped out of the kitchen, unable to still her shaking hands. The old woman didn't look back at her, eyes stuck on the TV, as if she'd never said a word.

"What did he want?" Alex asked. Her lips quivered now, too.

"He just talked a lot about the past. Really... strange things. I don't remember." The woman sounded like she was talking in her sleep.

"What did he look like?" The minute she asked it, Alex regretted the question. But she had to know.

"Oh." June shrugged, and her eyes wandered.

Alex knelt in front of the woman and put both hands on June's knees, blocking the TV. "This is important," she said. "What did he look like?"

Finally, June's glassy blue eyes settled on her. "What, dear? Who do you mean?"

Alex rose; she knew it was no use. June's mind wasn't what it used to be when they'd first met. She walked back into the kitchen, biting on her lip. She didn't know what to do. The smartest thing would be to leave right now, but she couldn't get herself to leave the old woman alone. Who would care for her?

"No one," she whispered; her hands still trembled when she picked up the knife again, and she had to put it down for a moment. She wanted to cry, but she hadn't let herself do that in a long time. Alex had learned to be strong.

Could he really have found her? Everything pointed to the fact that yes, he had. She poured water into a cup and added a tea bag.

"Very strange man," June repeated from the living room. "Very young. Good-looking. You would have liked him, Jesse." That was just the way the woman worked, like turning on a light switch—one moment recalling what she'd done twenty years ago, the next minute forgetting her own name.

Alex turned with the cup in her hand.

"He had the strangest eyes. Unusual color, you know? Almost... *purple*." June laughed. "Oh, that can't be right, dear. Purple eyes? I must have imagined that bit. But he was dressed like you, all in black. A... red patch on his shoulder. You would have liked him, Jesse, dear."

Alex hadn't realized she'd dropped the cup of tea until she heard it shatter at her feet. June didn't react at all, apparently back in her own world again where almost nothing could reach her. When Alex peered into the living room again, June was once again transfixed by the images on the TV, as if they were real people.

Hurrying to the pantry, Alex got the broom and dustpan and quickly cleaned up the mess. Then she grabbed another cup from the cabinet and another teabag with hot water. She almost spilled it all over herself just walking back into the living room, and June mumbled something else she couldn't understand. This happened all the time, too, the old woman often talking to someone who wasn't really there.

Alex placed the cup on the table next to the couch, and June glanced at the cup of tea. Then she smiled, took the cup, and blew on it before testing it with a few small sips.

He had found her—Alex was sure of it—and she didn't know how. But he had, and now he was probably lurking, waiting for his chance to grab her. And her memories came back with full force.

"Did you know that Romulus founded Rome?" he'd asked her. "It's said that he and his twin brother were raised by wolves. In his claim to power, he raided, abducted, and raped the village women."

"Just like you abducted me," Alex had muttered.

He'd grabbed her chin; her next words had frozen on her lips, then he'd released her and caressed her cheek. "How can I abduct my own wife? I love you." He'd sneered at her then, and Alex had hated herself for thinking those lips had been so inviting.

"Wife?" She'd laughed in his face. "I was never given the choice. And your *passionate lovemaking* is nothing more than fucking. There's no love involved."

He'd pulled her closer, their lips just inches apart and their bodies pressed tightly together. "Maya, we're going to have to do something about that dirty mouth of yours. And still, it's the filth coming out of that mouth that's always made me want you so much." His grimace had made her tremble. "Admit it. You like it when I *fuck you*."

Her body had always betrayed her with him, and she'd melted in his arms, kissing him first. Her self-loathing had grown even more for falling into his trap so easily.

Even now, in June's house, she felt him—sensed his presence, smelled him on her own skin and hair. It was all she could do to keep breathing.

'*Maya,*' his voice called in her mind, '*I need you...*'

"Tell me you want me!" he'd ordered as he forced her onto his bed. She'd been under his spell just like that. Now, she wanted him again.

No. Alex shook her head. She wouldn't. Not this time. But she felt him so close now in June's house.

She held her wrist, clutching the bracelet; it glowed red now, and the voice returned. June never once looked at her, lost in her tea and *The Bachelor* on TV. She didn't understand that soon, Alex might not be around anymore. Not if the man were to return. She didn't want to, but Alex would be forced to leave.

When she went back into the kitchen, she grabbed her bag and got ready to go herself. She stopped in the living room once more and looked at June there, unchanged, completely unaware of her. The old woman would be fine, Alex thought. Right now, she had to do something she'd been putting off for too long. Before she ever lost this chance again, it was time to see her son.

19

THE EERIE SOUND

A FEW HOURS AFTER SCHOOL LET OUT, MR. RANDAL PETERSON sat at his desk, checking over the remaining items on his lesson plan. When he finished, he cleared his desk and gathered the pencils and loose pens into a cup. Only then did he notice the ragged marks drawing across the end of his desk. For a minute, he wasn't sure what could have put them there. Then he remembered Tina's fingernails gripping into the wood. He hadn't realized her nails were sharp enough to leave a scratch like that, but apparently, they were.

That girl was the devil, he thought. There was something unnatural about her. But then this whole school seemed unnatural. How many times had he said that over the years? Dr. Edwards had never believed him, but then, Dr. Edwards had never been someone he could trust, either. The late principle had had a touch of something unnatural himself. And now, that granddaughter of his ... She looked like an ordinary girl to the untrained eye, but Randal knew better. He could almost sense trouble before it arrived—that peculiar evil. And ever since Dr. Edwards made him take his cross off the wall of his classroom, Randal had begun to no longer feel safe even there.

He caressed the rough, metal edges of the cross dangling from his neck—his only comfort. Prayer was needed; these kids no longer had any respect for adults. Prayer and punishment. That was what this school required. Nowadays, no one could strike a child without having the authorities at their doorstep and sending them off to prison. Didn't they see that discipline was the only chance of saving these kids and keeping them out of trouble? If Randal were in charge, things would certainly change around here.

Pausing in his end-of-day routine, he looked up at his classroom doorway. The last student had cleared out of the school a long time ago. He should be on his way out too, but he always wanted to be perfectly sure everything was ready for the next day of class. As far as Randal was concerned, he was the only functional teacher left. The new principal would see that about him. Though Randal hadn't quite figured the man out yet, he'd see how Dr. Müller fit into all this soon enough. Maybe Müller was the change this school needed. The man's nephew seemed a bit odd, though, always lurking in the hallways.

An odd sound drifted toward him from the hallway. Was that ... scratching? Randal rose, putting down his lesson plan, and tried to make out the sounds. He thought he heard someone's squeaky shoes, or maybe it was the janitor's noisy cart making its rounds.

He stepped toward his classroom door and poked his head out into the hall. There it was again. Randal looked up and down both ways, but he saw absolutely nothing. Then the noise stopped completely, followed by an eerie silence in the air.

It was definitely time to go home. He grabbed his lesson plan from the desk and reached into the drawer to grab his keys from among the clutter. But when he turned back around, his hands were shaking so badly, he dropped the keys. Quickly, Randal knelt to retrieve them, and the loose papers of his lesson plan spilled from the folder in his hands and scattered across the floor.

Muttering in frustration, he gathered them up again. Then he heard the noise again, only it was much closer now. When Randal slowly looked up, he saw her as clearly as he saw the last paper bending beneath her sneaker.

Tina? Her fingernails were making a scratching sound. She smiled down at him, but it wasn't in greeting.

20

INVITED GUEST

WE GOT HOME A LITTLE LATER THAN NORMAL; MICHAEL HAD wanted to stop for groceries. Even when he slowly emptied the bag in the kitchen now, I could tell there was something on his mind, but I didn't want to intrude into his thoughts. Clearly distracted, he folded the bags and put them in the pantry, moving almost like a zombie.

"So, Michael," I started, emptying the last plastic bag, you bought a lot of stuff. Are you by any chance making your famous chicken casserole? Maybe enchiladas?" I put the last few things into the fridge, and Michael just turned slowly to face me.

"I invited a guest over for dinner," Michael announced without meeting my gaze.

"Who?" I asked.

I was surprised I hadn't noticed it before, but now he didn't have to say anything; as soon as I'd asked, I read it in his mind. "Dr. Müller?"

"Yes, I invited Dr. Müller and his nephew John for dinner." He said it with a smile, but when I glared at him in disbelief, he cringed. It also might have been a little too soon for me to pull the words from his thoughts before he had the chance to speak them.

Those were the last people I'd ever expected him to invite to dinner. "You did?" I asked.

Michael tried to smile and failed miserably. "I thought you'd be happy about it."

Happy? Was he serious? But he didn't know anything more about either Dr. Müller or John; I knew that much. He had no idea what had happened in that office when I'd first met them, or anything else after that. John grabbing my arm in the hallway, the kiss—I doubted Michael would like that, and I wasn't going to tell him about it now. "Why would you think I'd be happy about it?" Instead of waiting for an answer, I walked out of the kitchen.

Michael followed, still not sure what was bothering me. That part radiated from him. I didn't want to talk about it. I didn't want him to ask. What could I possibly tell him?

"I thought dinner would get us all a little better acquainted," he said. "It might be nice. So we can get to know our new principal. It helps break the ice, Claudia. And Dr. Müller may be able to offer some assistance in finally getting all those repairs we badly need at Milton." I just stood there in the hall, unable to say anything. "Was I wrong?" he finally asked.

"No," I replied. "Of course not. It's just..." What could I tell him? Nothing right now made any sense, even to me.

Michael studied me, then took a deep breath. "I think I know what it is."

I looked up at him. "You do?"

"Yeah. Dr. Müller's taking your grandfather's place at that school, and... well, your grandfather's position there represented a lot of things. You're still mourning him. And here's a new principal moving in so shortly afterward. I imagine that only makes it harder to accept he's gone."

I blinked. "Yeah. You're right. I guess."

"Honey, if you don't want me to invite him over, I won't. I don't want you to be unhappy. Okay?"

"No, it's fine. I get how it'll help the school, too."

Still, he frowned, looking even more uncertain. "Are you sure?"

I nodded. "Yeah, I'm sure."

"All right, then. Why don't you go upstairs and get ready? Who knows? Maybe you can get to know John Müller, too. He seems like a nice kid."

By the time he'd said this, I'd already reached the bottom of the stairs leading up to my room.

"Prom's coming up," Michael added. "I wonder if he has a date." He turned around just a little, smiling before heading back into the kitchen. Did he just suggest I go to prom with John Müller?

"I'm sure he already does." I made sure I sounded as uninterested as I possibly could. Michael looked back at me, I flashed him a quick grin, then I raced up the stairs.

☀

The startling tug I felt in my bedroom took me completely by surprise. Then I heard the doorbell ring, and I knew it was him. He was here. Dr. Müller didn't bother me nearly as much as his pretend nephew John. I knew what they both were—well, at least I knew John wasn't who he said he was. But I still had no idea who or what Dr. Müller was or what part he played in all this.

I wasn't sure what to expect from this dinner, which Michael seemed determine to have just to break the ice with the new principal. The poor man had no idea that neither of his guests were even remotely who they said they were. I didn't want to be the one to tell him, but I wondered if anyone else ever would.

Now, all I wanted was to hide in my room and never come out. The doorbell rang again.

"Michael, someone's at the door," I yelled. Normally, he would have at least replied to that, so it was strange when he didn't. I opened my bedroom door to poke my head out into the hall. When I looked downstairs, I saw Dr. Müller's outline through the glass window in the front door.

Michael's bedroom was just at the other end of the hallway, so I went there next and gently knocked. "Michael, someone's at the door." There was no way I was going to get it and be the first one to greet "our guests." Really, they were Michael's, not mine. I didn't want to see John at all.

"Will you get it, please?" Michael called, stopping me from knocking a second time. Frowning, I slowly backed up and headed toward the top of the stairs, glaring down the staircase. "Just until I'm finished," he added.

I sneered in irritation. "You owe me, Michael," I whispered and slowly made my way down the stairs. Michael stepped out of his room just then, adjusting his tie when I turned to look back at him.

"What do you think?" Michael asked, gesturing to the tie.

"Lose the tie," I suggested with a smile. "You're not going on a date with him."

He smirked, his eyes darting toward the doorway when the doorbell rang again. Then he took off the tie and headed back into his bedroom. I huffed and slowly walked down the stairs.

I basically dragged myself to the door, where I saw Dr. Müller's face through the glass pane. He waved, and I promised myself I'd try hard to be on my best behavior. I didn't see John right away, and for a moment, I thought maybe he hadn't come. Then I felt the tug that always came with his presence, and I spotted him just to Dr. Müller's left.

I opened the door and just stood there, glaring at both of them.

John didn't look up at me, doing his best to keep himself under control. I could feel him resisting whatever it was I also felt radiating from him. Sweat formed on his brow as he focused on the tips of his dress shoes.

"Hello, Miss Belle. How are you?" Dr. Müller asked politely. I glanced down at the brown bag in his hand, which looked like a bottle of wine. But I was more focused on the strange distortions I heard in his mind, which were really hard to distinguish from his actual thoughts there. I could pick John's thoughts out easily enough, just not Dr. Müller's. So I tried not to listen to anything that sounded like a radio.

Still, I knew something was different. I'd heard something like this before coming from the both of them, but this time, John seemed different and far more in control.

"Sorry for being a little late," Dr. Müller added.

I forced a smile for the sake of pleasantries.

"And I brought some red wine. I hope it's appropriate for the dinner."

I didn't know. I didn't drink.

"She doesn't drink, Joseph," John said. "How would she know about wine and food?" Now he finally looked at me through the doorway, and I'd never seen him look this confident or in control of himself before. More than that, he looked fearless—self-absorbed.

"Of course not." Dr. Müller grinned and chuckled in slight embarrassment. "I meant for Michael and me, John."

"My uncle and I really appreciate your invitation to dinner," John told me.

I forced another smile and had to lower my gaze. There was that tug again, but it couldn't have been from John. That pull had always unraveled him before. Was it coming from me this time instead? I couldn't help but wonder where his sudden confidence had come from, and then I found myself studying his clothes.

He wore a dark sports jacket, black slacks, and well-shined black shoes. A blue silk shirt popped from beneath his jacket. Honestly, he looked like one of those teen-fashion magazine models. His piercing green eyes were anything but normal, even without the gold dancing in the center now. They still didn't quite look like they belonged in a human face.

I hated to admit it, but he looked quite handsome. And now his strong presence was actually intimidating. I cursed Alex for putting such crazy observations into my head. Now I knew I wouldn't be able to look at him without blushing or feeling sick with nerves.

"Can we come in?" John asked.

I moved aside, my face growing hot at the fact that he had to ask. "Michael should be down soon," I said. My lip quivered as we all stood awkwardly together in the entrance.

"Such a large house for just you and Michael," Dr. Müller mused, looking around.

"It was my grandfather's house, Dr. Müller," I replied, avoiding his eyes.

"Please, Miss Belle. Call me Joseph."

"Makes him feel old…" John told me with a smirk.

"Old isn't all, nephew. I can relate better with people on a first-name basis. The title makes me feel restricted. I don't want you to think I'm a stick in the mud." He chuckled, but there was no way I'd buy into this game of theirs, even if Joseph—as he called himself—didn't know that I already knew their secret.

John could tell I wasn't entertained in the least; I heard in his mind clear enough. He seemed to agree that no amount of Joseph's friendly banter was going to persuade me to warm up to them. I glanced briefly at John and thought it was strange that he looked so concerned about it.

"So how are you doing?" Dr. Müller asked me. "In light of the circumstances, of course." He shifted the bottle of red wine in his hand, not sure where to put it, but he honestly seemed more focused on me than anything else.

"Fine," I whispered, unable to offer much. I bit down on my lip to the point that it actually hurt.

"That's great. I'm happy to hear that." The man grinned, and I tried to return the smile but failed miserably. The silence deepened, and I prayed Michael would hurry.

"Things will get better," Dr. Müller added. "I promise. It may not seem like it now, but it will." His eyes were wide, warm with reassurance as he tried to offer kind words.

"I heard you love to paint," Dr. Müller said. "What else do you like to do?"

Did he *really* expect me to answer that?

"Joseph..." John shot the man an irritated look.

"Sorry. I guess I talk too much."

Michael finally came down, and I was incredibly grateful to see him. I was hoping not to have to answer any more of their questions or wonder why John was so silent this evening. At least, his mind was silent. Still, I couldn't ignore the occasional tug I felt, the drawing, the energies between us stirring up even more need and connection.

"Dr. Müller, I'm sorry for keeping you waiting," Michael said politely as he came down the stairs toward us. "John."

"Nonsense, Michael. We had the best company," Joseph said. I tried to smile.

"Ah, good. Shall we?" Michael directed us into the dining room.

"I brought a bottle," Joseph said, lifting the paper sack. "I hope it isn't too off for the occasion."

"Absolutely not," Michael replied. "Thank you. This really wasn't necessary."

"It was the least I could do." Joseph removed his jacket. "So, I hear Claudia is a great painter..."

Why did he keep asking about this?

"One of the best," Michael boasted. "I was impressed to see her sketches. Even more when I had the honor of seeing some of her paintings."

My face flushed hot again. "Michael," I said, grinding teeth. "I'm sure they're not interested."

"You're too modest, my dear," He said.

"I want to see..." John's voice was quiet, and when I glanced back, I found him looking at Michael. "I'd like to see them. I mean, if it's okay." He gazed at me then, eyes wide with innocence, and it almost looked real.

"My nephew has always been interested in taking art as an elective," Dr. Müller said. "But my brother would rather have him concentrate on his major studies. The man's a General Surgeon. Kind of wants John to pursue the same line of career."

"Wow, I see," Michael said.

"Right," I whispered. Joseph gave me an unsettling look, forcing me to look away.

"Claudia, why don't you show John your work?" Michael asked.

I narrowed my eyes at him; we didn't have any signals I could give him to say, '*No, please don't make me do that.*' I'd hoped just a hesitant glance would get the message across, but no luck.

"Dinner's almost ready," he continued. "You kids go upstairs. Let Claudia show you her artwork, John. You tell me if she isn't the best."

"Yes, sir," John said, already headed for the staircase. When I turned to look at him, he shot me a clever smile. I huffed and moved with the quickness of a turtle as he hurried up those stairs ahead of me.

Joseph handed Michael the bottle of wine. Michael walked ahead into the dining room, admiring the bottle and its label.

"Play nice, kids," Joseph called after us. When I looked

back, he smiled and winked, then joined Michael to correct him on pronunciation of the label name.

"We got it, Joseph," John called down the stairs, clearly annoyed.

Why were they here tonight?

Michael caught me looking back at him and shooed me up the stairs. Seriously, wasn't he at all concerned to leave me alone with John—or any boy? John was looking down at me again, now on the second floor, running his hand over the railing.

"You coming, Miss Belle? We have a lot to discuss..." He beckoned me closer with a single finger, then winked at me. The minute I stepped onto the second-floor landing, John disappeared into my bedroom. I found him in the back of the room, looking at the sketchbook I'd always had with me before I lost my parents.

"Close the door," he said without turning around to look at me.

I wrinkled my nose at his back. How dare he order me around like that? This was my house. I felt the tug again, and I searched for anything that might have been either causing or blocking it, like a circuit not quite making the full connection.

"Excuse me?" I replied with enough attitude for both of us. "Michael won't like the door closed,"

"Don't worry about Michael. Joseph will take care of him. It'll be okay. Now do as I say. Close the door and come here."

I frowned. Why was he *here*?

I wanted to defy him, but I was afraid of what he and Joseph might do to Michael if I did. So I obeyed.

When I closed the door, I turned slowly and took a few more steps into my room. "He's not going to hurt Michael, is he?" I asked. "Michael's completely innocent. He hasn't done anything to you."

John just kept flipping through my artwork. "These are very

good. You did all these?" He shuffled through the scattered drawings on my desk now, too.

"Yes," I said.

"Michael, your guardian... Does he know what you can do?"

It seemed were about to finally have this conversation, but I hesitated. Replacing the drawing he'd lifted from my desk, John turned around to look at me. "That's none of your business," I told him.

He narrowed his eyes at me, a slim smile spreading over his beautiful lips. "I asked you a question. Does Michael know what you can do? It's very simple."

"Does it matter?"

When he grinned, he seemed on the verge of laughing. "Well, I guess it doesn't."

"So what do you want?" I snapped.

"I don't know." John blinked, as if he were just as surprised by those words as I was. Now it seemed neither of us knew what was happening. "I don't know why I'm here, or why it is that I need to be here with you. How have you bewitched me like this? I can't understand this force, driving me to seek you. But I needed to see you again." He looked around my room again, then turned through the pages of my drawings. Moving to the easel, he ran a finger down the dry paint of the last thing I'd created there. "You paint so beautifully."

I crossed my arms annoyed. "How can you tell?"

John flashed me another innocent grin, then apparently had to return to studying my art.

Downstairs, Michael and John's pretend uncle made nauseating small talk while Michael finished setting the table for dinner. It felt like I could hear everything, though I still strained to pick up anything that would point to Michael being in trouble now.

"Don't worry," John said, turning back toward me. "Joseph

isn't going to hurt him. I promise you that. I'm not planning on hurting either one of you. I just wanted to see you again."

How nice of him. I wanted to say that to him with all the sarcasm I had, but instead I just asked, "Why?"

"First, you're incredibly intriguing," John said almost immediately, then bit his lip. Apparently, he hadn't meant to say it out loud. "Like I said, I don't know... Something beyond my own understanding has brought me here. Perhaps by sheer luck or coincidence, I was able to see you through this arranged dinner. Maybe it was meant to be."

I wanted to ask what in the world he meant by that, but he just kept talking.

"These are very, very good," he said. "You're very good. I've always been interested in art, but I just don't have the talent."

All I could do was watch him, unable to *feel* him the same way I had in the principal's office or the school hallway. I wanted to know why.

There was that tug again. John dropped the drawing and laughed.

"You keep pulling at me..." He chuckled. "Seeking me. You want to know why you can't read me, don't you?"

Admittedly, that surprised me.

John turned toward me again and lifted his wrist to tap his fingernail on the dial of the watch there. "This helps keep what's in here private," he said, then tapped his temple. Apparently, he'd also replaced the broken watch.

"Are you afraid of me?" I asked. That was the only thing I could think of to say, because he'd always been just a little ... off.

He smiled and stepped toward me. "I'm only afraid I'll hurt you if I lose control, Miss Belle."

Hurt me?

"You enhance my abilities in a way I don't understand... Perhaps 'hurt you' is the wrong phrase for what I mean." His eyes flashed that lovely green—an unnatural green—but without the gold in them. Had I been responsible for putting that swirl of gold there in the first place?

John stopped to adjust the dial on his watch, and the next second, I felt him. He was nervous and confident at the same time—was that even possible? His thoughts raced toward me; he didn't want to scare me, and he was trying so hard to hold himself back. That connection between us had reappeared, faint and not nearly as strong as before but there nonetheless.

"I want to be honest with you," he said, taking the last few steps toward me to reach out and touch my cheek. The minute he did, the gold spread from the center of his pupils again, coming to life exactly the way I remembered it.

I pulled away, and I felt his pain in response. I also felt that same current still pulling him toward me. When I'd backed up all the way to my bed, I sat down on the mattress.

In the silence, both Michael's and Joseph's muffled voices seeped up through the floor. "So, who is he?" I asked.

John frowned, then approached the bedside table and picked up the picture of my grandfather. He examined it briefly with keen eyes, and another smile lit up his already gorgeous face. Then his eyes flashed, and I felt the current of emotion—some strengthening sensitivity—growing stronger between us. I pushed it away, clearly feeling the new wound it left on John's pride and hope. I could feel his reaction. I could *see* it. It was so odd to know he felt very much the same as I did.

He turned. "You mean Joseph? He's a friend."

"A friend?" I glared at him. Liar. The minute I'd thought it, John blinked, apparently having heard my thought as clearly as if I'd said it out loud. Then I stood, walked toward him, and snatched the picture from his hand. John didn't seem surprised at all but merely grinned. "The least you can do is be honest with me," I said. "I know what you are."

"Fair enough."

I hadn't expected it to be that simple.

"Joseph is a guardian," John added. No, I had absolutely no idea what that meant. "And you know I'm a hunter."

I walked toward the other side of the desk beside my bed and set down the picture. "A guardian?"

"He's sort of my bodyguard. Not that I need one, of course."

"You sound really sure of yourself," I muttered, and he just kept smiling. I was really starting to hate it, mostly because it looked so good on him. I bit my lip. "You make it sound like you're the best or something," I said, returning to my seat on the bed.

"I am."

So, he was handsome *and* arrogant, I thought.

"Joseph is there to make sure I get the tools I need to do my job without interruptions..."

"Like a personal secretary," I volunteered.

John laughed. "He wouldn't put it that way, but yes. Something like that."

"Why is he pretending to be your uncle? Why are you both really here in Milton?" I narrowed my eyes at him, wanting to remind him that I could read his thoughts. But we both knew that he was volunteering this information now, and if he wanted, he could easily move that dial on his watch again and block me out. "Are you here for me?" I added.

John's eyes softened. Then he exhaled, stepped forward, and knelt in front of me. I didn't know whether to back away or stay there. My first thought was to shove him back with my mind, but I caught his wish to reassure me—to convince me I didn't have any reason to be afraid.

"No, I'm not here for you," he said. "You... well, you were just... an unexpected discovery." His brow furrowed, and he ran a hand over the back of his neck. It was hard not to feel so many jumbled emotions racing through him. When he looked up at me again, that connection between us strengthened, and I felt his emotions shift to fear, sympathy, concern. "I'm not even supposed to be here with you," he added. "I'm supposed to tell Joseph about things like this." It seemed to truly pain him that he'd been hiding something so huge from his friend, or guardian, or whatever Joseph was to him. "And I can't be sure why I haven't. I just can't do it…" Then he stood and sat beside me on the bed.

My heart pounding in the back of my head, and I had a feeling John's beat now in pretty much the same way. "You haven't told him about me?" I asked.

"No." He leaned closer. There was something beautiful in his eyes, dancing again with that lovely gold. John reached out to touch my cheek again, sending an electric current racing through us both. He smiled, and now so did I. "I've never known anyone quite like you, Claudia. I was curious at first. Now, I can't begin to understand my need to be around you. Close to you. This feeling"—he gestured between us—"this connection… I feel the circuit. It can't be broken. I can't pull away. I don't want to, even when I know it's getting stronger. Don't you feel it?"

I nodded slowly, then glanced down at his watch. They sounded like whispers rising from the watch's face as the hands spun to the left and then the right.

"I used to fear it. Now I know I have nothing to fear." John cupped my cheek and leaned even closer. I didn't pull away. What was I doing? John was the enemy…

Before he kissed me, I slipped away from him to stand and walk to the center of my room. What was happening? Yes, I felt everything John had just described. I knew something powerful existed between us, but I refused to admit it was important. I didn't want to trust him.

"What are you doing?" I asked. Really, though, I was asking myself.

"I'm sorry," he said. "I couldn't resist... I can't. Every time I'm near you, something pulls me closer. Don't you feel it?"

Of course I did, but I couldn't tell *him* that. John watched me from the bed, the need in his eyes growing beneath the dancing gold, though it had dimmed a little.

"Forgive me for frightening you in the hall earlier today," he said.

"You didn't frighten me." I felt stupid for thinking I could convince him of that. He smiled, and I bit my lip again.

"I didn't mean to be so fierce," he continued, "but you surprised me when you ran. It... triggered my hunter instincts, and the only thing I could do was run after you. Your energy opened this other... force inside me."

My energy. I didn't believe him.

"You pulled at me, just like you pull at me now. You tug... and you tug so hard. It's not easy to resist or to fight this desire to go to you. The watch makes it easier not to lose myself in your energy."

So that pull *had* come from me, as far as John knew.

"I have never lost control like that before. You were all I wanted. I had to be close to you, to protect you. I knew it as fiercely then as I know right now that you are so very special... to me."

I turned my head slightly away, and there was that pull again.

John's laughter filled the room. "Your actions reflect denial, but your emotions reveal the truth of what you really feel. Your energy tells me exactly what you want."

I whipped my head toward him again and glared. "You don't know anything about me."

"You're right. I don't." He stood from the bed and stepped toward me again. "I want to..."

A spark flared inside me, lighting my heart and filling me with something I couldn't name. I felt alive. Even then, I bit my lip and bottled it up, because it still terrified me. A flash of that shadow looming over us in my vision entered my mind, those tentacles reaching out toward us. I gazed and looked up into John's blazing eyes.

"If you're not here for me," I said, "then why did you come to Milton?" The hair on my arms stood straight up, now, the pull between us and the rising spark running through my veins. His eyes flashed with that gold again, but he seemed to be in control of himself. "You hunt things for those people in lab coats," I said.

"I feel you wanting to push me away," he said, still smiling. "But you can't. Just like I can't resist your pull on me."

Then he turned to pace slowly in front of me, fighting with himself to be honest, but he knew he couldn't hold secrets from me. The struggle I felt in him was intriguing and incredibly satisfying.

"I can't believe I'm going to reveal this to you," he whispered, then stopped pacing and faced me. "I've never told anyone this." Then John returned to sit on the edge of my bed and patted the mattress beside him.

"Come sit beside me... please."

When I did, another jolting wave of connection overwhelmed us both.

"I work for a secret corporation only known as the Company," John continued. "This organization is divided into several parts operating different divisions. Military, space, science, and most importantly, pharmaceuticals. But what I do takes place within an academy."

"The academy?" I said. quizzically glaring over at him. It clearly took a lot out of him to reveal something as secretive and important as this to me.

"It's a school were recruits like me are trained."

"Wait. There are others like you?"

"Not... exactly like me." He grinned. "I'm the only one... like this. They call me an anomaly."

I wrinkled my nose at him.

'At least, that's what Dr. Nicholson called me,' John thought. When I picked up on it, I recognized the name instantly. I'd heard it in Josephs' mind too.

"Who's Dr. Nicholson?" I asked. John glanced quickly at me with a frown of surprise and curiosity. Then he seemed to remember he was talking to someone who could do the kinds of things I did. "Is he real?" John nodded. "So who is he?"

"How do you know of him?" he asked.

"I heard the name in your uncle—I mean in Joseph's thoughts."

"You heard Joseph's thoughts."

"Yes..." As if in reflex, John looked down at his watch, and I followed his gaze. "I think there was something wrong with his watch when I heard it," I added. "It was making a lot of weird sounds that day. Who is he?"

John hesitated, and I waited. "He's sort of my boss," he finally said. "He's the one who sent me here."

"Should I be afraid of him?" I asked. When I'd first heard the name from Joseph, the man who seemed pretty difficult to scare had been worried about what Dr. Nicholson would say. Now, John spoke about this mysterious doctor as if the man were someone to be feared.

John's silence when I asked concerned me even more.

Then he reached out to take my hand tightly in his. My own rising anxiety faded at his touch. "No. You don't have to be afraid," he told me. "You have nothing to worry about. He's looking for some creature... with a strong force. I was sent to find it and bring it to Dr. Nicholson. And that will be the end of it."

"Then what happens to you and Joseph?"

He was quiet for a moment and dropped his gaze from my face.

"Are you going to leave?" I asked.

"After everything's finished? Yes."

Why did that suddenly bother me? If they found whatever they were looking for, then he and Joseph would be gone, and I wouldn't have to deal with either of them anymore. I wasn't sure that I liked that. Not after all this. I'd always known there was something between John and I, and I'd never wanted to admit it until facing the fact that he would leave when he'd completed what he'd been sent here to do.

"I know it's a lot to take in," he continued. "I have abilities that others don't have. I move faster. I'm stronger. I was born with these abilities, and that's why he sent me. The academy is all I know."

"You grew up there?"

"I've been there all my life."

I frowned. "What about your parents? Family?"

"I have none." He sounded proud enough when he said it, but I felt him picking up on my own sadness, which seemed to make him reconsider his words.

"What's it like?" I asked, trying to imagine such an empty-feeling place. Honestly, it wasn't too hard. I didn't have any family, either. "The academy, I mean."

"It's a military base," he said. "We train, exercise, eat in groups, sleep in the barracks, wake up every day at dawn. Repeat."

"Do you have school?"

"Of course. Except my studies are a little different than what you might learn at Milton. Alchemy, chemistry, biology and medical training, and a variety of languages. One of the first things we learn is the proper use, assembly, and disassembly of firearms. Then we have target practice and run simulations—"

"What?" This was starting to sound more like an academy from the future, now.

"Training games," he said. "Both computer and life simulations where I hunt my targets. Sometimes I go in with a team, sometimes I'm on my own."

I stared at him for a minute. "Do you get to go out?"

John frowned at me. "Go out?"

"You know, have fun. Time for yourself."

He blinked. "Yeah, of course. We get leisure. I end up at target practice anyway, or I pass the time reading the medical textbooks I haven't fully finished yet. Sometimes it's language studies on my own."

I smirked. "That's not fun."

He laughed, then studied me with a soft gaze, like he was just taking all of me in. That warmth radiating from him made me blush. Why did I have to be this sensitive? "It is for me," he said.

His explanation didn't make it any easier to imagine what his life must have been—without family, growing up in an academy and drilled by military officers in uniform, not knowing much at all about the outside world. That golden light danced in his eyes again. "And you hunt others like me?" I asked, my voice barely rising above a whisper.

"I hunt extraterrestrials. What the Company calls ET Product. I've never come across anyone… like you before."

"I had a vision of the girl you took captive. She could read minds like me."

John's eyebrows lifted above his wide eyes. "You saw all that?" I nodded slowly. He lowered his head and folded his hands together on his lap. "They're called mindsifters. Or mindbenders," he admitted. "And she was one of a few who escaped the Company thirty years ago."

"Escaped?" I asked. Now the place was starting to sound like a prison.

He nodded. "They were products created by the Company. There was a fire, and a lot of equipment and research was lost. As well as quite a few company products." Apparently, I still looked completely lost, because he added, "The Company also dabbles in creating new lifeforms to help the human race develop possible cures for diseases like cancer and HIV. They've successfully created suitable solutions for lost limbs, body replacements, and organ transplants. Dr. Nicholson is one of the top research scientists in that department."

"So he's definitely important," I said.

"Yeah, he is. The Company has achieved a lot of successful accomplishments because of him. And they continue to progress..." His gaze roamed across my room for a minute before he looked at me again. "The girl you saw. She was the only one left of her kind. And now there's you. But *you* are unlike anything I've ever seen. You're... different. Extraordinary..." He leaned toward me again. "I can't believe I'm telling you all this. But you're nothing like her."

"It sounds like I'm a lot like her," I replied. "She can read minds. So can I."

"No, she was created in a lab, just like the rest of her kind. I was trained to bring them back to the men in the lab coats, as you put it. That's what I do. Now you know."

He stared deep into my eyes, the dance of gold specks expanding across the green of his eyes. I wondered if he actually felt the difference when that gold sparkled. John leaned forward toward me even farther and touched my cheek.

"I can't deny what I feel when I look into your eyes or when I'm close to you," he told me. "You give me strength and make me weak at the same time, and still, I just want to be near you." He laughed. "I know how that must sound. But it's what I feel. I don't understand what this is or what's happening to me, but I know I don't want it to stop..."

He took a breath, then his eyes flashed again when he

exhaled. "You're afraid?" he asked me, as if he'd just found that growing sensation inside me and it pained him. "If I scare you, I won't say any more. As hard as it is to stay away from you, I will, if that is what you wish..." His brows drew together, and I felt the tentative hope flaring inside him that I might tell him to stay. "Is that what you want?" he asked.

"No." I said it quickly and without thinking, which definitely surprised me. "I think I'm only afraid because I feel the same way," I admitted. "I don't understand it. I've never met anyone like you before. I feel safe with you. I just met you, but you make me feel... protected. It's strange."

"No, it's not," he replied.

"I'm glad you were honest—"

Then his lips were on mine, and my heart pounded in my head again. I had to tell myself to breathe, even as I felt the warmth of his soft mouth against my own. Then I saw an image of us in his mind; he was holding me in a tight embrace, vowing to protect me. Now, it seemed, the hunter had become the defender.

"Dinner!" Joseph's voice startled us both. I pulled away and rose from the bed to face the door just as it swung open. Joseph poked his head into my room, and John leaped to his feet, rubbing the back of his head. He looked like an entirely different person when he blushed in embarrassment.

"What are you two up to?" Joseph asked with a wide grin.

"Claudia was showing me her artwork."

Joseph stepped into the bedroom and around us toward my art table to flip through the scattered pieces—a few pictures of the school, fruit bowls, and the portraits I'd done of the assistant principals, Mr. Claypool and Mr. Vasquez.

"Wow. I'm impressed, Miss Belle." Joseph acted like everything was fine and normal, but I couldn't stop thinking that he already knew what John was trying to hide from him.

John glanced at me and tried to smile, but he was too

nervous and embarrassed by Joseph's interruption. I wondered why. "Uh… did you say dinner was ready?" John asked.

Joseph turned and walked across the room again to stand right in front of John. Then he put a hand on his fake nephew's shoulder. "Yes."

John pushed his hand away and moved past him, then gestured for me to step into the hallway first. They stayed behind in my room for a bit longer, and I glanced back to see John motioning to Joseph to stay back. Joseph scowled, clearly upset by something. Then John joined me in the hallway.

"Is everything okay?" I asked.

"It's nothing," he replied with a smirk. "He's just being Joseph." I had no idea what that meant, but I doubted John would explain it any more than that with Joseph standing right on the other side of my door. Then he grabbed my hand and had my undivided attention again. "I'm going to ask you something," he said. "I want you to consider it first before you dismiss it or answer."

I tried to pick his mind, but he'd already turned the dial on his watch again to block me out. "Ask me what?" I said.

John only smiled and moved toward the top of the stairs. "You'll see."

I followed with Joseph, who stepped right in front of me as we walked. Then he stopped, and I almost walked right into him. "Please," he said. "After you, Miss Belle."

I moved to the stairs first.

John turned back to frown at him, then grabbed my hand. It surprised me, but I let him lead me down the steps, and I had no idea why or how I still felt so calm and at peace with it.

When we stepped into the dining room, John and Joseph reached for the same chair. Then Joseph seemed to realize his fake nephew's intentions, and when John pulled the chair back, he gestured for me to sit in it. I'd wanted to sit at the other end of the table, but I couldn't just tell him, 'No, thank you.' So I took the seat reluctantly, feeling Joseph's gaze on me from where he'd picked a different chair across the table. I couldn't read his mind or sense any kind of emotion coming from him. That didn't make his keen observation of me any less noticeable.

Then Michael joined us at the table he'd already set. The man had made chicken casserole with buttered bread, green beans, corn, mashed potatoes, and gravy, but he'd bought the apple pie for dessert.

Joseph did his part by opening the bottle of red wine and pouring a glass for Michael first and then himself. John grabbed the pitcher of lemonade and filled my glass, then his own.

Dinner was quiet—except for Joseph and Michael talking almost nonstop about school. I didn't pay attention to any of it, thinking instead about what John had revealed to me and the truth of who he was. If he trusted me enough to tell me all that, maybe I could trust him with my own secrets, though I didn't think I had nearly as much to reveal as he did.

Michael and Joseph seemed far too busy in their discussion to even glance in our direction. Michael brought up the repairs Milton needed, asking Joseph for his opinion on how to approach the district for funds. They talked, and I drifted until I felt John's hand touch mine. A surge of energy raced up my arm; my first thought was that he'd turned his watch's dial down enough for me to feel a little more from him. I felt him connecting to me, but his specific thoughts remained a blur. How did he do that?

"I can feel you," I whispered to him, "but I can't hear you. How does that watch work, exactly?" John glanced across the table. We were still essentially being ignored.

He pulled up his jacket sleeve just a little, exposing his wrist and the watch under the table. The dial was movable, the head looked like it came loose, and the clear face revealed all the inner mechanicals that made it look like nothing but a normal timepiece. It was beautiful, with silver along the outside of the face and gold on the inside. Every piece of it looked old, but now I knew it wasn't anything like what it pretended to be.

"The dials have different frequencies," John whispered. "They each perform a different function." I reached out to touch it, and when I did, the dials moved rapidly. John pulled back his wrist a little and adjusted one of the dials again.

"I don't want to break it..." I said softly, glancing sideways at him. He grinned, and I blushed.

"You won't. I just lowered the frequency. It should be all right."

I reached for it again, and the dials moved much more slowly this time. Whatever direction I moved my fingers over the watch's face, the dial moved in turn, following me left then right.

"You're amazing..." he said, watching this effect I had on his pretend watch.

I couldn't help but smile. "Why does it do that?" I asked.

"Your energies are off the scales. It's designed to read surges, circuits, and *sources* of energy. All kinds..." His whisper softened even more, and he blinked at the watch for an odd few seconds of seriousness.

"What's wrong?" I asked.

"Nothing," he whispered.

He looked so lost when he glanced up at me again. I lifted my hand and hovered it just above the fork beside my plate, then I checked to make sure Michael and Joseph were still too busy to pay attention. John shot me a curious frown, and I lifted the fork from the table without ever even touching it. It was just a parlor trick. My father had done the same thing to impress his co-workers; people thought he was some sort of a magician. The best part was when I made the napkin move and walk around the table like a tiny person. Then it danced with my fork.

"My father used to do this for me when I was a kid," I said. Still, I vividly remembered him being ashamed of the exact same thing when he did it at work. That was the one and only time he'd ever brought me into the office with him, and I'd never gone back.

John smirked, then snorted, and we both burst out laughing. Of course, it brought us all the unwanted attention from the two men sitting on the other side of the table. I grabbed the fork and John grabbed the napkin. We both smiled as Michael and Joseph studied us, then they went right back into their conversation and drinking up all that wine. I couldn't help giggling again, and apparently, John couldn't, either.

The next time I looked at Joseph, my gaze met his. I didn't think John noticed at all; he seemed to be having more fun than he'd had in a long time, which was probably true after everything he'd told me in my bedroom. But it didn't make me stop laughing.

John pulled my hand into his one more time, and for a brief moment, I felt all his desire and longing. His eyes flashed in that golden dance again. "I don't want this night to end," he admitted. Just hearing him say that made me tense up again. "Why are you scared, Claudia?" he asked. "Don't you trust me? I've been nothing but honest with you. I can't hide anything from you, and I don't want to. I want you to trust me." His brows drew together in pain as he studied my gaze. "I'm not going to hurt you. Let me prove it to you."

I narrowed my eyes, wondering how he'd ever prove something like that. "Why?" I asked.

He cupped my cheek. "I want to be close to you. I'm falling for you."

Now I had no idea what to say. I closed my eyes, feeling his energy connect to mine, and I knew he'd told me the truth.

Only when his hand pulled away from my cheek and the connection faded did I open my eyes again.

"Mr. McClellan," John said. Michael and Joseph stopped talking to look at us in curiosity. "I wanted to ask, sir—"

"Please, John, call me Michael."

I tapped my foot against John's leg, trying to stop him from whatever he was about to do. He grinned at me and grabbed my hand again, curled his fingers around my palm with a tight squeeze. My cheeks burned.

"Michael, with your permission, I wanted to ask if I could take Claudia to prom."

That was the last thing I'd expected. I blinked up at John, completely speechless, but he didn't look at me. He just held Michael's gaze, and even Joseph looked entirely puzzled.

Milton's new principal cleared his throat and spilled his wine all over his lap. "Excuse me," he said. He put the glass down and wiped his pants with the table napkin. He forced a smile, clearly unhappy with John's request. I still couldn't hear anything from his mind through the aggravating distortions.

"Well, that would be up to Claudia, John. Of course, I would have no problem at all with you asking her or, for that matter, actually taking her." Michael looked at me, and now I was on the spot. All three of them waited for me to say something, and then a loud wave of thought burst through the distortion coming from Joseph.

'He's never been interested in any girl as much as this one. If he compromises this assignment, he'll be explaining that one to Dr. Nicholson all on his own. Then I'll end up being the one who has to clean up the mess.'

Now that I'd heard Joseph's thoughts, apparently, I didn't know what to do. I got up, then looked down at John. He frowned in concern, obviously not wanting me to leave. He wanted to say something, but he sat rigidly in his chair and waited. With Joseph and Michael watching, I guessed he didn't want to reach out to me for them to see what happened when he did.

"I'm sorry," I said. "I'm going to bed. I'm tired and... I'm just not feeling well today. Excuse me. Nice meeting you." It didn't make any sense at all—especially when I'd already met them— but I left the table and ran up the stairs. When I got to my room, I closed and locked the door behind me, waiting for the sound of footsteps coming after me. There were none. For a second, I was relieved. Then I couldn't figure out why I'd just run away.

Did I want to go to prom with John? No. Did I like him? No. Yes. A little.

"Oh, god," I groaned and rubbed my face. "What's wrong with me?"

21

THE MYSTERIOUS QUENTIN

I TRIED TO REANALYZE WHAT HAD HAPPENED DOWNSTAIRS. JOSEPH obviously suspected something. John's interest made him suspicious, and the man had been thinking about cleaning up the mess. I had a feeling that was me.

The weirdest thing was that I'd picked up on Joseph's thoughts even though he'd been wearing his own version of John's strange watch. Did I also have the ability to make it through their devices? If I did, I had no idea how to control it. Then I wondered if I should even tell John at all about hearing Joseph's thoughts. He trusted Joseph. Would he even believe what I told him?

I must have sat in my dark room for an hour before I heard the front door open. Then nothing. Finally, footsteps moved slowly up the stairs. My first thought was that Joseph was coming for me, and I jumped under the covers like a scared little child hoping the boogieman wouldn't find her hiding.

I peered from underneath the sheets and clearly saw a shadow stop outside my closed door. It stayed there for a moment, then moved on. Another door at the end of the hall opened, the hallway went dark, and the door closed again.

Throwing the sheets back, I realized childishly that it had only been Michael, and as I lay there, I watched a breeze push back the curtains and smelled the scent of pine wafting into my room.

For a long moment, I lay there on my side, watching the curtain move, catching a few stars in the visible night sky. John had said there were more people out there like me who could read minds and move things with their thoughts. The idea both delighted and terrified me. John had also revealed that he'd been responsible for capturing most of them. So why hadn't he done the same with me? I got it that he'd never felt whatever pull existed between us with anyone else, but I still didn't know why—or why he still hadn't told Joseph about any of it. Maybe he was trying to keep this Dr. Nicholson from finding out about me. I still hadn't decided whether or not I'd ask John about this mysterious doctor.

I blushed just thinking about talking to John again. My god, what could he be thinking right now after I'd left him at the dinner table in a panic? It hadn't been because of John. I'd left because I'd felt Joseph's animosity toward me, and it made me more than a little wary. I wanted to call John and try to explain, but he might not be able to talk. He might have someone listening in on all his conversations. It wasn't like he was a normal high school guy whose parents mostly respected his privacy. At least I didn't feel so alone now. Then I remembered that I'd never actually gotten his number.

How would that conversation go, anyway? 'Hey, John, I somehow read Joseph's thoughts, and he doesn't like me. He's thinking about having to clean up your mess if you don't do your job, and I'm pretty sure he was referring to me.' What would he even do after hearing something like that? What *could* he do?

I thought I wouldn't ever be able to fall asleep, but after what felt like hours of lying there, I finally did.

☀

Something was chasing me through the halls. No matter where I went, the shadowy figure loomed closer and closer, spilling like black ink toward me. It emerged from every crack in the floor and dripped down every surface; its wavering arms reached for me from every direction. I knew it wouldn't stop until it had me, and I had no way to escape. Nowhere, really, to run.

The halls extended in front of me, long and endless, offering nothing for me to grab a hold of or use to hide myself. Those looming arms stretched closer and closer, then bony fingers wrapped around my arm. I screamed, but when I whirled around to face the shadow, I saw my young rescuer's face instead.

He smiled at me, and the warmth I'd felt that day in the pool Milton High didn't have, once again consumed me. Now I was safe—protected. He took me in his arms and held me with a sigh, pulling me closer against him. *"You are safe now, my pet,"* he whispered.

I opened my eyes, blinking around my room after such a sudden awakening from the dream. Then I saw the figure sitting on my window ledge. My first reaction was to scream, but before I could, I realized there was nothing to be afraid of.

He was here. He'd finally come back for me.

"It was you that day, wasn't it?" I asked, nervously waiting for his reply. The room's shadows obscured his face, but I recognized him with every part of my being. I knew it was him.

He leaned forward slowly, his face entering the moonlight streaming through the window. His coal-black mane glimmered against his ghostly pale skin, lighting up the line of his nose and his cheekbones. Those strange, beautiful violet eyes sparkled at me.

"Yes," he replied, then grinned. "I must apologize."

I sat up in my bed, unable to say a word. Seeing him again made me think of my grandfather, but through that mourning I realized how happy I was to see my protector here now. It meant he was real, and I wasn't crazy.

"For what?" I asked with trembling lips.

"For not coming sooner when you needed me." He leaped off the ledge and slowly stepped into the room. His black jumpsuit looked like some kind of uniform, the various pieces of it shimmering like scales in the moonlight. A patch of purple covered his right shoulder, but that was the only color.

"I don't understand," I said, then slipped out from beneath the covers and scooted toward the foot of the bed. "Whatever it was... whatever was trying to get me that day... you stopped it."

That man with the red tie flashed again in my memory— the way he'd looked at himself in the mirror and *changed* from behind his own eyes. It unnerved me just as much to think of it now.

My rescuer bowed his head and dropped to his knees at the foot of the bed. Then he slowly gazed up at me.

I could feel his sadness; his large purple eyes overwhelmed me. I knew he was genuinely sorry for what had happened, though I really had no idea what had happened. Only that I'd been protected.

I felt him now as clearly as I'd felt John. But it was so much different with this guardian of mine kneeling in front of me. He knew why he was here and what he wanted. I blushed when I realized that was me. His connection was so much fiercer, and I couldn't even try to question the things I felt radiating from him. He wanted me back.

'*I need you, Pet-tricia,*' he thought directly to me. That definitely wasn't my name, but he didn't give me time to ask. '*You have to remember,*' he added. '*You have to remember who you truly are…*'

His eyes pulled at me, assuring me he wasn't a stranger at all and I could trust him. I wanted to resist, but his tug on my memories convinced me even more that I'd known him once, a long time ago. I had no idea how to find that truth inside myself. I shook my head, trying to clear my mind.

"No," he said aloud and dropped his head again between hunched shoulders. "I failed you, and for, that I apologize."

I extended my hand, hoping to feel his face. When he glanced up at me—broken, sad, and so beautifully mysterious —I paused. I longed to know the man behind those eyes. The memory he claimed I'd lost.

"You saved me," I whispered, realizing I was shaking now. He rose immediately, pulled away, and went to the window again. The moonlight glowed on his face. "What was that thing?" I asked, though I had no doubt I already knew the answer—that I knew the true name of the shadow in the black suit and red tie.

'*Death…*' the wind whispered. Suddenly, it didn't feel like we were alone; it felt like Death itself now lurked just outside my window, teasing us both.

My protector looked around as the voice in the wind faded. Then he approached the bed again. I trembled. His eyes danced over me. "Don't be afraid. He can't hurt you as long as I'm here. I've made a bargain with him. Unfortunately, as an agent of death, he knows the role quite well. The energies... draw him to you." He paused, as if his own thought had distracted him.

"Who *are* you?" I whispered, intoxicated by his presence in a way I could never understand. Before I realized it, I rose from the bed and stepped toward him, staring into his deep, hypnotic eyes. My face grew warm. His beautiful purple eyes sparkled like clusters of light, all dancing at once. I couldn't move any closer, and all I could think of was being with him. Then, almost immediately, I knew everything he knew.

He pulled away from me once more before leaping onto the window ledge. Whatever spell had captured us, it had now just lifted. If I could remember what I'd meant to say, I'd be able to speak freely now.

'Quentin,' his voice repeated in my head.

"What's happening?" My voice shook now as much as my body. "How is this possible?" That was really what I'd wanted to ask, but deep inside, it felt like I already knew. So why was I resisting the obvious?

"Anything is possible," Quentin replied with a smile. "Come. I want to show you something." He beckoned me with an outstretched hand.

I hesitated, looking back at my room and wondering if Michael had heard anything.

"Don't be afraid," he said with raised eyebrows.

"I'm not afraid of anything," I stated.

"Then take my hand." His reaching fingers looked exactly the same as the day he'd offered them beside the pool. But this time, the choice was entirely mine. "Trust me," he added with a tender smile. "Take my hand. I want to show you something wonderful."

Still hesitating just a little, I made the decision and took his hand.

He whisked me toward him until our bodies were achingly close and frowned. "Don't you trust me, my *pet*?" he whispered.

That made me pull away to gaze at him. "Yes." Even that surprised me. Quentin had saved me, I knew. So how couldn't I trust him now? If he'd wanted to hurt me, he could have left me for the shadow to consume beside the pool.

But before the word could leave my lips, I exhaled, closing my eyes. Then my stomach lurched, and a tiny scream almost escaped me. When I opened my eyes, we were in the sky. The drop had left me breathless, and my heart pounded with alarming speed. I couldn't control the sensation overwhelming my entire being. The air blew through my hair as Quentin held me close against him; his eyes glittered at me as he said, "Hold on."

His grip tightened, and we moved faster. Now I couldn't see anything but a bright light, consuming us entirely, and I had to close my eyes. Then, just as quickly as everything else, the rush of our movement disappeared, replaced by incredible peace.

We were standing on a beach, the white sand gathering at my feet. Seagulls filled the blue skies above. Behind us, a vast blue ocean expanded along the horizon as far as the eye could see. I looked up at Quentin, breathing quickly. "Where are we? How did you *do* that?" I pulled away from him to walk toward the ocean, then I found myself running to the edge of the water and grinning at all the freedom and beauty in front of me.

"This is Demos. My world. Here, I can do anything I want." Quentin lifted his arms to the sky.

I raced into the water until it was up to my waist, looking far into the ocean and wishing to go farther, to explore the beauty before me. When I turned back toward Quentin, I saw everything else—a vivid jungle and a landscape of mountains in the distance; tall green plants; birds of every color flittering through the branches.

However I'd gotten here, I never wanted to leave.

Something splashed in the water behind me, and I spun around to see a tailfin glistening above the water's surface before it disappeared. Then again, the tail appeared, and when I whirled around to see what it was, I caught sight of a woman's face in the clear ocean water. I nearly fell back, but the woman emerged and caught my arm before I lost my balance. She was beautiful, with flaming-red hair falling over her naked torso, and now I had no doubt that the tail belonged to her. I couldn't stop staring at it.

"You're...you're a...." I felt stupid for stuttering and immediately put a my hand over my mouth.

"I did not mean to frighten you, miss," she whispered. "I had to see you for myself." Then she grinned and called over her shoulder, "It is *she!*"

Behind her in the distance, a few heads appeared above the blue water to gawk at me.

"To see me?" I whispered.

Something must have startled her; she dove back under the water and disappeared in seconds.

"Wait!" I shouted. The woman reappeared, but now she looked up into the sky. I startled when I saw Quentin hovering just beside me, *kneeling* on the surface of the water.

He gently beckoned the woman back toward us with a wave of his hand. "Say hello, Selena," he whispered to the mermaid, and she lowered her head. Only then did I realize that another had been with the redhaired woman, and this second one emerged to greet me.

She might have been more beautiful than the first, rising from the waters with her long blonde hair draping over her shoulders and chest. She smiled and bowed to Quentin. "Greetings, mighty one," she said, then turned her intense gaze onto me.

"Say hello, Selena," Quentin firmly repeated.

"Greetings, miss. It is an honor to finally meet you." She bowed her head to me, as did her companion, and many others emerged to do the same. I could only stare at them, mesmerized and unable to speak.

The blonde-haired mermaid smiled. "We've heard—"

"So what do you think?" Quentin interrupted with a smirk, though the question was clearly directed at her and not me.

"She is beautiful, mighty one," Selena replied. But when she glanced at me again, it wasn't hard to see all the hate behind her eyes.

My face felt hot under so much attention from her and all the others gathered around us.

"You found her," Selena added in a whisper. "Just as you said you would." She offered a weak smile and looked a little disappointed.

Quentin merely laughed, apparently ignoring the mermaid's growl in response.

"This is unbelievable," I muttered, feeling like a little kid gaping at presents on Christmas.

"Not in my world," Quentin said. When I looked up at him, his gaze was so intense, I felt how much he was enjoying my curiosity—and my innocence.

"They're so beautiful," I whispered. The blonde mermaid named Selena frowned and boldly approached me again.

"You're beautiful," Quentin said with a smile, reaching down to caress my wet cheek. My lips trembled, and a breeze rushed over my back, whipping the wet strands of my hair into my face until they clung there. He peeled them away.

"The Spider Queen has inquired about your return, mighty one," Selena said. She spoke sternly now, and it wasn't that hard to imagine she didn't like me.

"I'm not interested in the Spider Queen," Quentin said. He left his palm against my cheek when he turned to shoot Selena a warning glance.

"She has prepared a great feast in your honor," Selena argued.

"I said I'm not interested!" Quentin snapped.

The mermaid flickered backward through the water, her eyes wide, and bowed until her face almost touched the waves. "Forgive me, mighty one," she said again. "I only thought—"

"You thought what? I take a moment of my precious time to allow you this honor. To see *my beautiful Pet-tricia*. To be the first to see me triumph over my suffering. And you speak of nothing else but *her*!"

"Forgive me," Selena whispered. "I only thought she might look upon what you sought for so long. And that you are victorious... where the others have failed."

Quentin frowned at her, but it quickly shifted into a smile. He rose from where he knelt on the surface of the water and placed his hands on his hips. "What she thinks makes no difference," he said.

"What of your brother, mighty one?" Selena asked, and she shrank into herself when Quentin looked down on her again with a sharpened scowl.

"He knows. But he doesn't believe..." Quentin stared off across the ocean, then turned to look down at me. "But he soon will."

I had no idea what they were talking about—no idea who the Spider Queen was or that Quentin even had a brother. I still wasn't entirely sure I'd been speaking to actual mermaids. Only when Quentin offered his hand to pull me from the water did I realize I was shivering. Now, I stood on the surface of the water beside him, wondering how that was even possible.

"Can he be convinced?" Selena asked, apparently having found her courage again. The other half-human creatures around her moved back, away from Quentin as he glared at her over his shoulder. It seemed she was the only one of them who ever questioned him.

His lips pulled back into another grin, and he gazed at me, cupping my cheek again before stroking my wet hair. "My *Pet-tricia* must awaken from within. Only then will he realize his mistake." He studied my eyes, pulling me closer against him as I shivered. "But all in due time. First, I must do what I can to make you remember," he told me.

"Who's Pet-tricia?" I whispered, staring up into those sparkling eyes. He obviously thought that was my name, but it wasn't. I couldn't think clearly enough in this place to imagine why he had me confused with someone else.

"No one," he softly replied. Then he pulled me closer, wrapped his arms around me, and we shot back into the sky. Below us, a few of the mermaids waved; others, especially Selena, merely disappeared beneath the waves.

We flew over a landscape much different than the ocean and white sand of the beach. The mountain range I'd seen in the distance was now just below us, most of them covered in inches of thick, pure-white snow.

"It's incredible," I said, gazing in awe at the landscape. When I looked at Quentin, he was smiling again. A group of women on broomsticks joined us in the air. "Are they real?" I asked. The women—all with long, flowing dark hair, dressed in glittering gowns, and dazzling with jewels and gems—giggled and sped away ahead of us. A few of them waved, and I waved back.

Quentin took us through the clouds gathered above the mountain range, and we broke through them over a vast forest. I caught sight of a grand city built within the trees, where people gazed up at us in surprise. Staring, motionless, they almost seemed panicked as we sped past. There was only a glimpse of them before we were gone, flying in and through the forest's tallest trees. Strange animals I'd never seen before leaped from branch to branch beside us. The forest opened for us again before we rose high into the sky.

Then I saw what looked like a door—a haze of brilliant colors opened in the pastel skies. Quentin headed straight for it, and in seconds, I realized we were back in the real world—my world.

Quentin carefully brought me down through the open window of my room. In the darkness, we stood there, still holding onto each other. My room was so quiet, the night as peaceful as it had been when we'd left. Nothing had changed, almost like we hadn't just flown through a completely different world.

Quentin nearly collapsed against me, looking suddenly exhausted. I held him up, unable to pull away. "That was unbelievable," I whispered. "I mean, I believe it. I was there. But it was just... incredible." Then I realized he still hadn't moved, and when I looked up, I found him gazing down at me again. His smile widened, and the way his eyes bored into mine made me flush. And then I sensed it—his will once more holding me without touch and without force.

In that moment, I knew I wanted to be with him, no matter what. Whatever he asked of me, I'd probably find impossible to resist.

"I'm glad you liked it," he said.

"Why did you show me this?" I asked.

"I wanted you to see my home." Quentin still smiled, but his face looked just a little paler now.

"Why did you come here?" I whispered, hypnotized by his dark eyes.

"To find you." He leaned closer, and I felt his breath against my face. I thought he would kiss me, but at the same time, he resisted.

I took a deep breath. "Why me?"

"You are incredibly special to me. And more important than you realize." He brushed his hand against my hair and leaned toward me again. I closed my eyes, longing for his lips to touch mine, but they didn't. When I opened my eyes to look at him again, he was gone.

I rushed to the open bedroom window; the curtain flapped against the window ledge, and I leaned my head out to look for him. All I saw was the yellow moon perched in the endless night sky. My rescuer was gone. Again.

That night, I could barely sleep. When I did, I dreamt of mermaids, witches darting through the brilliant skies, and blue oceans teaming with sea serpents.

22

THE MORNING AFTER

MICHAEL'S VOICE WOKE ME FROM THE OTHER SIDE OF MY bedroom door. Then I realized I'd fallen asleep on the bedroom floor beside the open window—or at least I'd gone back there sometime during the night. I sat there for a moment, wondering if I would ever see Quentin again. Somehow, I knew I would. And the desire to see him again—to feel his arms around me and his lips finally pressed to mine—still drove me insane. I had no idea why I felt this way, especially because it wasn't like me to lose control of myself like this.

Disappointed, I rose to get ready for school. I found myself thinking about Joseph at dinner, then John. I'd left him at the table without any explanation, and I didn't have a clue how to explain why I'd run away from him. What *could* I say? I knew I liked him, but this thing I felt for Quentin was tugging me in a different direction. Just thinking his name made me feel like he was close again, watching me.

· · ·

At breakfast, Michael watched me as I sat quietly at the kitchen table. He worried too much, like he was my father or a nagging babysitter.

"You okay?" he asked.

I knew I looked as tired as I felt, sitting there poking at my eggs. He poured himself some orange juice and just kept staring at me.

He was going to ask me about the night before. I could hear him struggling to come up with the best way to say what he wanted to say. "What happened last night?" he finally asked. "John was pretty worried about you. He thought he'd upset you somehow. Was it because he asked to take you to Prom?"

I looked up at him. I'd forgotten all about John asking me to prom. But that wasn't it.

"Did someone else ask you first?" Michael pried.

I wrinkled my nose. "No. It's not that." I sighed. "Look, I'm sorry about last night. I guess I'm just a lot more tired than I thought. I didn't mean to just disappear. Nobody said anything that upset me. I just… I don't know."

"If you don't want to go to prom with him—"

"No, it's not that at all." I said, but I didn't sound that convincing. And I knew Michael wanted more from me. I couldn't tell him Joseph gave me the creeps, could I? Or at least that he'd been pretty wary of me, which made the feeling mutual.

"Then what happened?" Michael asked with a frown. I stared at him, wondering if I could tell anything remotely close to the truth—what I feared and what I felt. "If you like," he added, "we can go shopping for a dress. I know how crazy you girls get about the dress. Believe me, I know." I supposed, being a teacher in a large school, he'd seen his fair share of teen dances. "Joseph asked for my help," Michael added. "James and Richard will have to attend as the assistant principals, of course. I thought it would be nice to volunteer too."

I glared at him as he drank his orange juice. He was normally in good spirits, but I couldn't blame him for not being able to keep that up after last night.

"I really haven't thought about it much," I muttered.

He blinked at me with wide eyes. "Honey, it's one of the biggest nights of high school. I remember my prom."

I wrinkled my nose at him, really not wanting him to get into any details about it. "Oh, yeah?" I said, trying just to brush it off even though I wasn't actually curious.

"Are you sure you're okay? You haven't touched your breakfast. Did I make the eggs the wrong way?" He tried to smile again, but it made him look like such a dork.

"Oh, no. They're fine," I said. "I'm just tired." This time, it was the truth. My trip with Quentin and being unable to sleep after he left was already catching up to me. Just thinking about him made me smile.

"Did you have trouble sleeping last night?" Michael asked. "Bad dreams?" He came to sit at the table with me, and I immediately regretted opening the conversation for him to ask those kinds of questions. I didn't want to lie to him, but I couldn't tell him about Quentin.

"Yeah." I looked up at him with a strained smile. "I guess you could say that." I shouldn't have said anything.

"Well, don't forget I'm always here if you need to talk to someone. Okay?" He picked up his cleared plate and took it to the sink.

"Okay." I just hoped he wouldn't keep asking about it.

"So, go with John to prom. I have a good feeling about him. He seems well-rounded."

I stared at him and gulped down my own orange juice.

"Get to know him," Michael added. "You might like him."

"I don't think his uncle likes me very much." The minute I said it, I wished I could take it back.

Michael's fork clattered into the sink, and he turned around to face me. "What makes you say that?"

"I don't know. Maybe he thinks I'm not good enough for his nephew."

"I didn't get that feeling from him, but you're better in tone than I am..." He frowned. "Maybe you just read him wrong. He said nothing but nice things about you. And he was only asking after you out of concern. Just like John."

I had no idea what Joseph had asked about me, but I didn't want to keep going down this road with Michael right now. So I just shrugged.

"I think John might have a little crush on you, Claudia. I mean, why wouldn't he?"

I blushed. Were we really having this discussion right now?

"Just go with him. He's a good kid. You'll have a lot more fun with him than spending your prom night with a bunch of principals."

I must have looked disgusted at this point, or extremely uncomfortable, or both, because he finally dropped it. I quickly finished my breakfast, rinsed off my plate, and stuck it in the dishwasher. When I turned around, Michael was packing his lunch and taking a brown paper bag out of the fridge.

"I made you a little something," he said, looking a little too proud. I tried to smile back, realizing that not taking the sack lunch would most likely just hurt his feelings. "The cafeteria food's pretty foul, isn't it?"

He was right about that, and I snorted. "Thanks." I took the bag, and Michael grinned, like I'd just given him some kind of award.

"Well, I guess we'd better get going," he said and finished wiping up the table.

. . .

We were almost at the front door when a car horn honked so loud, I jumped. Then I saw Alex had just pulled up in her red, 1969 Mustang convertible to get me. She'd insisted on giving me a ride to school, even though Michael and I were literally going to the same place.

"Who's that?" Michael asked as he peered out the window.

"Oh, that's for me," I said, slinging my backpack over my shoulder. "I forgot to tell you. This girl from school offered to give me a ride. I hope it's okay."

Michael pulled the curtain open a little farther, and I saw Alex finish putting on her lipstick then turn to wave at us. He nearly returned the wave, then seemed to realize this was the girl I was talking about. "Alex Burton? You're friends with Alex Burton?"

"Yeah, I guess," I said. I could hear it so clearly; in his mind, Alex was nothing but trouble. His thoughts were always this easy to read.

"Okay," he managed. "Go ahead." Clearly, he didn't want me to, but he wasn't about to stop me.

"Are you sure?" I asked.

"Of course. You need to make friends. I'll see you at school. Just be careful." He opened the door, and I gave him a smile before racing out to Alex's old mustang. "Drive safe," he called after me, stepping just outside the front door. When I opened the passenger door, I turned back to see him examining Alex's beat-up car from top to bottom. I could hear his mind; he was trying to see if the tires had air and whether she'd updated the registration. I think he would have asked about it if given the chance.

"Don't worry, Mr. McClellan," Alex called through the open door. "I'll get her to school in one piece." As soon as I got in and shut the door, she peeled out of the neighborhood. I tried to shoot Michael a reassuring smile as we sped away, and I saw him take a step off the front porch as if he'd changed his mind.

"Did you really have to do that?" I asked Alex.

"I couldn't resist," she said, grinning. "Sorry."

"He already doesn't like it that I'm hanging out with you," I told her.

Alex laughed. "Oh, really?"

"Yeah. You want to give him another reason?" I didn't think it was that funny at all.

"So, have you asked yet?" Alex said, driving right through a stop sign.

I braced myself against the frame of the door. "What are you *doing*?"

"Relax," she said, rolling her eyes. "I checked first."

I shook my head and stared out the window, trying to pretend I wasn't going to get it from Michael when I got home. Maybe he'd even bring it up at school. I could already imagine scolding, and I was sure he'd never let me ride in the car with her again.

"Well?" Alex asked.

"Well what?" I turned to look at her as she sped right through a yellow light.

"What do you mean what? Did you ask about the party yet?"

I'd completely forgotten about the party this weekend, and I hadn't even brought it up with Michael. I had a feeling he wouldn't let me go, especially now that he knew I was hanging out with Alex Burton. "Not yet..." I said.

Alex whipped her head toward me. "What? Claudia, it's in two days. You have to ask." She drove like a madwoman down Broadway until we came to a screeching halt at a stoplight, just a turn away from the school.

"I know," I said, glaring at her. Her driving had made me physically nauseous, like she'd only just learned how.

"Afraid he's not gonna let you go?" she asked, raising an eyebrow.

"Maybe," I admitted. I opened the brown paper bag he'd given me for lunch, then shamefully stuffed it into my backpack.

"He made you a sack lunch? What a dork."

I frowned at her.

"Sorry." She smacked her gum and blew a bubble. When it burst, she added with a wink, "Look, just sneak out. No big deal."

"I can't do *that*," I exclaimed.

"Why not? I do it all the time. Piece of cake. And I'll pick you up."

"I don't know," I said.

"Okay, so what's the problem, then? Everything okay with you and old man McClellan?"

I frowned out the windshield. "It's not that."

"Then what is it?" Alex asked, shaking her head.

The light finally turned green, and she sped off, nearly running down two guys on the crosswalk as she careened into the parking lot. She honked at them and kept driving, looking for a space. There didn't seem to be one left, so she took us around the circle again. I thought she was heading back onto the street, but she'd apparently decided to take one of the teacher's spaces.

"Wait, you can't park here," I told her.

Alex shut off the engine. "Why not?" She shrugged and reached into the back seat for her backpack. Then she checked herself out in the rearview mirror one more time and wiped some dark lipstick off the corner of her mouth.

"You just parked in a teacher's space." Just in case, I pointed at the posted sign right in front of us.

"It's Mrs. Whitney's, and she's out today. Don't worry, I checked. I'm not stupid."

This time, I rolled my eyes at her and grabbed my bag from

the car floor. How would she know which teachers were out today?

"So, what's the problem?" she asked. I looked at her, wondering if I could even begin to explain anything to her without her thinking it was a huge joke. "Well?"

I took a deep breath and said, "Have you ever felt like you've been dreaming but were wide awake?"

She frowned, suddenly looking quite serious, and nodded. I almost sighed in relief until she said, "All the time. It's called acid." Then she burst out laughing. I opened the car door and meant to get out, but she pulled me back by the arm. "I'm just kidding. You can tell me what's going on." I waited for her to laugh again, but she didn't.

"Do you believe people can do things with their minds?" I asked her.

"What? You mean like move things and shit like a Jedi?"

"Yeah," I whispered, waiting for her to start thinking the word 'freak'.

"I do actually," Alex admitted, and I could sense she was being honest. "Wish I could do that. Can you imagine? That would be so awesome!" She laughed. "Don't tell me you can read minds."

I looked the other way, unsure if I could tell her or if she would even believe me. But it was too late; we were already having this conversation.

"Can you?"

"I can," I admitted, waiting for the reaction in her eyes and then her lips. Everything always happened with her in that order.

"No, really. Like actually read minds?" She spun toward me. "Are you serious? You're pulling my leg, right?" For a few seconds all she did was stare at me, and as if by mere examination, she could see it in me.

So, I did what was obviously the next best thing. I gave her a show and tell. I locked the doors, turned on the radio, and scanned through the stations until I found an 80's classic from Huey Lewis & the News, "The Power of Love".

"That radio's never worked," she muttered. "How did you do that?"

I tapped my temple, already convinced she'd either laugh at me or leap out of the car and run away screaming.

Instead, she smiled and said, "Awesome!" Then she danced to the music, like nothing had happened. "I'm thinking of something very interesting." She smirked at me, and the minute I looked at her, I knew.

"No," I told her. "I can't."

"Yes. Oh, come on, Claudia." She nodded and pressed her hands together, pleading with me. "This is amazing! This has to be exploited in every possible way." A giggle escaped her, then she froze. "Hottie at twelve o'clock..."

"What are you talking about?" I felt that familiar tug and whirled toward my window to see John, He turned toward Alex's car, and I ducked like an idiot.

Alex grinned, and I pulled her down with me onto the front seat of the car. "Oooh, hiding from hottie?" I shushed her. "Pocahontas, what are we doing? Did you already talk to him? Oh, you did? Do tell..."

"He asked me to prom," I admitted.

"So why are we hiding?"

I hushed her again. "I ran off in the middle of dinner."

"Wait, dinner? He was at your house, and you didn't call me? When?"

I glared at her. "Yesterday... I ran right after he asked. I don't want him to think I don't want to go..."

She stared at me as if she were watching a romance movie and batted her eyelashes. "Wow. Prom, huh? That's awesome. I don't get why you're hiding, though."

"Didn't you hear what I said?"

"Claudia, if I had a nickel for every time I didn't run off from some guy... jeeze."

"Whatever. I still need to talk to him..."

"Oh, you like him, Pocahontas." When I blushed, it only made Alex laugh. "I knew it."

The radio abruptly went dead.

"He has a nice car," she whispered, looking out the window.

"He has a car?" I wanted to see it for myself, but I felt the tug of him searching for me again and pushed it back at him. The way Alex looked at me made me wonder if she'd felt those tugs too. Only she *couldn't* feel them. Not like I could.

She turned back to admiring John's car. "Yeah. It's a nice one too. Looks like a new Jaguar."

"Yeah, his father has money. I think the man's some kind of doctor or surgeon," I said.

"Shit. Hot *and* loaded. Looks like you hit the jackpot. Oh, damn. I just saw Dr. Müller." She dropped back down onto the seat.

"Dr. Müller?"

"If he sees us, he'll make me move my car." She giggled.

Was that really the only thing she was concerned about? "I have to go," I said, nervously trying to open the car door.

She grabbed my arm. "You can't go now. Just relax. I don't think he saw us." Alex peered over the dashboard and lifted her head up, grabbing her school bag. "Okay, come on. He's gone."

I felt the tug again and looked around, but I didn't see John.

"Come *on*." Alex opened her door, I opened mine, and I nearly crawled out of her car to hide behind a truck in the parking lot. "Okay... Go!" We rushed inside the building just in time. I glanced back and caught sight of Dr. Müller making his rounds.

Alex grabbed me and yanked me along behind her, pulling me through a crowd of students and into the side stairwell to our left just as Dr. Müller stepped inside. I lost sight of him when we raced to the second floor. The bell rang just as we reached the top landing.

I wanted to find John, to explain myself to him and why I'd run off in the first place. I knew he was worried about me; I could feel it. The thought that he'd dialed back that watch just to sense me made me smile. *John...* The tug grew stronger, yanking me enough to make me stumble. He had to be close, somewhere.

We stopped, and I pulled out my phone to check the time. "Damnit. I'm gonna be late."

"Forget it. Let's just ditch class today." Alex wiggled her eyebrows. "Let's play with your new gift."

"I can't." The second bell rang, and now I was really late. John kept tugging and pulling at my mind, like an invisible rope wrapped around my waist. I wanted to tell him I was coming, but the feeling was enough to let him know I was near. Why wasn't he coming to me?

'The roof.' It felt like his warm breath had brushed against my cheek, as if he were standing right next to me, whispering those words.

John wanted me to find him on the roof.

The hallways slowly cleared of students, and I saw him down the hallway. *John,* I called to him with my mine. He turned, saw me, and motioned for me to follow. Then disappeared through a black metal doorway. I hurried away, leaving Alex behind before she even noticed I was gone. I ducked through the same metal doorway leading up a flight of steps to the roof.

Leaving Alex without a word made me feel just a little guilty, but right now, the only thing on my mind was John. Once I reached the roof, I saw him standing close to the edge, looking down at the street. He wore the same sporty jacket he'd worn last night; his brownish blond locks blew slightly in a breeze.

"John?" He turned, and where I expected to see his bright green eyes sparkling back at me, instead, his eyes were purple.

He smiled, and his entire appearance shifted. The sporty jacket melted into that scaly leather uniform, his light hair darkening into black, matted locks above a pale complexion.

"Quentin..." This discovery made me feel both guilty and betrayed.

"Is it him you want to see instead?" Quentin hissed, moving toward me. I was paralyzed by his words, terrified. I wanted to ask where John was, I knew what had happened. I hadn't felt John's tug in my mind, only Quentin's. "You don't belong with him. You belong with me...."

I couldn't resist his pull, stumbling toward him from the stairway.

"Why did you leave so quickly last night?" I asked.

He could sense me trying to resist him, I knew, and then all my resistance was gone. I needed to stand by his side, though I still didn't understand why. When I reached him, his deep purple eyes swam with the same fierce connection I felt, and he took one step toward me.

"Forgive me. I did not want to leave... but your world does not hold the capabilities I require to exist. That is why I often must go."

I gazed at him, perplexed, but none of it really mattered. I just felt the need to be near him. "You mean to the place you showed me?"

"Yes. That is my home. I cannot exist beyond its walls unless I acquire energy from another *source*." He leaned forward, almost stumbling toward me, until we were holding each other there on the roof. His eyes grew heavy with desire at my touch, and the same swirl of gold I'd seen within John's eyes now flared in Quentin's. "You're my angel," he whispered. I touched his cheek, and he let out a huge sigh, closing his eyes while my fingers brushed across his cold skin.

"Are you all right?" I asked, trembling.

He grabbed my hand, keeping it on his cheek. "Believe me when I say I did not want to leave." When he opened his eyes again, he looked completely overwhelmed.

"Tell me how to help you," I pleaded. His lips quivered when they parted, releasing an almost orgasmic moan.

"You already have, my pet." Quentin took another deep breath, then slowly released me and leaped onto the ledge, extending his hand out to me. He seemed suddenly alive, radiant and full of vigor. "Come with me."

I looked back at the door to the staircase and hesitated. A feeling that someone was trying to reach me from beyond just wouldn't leave me alone.

'Come to me...' Quentin whispered in my mind.

I felt another tug, trying to hold me back.

'Forget him.' Quentin grabbed my hand. 'Come with me.' When still that didn't change my mind, he frowned, studying my concern. "You are not pleased to see me?"

"Yes," I forced myself to say.

"Then come with me, my pet! Let me take you to my world. I have so much more to show you."

I stumbled closer. "But... Michael. He'll be worried about me."

"He means nothing, does he, my pet?" Quentin whispered. "Come. I want you near me! Let me take you away!"

The words died before I could say anything else. I felt powerless and at the same time stronger than I had ever felt before when he was near.

"I couldn't bear being away from you." His grip tightened on my hand. "Nothing, no one, can keep me away from you. Come with me."

The feeling of being searched for filled me again, pulling at my heart.

'Where are you, Claudia?' Finally, there was his voice, calling desperately. 'Please be safe. Where are you?'

"John?" I exhaled.

'Yes! Where are you? I want to see you. I'm sorry if I said something to frighten you... Claudia?'

Quentin yanked a little hard on my hand, frowning at me until John's voice disappeared. "He means nothing." He pulled me toward the ledge, then dropped over the side and nearly took me with him.

I screamed and closed my eyes just before someone else's hand grabbed my other arm and pulled me to the floor. When I opened my eyes, I saw Alex staring down at me, trying to wake me up.

"Claudia!" she screamed.

I blinked up at her and realized Quentin was gone. "What happened?" I asked. "Where—"

"What happened? You almost fell to your death, you idiot!" Alex grabbed my hand and lifted me to my feet. I stumbled but managed to regain my balance with her help.

I staggered beside her toward the entrance to the stairwell, only glancing back once before we disappeared through the door.

23

THE ABSENT

THE BELL RANG FOR THE LAST TIME WHEN MICHAEL LOOKED across the classroom. The teacher he was evaluating and the students were all busy working on a project she had given them to last the entire period. The new principal, Dr. Müller, had given him quite a few teachers to evaluate, since Michael was good at the job. He looked toward the doorway and saw Mr. Claypool peeking his head up beside the door's window and signaling for Michael to join him.

"Mrs. Robertson, please continue with your assignment while I step out for a moment," Michael said.

"No problem, Mr. McClellan." The mousy-looking woman with brown hair and a pink pantsuit nodded.

The class remained quiet, as if he had never said a word, while the teacher continued writing her lesson on the chalk-board. A few students barely glanced up, uninterested. Michael stepped into the hallway to find Mr. Claypool's worried face looking back at him.

"Anything?"

The tall, blond assistant principal shook his head.

"Did you look everywhere?" Michael asked.

"Michael, I'm beginning to think she's not in school at all," Mr. Claypool said.

"That's impossible. I saw her leaving with Alex Burton."

"Alex Burton?" Mr. Claypool raised an eyebrow.

"Yes, I know. That's why I'm worried." Michael glanced back into the classroom.

"Knowing how Burton behaves, I'd say they're at the mall," Mr. Claypool said.

"Well, I need to finish all these evaluations Dr. Müller gave me," Michael said pacing the hallway.

"You want me to send Vasquez?" Mr. Claypool pulled out his radio.

"No. If Dr. Müller hears I sent him on an errand to find Claudia, it won't look good for either of them. I don't want Dr. Müller to think this is how we handle things around here. I just had dinner with the man last night. And now this... He plans to pull strings with the district regarding repairs..."

Mr. Claypool put the radio down and smiled. "That sounds promising. So, what do you want me to do, sir?"

Michael frowned up at him. "All we can do is keep our eyes open... If she's with Burton, then the mall is our best bet. But that lady is gonna have a lot of explaining to do when I find her."

Mr. Claypool shook his head. "I'll tell Vasquez what's happening." He lifted the radio again, but Michael stopped him before he could use it.

"It's best we just keep Dr. Müller out of the loop. Tell Vasquez in person." Mr. Claypool nodded, and Michael returned to the classroom.

24

TROUBLEMAKER

I MANAGED TO WALK THE REST OF THE WAY DOWN WITH ALEX behind me, who gave me a strange, motherly lecture about safety. We stumbled out the door into the hall.

"What the hell were you trying to do?" she snapped.

"What are you talking about?" I still really didn't know what had happened. One minute, I was with Quentin, and the next, Alex was shouting at me while I was laid out on the roof.

"Claudia, you nearly fell over the edge. If I hadn't come when I did... Let's just say we wouldn't be standing here talking." She eyed me for a few seconds. "You don't remember, do you? Are you okay?"

"I'm not sure," I said, stumbling away. "I have to go. I need to find John..."

His voice was calling to me. Alex shouted for me to come back, but I didn't stop. Michael's troubled mind searched for me. He had Mr. Claypool and Mr. Vasquez looking for me too. When Michael found me, I knew I'd be in big trouble.

I raced down the second-floor hallway, turned the corner, and crashed into Mr. Thomas. He simply looked at me. "Everyone's been looking for you."

I bit my lip as he motioned for me to follow. Alex ducked back into the stairwell before Mr. Thomas led me away in the other direction.

25

AT THE PRINCIPAL'S OFFICE

I WAS EXPECTING TO SEE MICHAEL IN THE PRINCIPAL'S OFFICE. Mrs. Wallace wasn't at her desk. Dr. Müller's office door was closed. Mr. Thomas knocked, then narrowed his dark eyes at me. I knew very little about Mr. Thomas, only that he was pretty strict.

"Come in," Joseph called from his office. As the door opened, he saw me with Mr. Thomas and immediately dropped what he was working on. There was a distortion in the sound around us, coming from him—a wave in the air like a radio frequency. Whatever it was, it was malfunctioning, and I could hear it.

I gasped. I didn't want to be here. Mr. Thomas extended an arm for me to enter first, then we stopped in front of Joseph's desk. Joseph gave me a ridiculous smile. I couldn't meet his gaze. I was both embarrassed and scared that he would know there was something different about me. The man wanted to keep me away from John, and then I tried not to think of John at all. Instead, I took a deep breath and calmed the nervous, frenetic energy. Glancing at Joseph's wrist, I looked for the watch beneath the sleeves of his pastel-blue dress shirt. The silver body seemed to shine from the outer edges of the sleeve. I tried to see if the needle hands were moving, but it was difficult to tell from this distance. Then I had to look away before he caught me.

"Sorry to disturb you, Dr. Müller," Mr. Thomas said, "but I found her in the second-floor hallway coming from the roof. She was obviously skipping class..."

Joseph looked at me, the corners of his mouth curving slightly. *'Miss Belle, you are just the person I wanted to see.'* I tried not to look like I'd just heard his private thoughts, and then he gazed down at his wrist. Oh, no. Had I just made the watch move? He regarded his watch suspiciously, then he looked away both from the device and from me. *'What just happened? Another surge? I hope John is closer to finding the cause. Whether it's ET product or something else... At least the girl is here, away from him. She's far too distracting, but maybe she can offer something.'*

Offer something? I still couldn't look at him, my stomach tying itself into nervous knots, now. *Control yourself, Claudia.* That seemed to work a little.

"I see," Joseph finally replied. Then he stood and stepped around his desk to stand in front of Mr. Thomas. "I'll handle this, Mr. Thomas,"

"Should I inform Mr. McClellan?"

Joseph glanced at me. Michael would not like the fact that I stood in Dr. Müller's office now, or that I'd been skipping class.

"No. No, I'll do that myself," Joseph said, still staring at me. I glanced briefly at him, and he grinned.

Mr. Thomas didn't look pleased, especially because he'd known Michael a lot longer than both Joseph and I had. "She's not a troublemaker," he said, apparently trying to convince Dr. Müller of the same.

"I'll make that conclusion, thank you, Mr. Thomas. Now, please just make sure you lock the door up to the roof."

"There is no lock, sir." Mr. Thomas glanced at me, and his

gaze softened. *'Don't worry, kid. I'll tell Michael. I'm not sure about this guy.'*

Though his thoughts obviously weren't meant for me to hear, they still made me feel better. I hid my smile behind my hand, grateful that Michael would know where I was. But now I wondered why Mr. Thomas didn't trust Joseph, either.

"Well, we need to secure it," Joseph continued. "Get Mrs. Wallace to call a locksmith. Keep students from going up there. The last thing we need is a lawsuit on our hands." The man looked down at me again as he spoke.

Just breathe, I told myself. A tingle raced up my arm. My gaze settled on a pen in the cup of them on his desk; it popped free and rolled across the wooden surface toward the floor. Both Joseph and Mr. Thomas glanced at the desk, and I stared at my shoes.

Joseph knelt to pick up the wayward writing utensil. He examined it briefly then glanced at me. "Well, what are you waiting for?" He looked up at Mr. Thomas and waved toward the door. "Get that taken care of. I don't want anyone else wandering up there." Then he dropped the pen back into the cup.

"Yes, sir." Mr. Thomas went to the door but shot me a final glance. Then he was gone, and it was just Joseph and me, alone.

Breathe. I lifted my head slightly as Joseph turned to his side of the desk and sat. I just stood there, unable to look at him for a long time, concentrating on my breathing.

"Are you okay, Miss Belle?"

I looked up slowly and met his gaze. "Yes, sir…"

"Strange. It almost seems you're trying to control a bad habit." When I frowned in confusion, he smiled. "You don't have a bad habit, do you? I won't tell Michael if you tell me you smoke." Then he winked. "I'm kidding, of course. But please, don't smoke. It's quite bad for you." He gave me that same clever smirk he'd worn as a dinner guest last night.

'What's your story?' he wondered, still unaware that I could hear him. 'Why does John like you so much? Why? John doesn't like anyone. But you are occupying his mind more than anything else these days...' It was so strange to hear him ask what he never intended for me to hear. *This could be a good thing for him, though.*

I blinked at him, waiting for more, but the man seemed to have finished his private brainstorming. I didn't know what to say to him—or what to think. It felt a lot more like he was playing some strange game with me, only I didn't know any of the rules.

"Have a seat," he said firmly. I collapsed into one of the chairs in front of his desk.

'Claudia, where are you?' John's voice broke through my scattered thoughts again.

John?

'Yes. Where are you? What's going on? I feel how afraid you are right now. Are you okay? Tell me, please. I want to see you. Is it something I did?'

I didn't know how to answer that.

'Why are you scared? Are you in danger? Tell me. I'm coming.'

Again, I took a breath.

"Miss Belle, you don't have asthma, do you?"

I shook my head.

"Well, that's good. I don't want to be responsible for stirring your symptoms."

"Am I in trouble?" I interrupted. It was a bold move, but I needed to get out of here.

Joseph's eyes widened in surprise, but his smile widened. 'You are far more than just in trouble, my dear.' "More or less," he said. "What were you doing on the roof?"

"Nothing."

I was never really good at lying. By the way Joseph just

wrinkled his nose and kept smiling, I figured he'd been properly trained to deal with this sort of thing.

"Oh? Would you rather I ask Michael? Mr. McClellan is a nice man, and I had fun at his home last night. I like him. So I don't want to disturb him with this news about you, Miss Belle." He glanced down at his wrist again, pulling lightly at the sleeve of his dress shirt. "Which makes me wonder... Why did you leave dinner last night? Is there something going on that I should know about?"

I stared at him, not really surprised that he was bringing that up. This just seemed like an odd time to have that conversation. I wanted to tell him the same thing I'd told John—that it was none of his business. But I had a feeling Joseph wouldn't let this go as easily as John had.

"Did you being on the roof have anything to do with what happened last night?"

"Last night?" I saw him tap the face of his watch, though that was as much as I could see from where I sat. "Do I make you nervous?"

I shook my head.

"Did my nephew say something to upset you last night?"

"Why would he?"

"I don't know. You left abruptly, Miss Belle. Maybe he said something ungentlemanly."

"No, he was nothing but nice to me." What was he getting at.

Joseph stood again and sat on the front corner of his desk, looming over me with that undying smile. "You were alone in your room with him, weren't you? Maybe he wasn't polite. You can tell me. If my... nephew said something to upset you, I need to know."

Now this felt like an interrogation, and it really didn't seem right. "No," I told him firmly. "John's always been polite."

He challenged me with another smile. "You like him?"

The butterflies in my stomach swarmed, and my cheeks flushed with heat.

"John can be such a romantic," Joseph continued. "He gets it from his father."

Father? I knew that was a lie.

The principal tapped his watch again. "Just be honest, Claudia."

"Yes," I said. "I like John."

After staring at me for a few more seconds, he shrugged. "Well, do you know how he feels about you?" he asked. "Because I want to be honest with you, Miss Belle. My nephew has had many girlfriends. I just want you to know that. He's wowed them and dazzled them. You're not the first."

My heart ached.

"I know what you're thinking. You're different. But my dear, I'd hate for you to get your heart broken. And with his father's line of work, there is always the potential of finding another position in another state. We move a lot..."

I swallowed the lump in my throat. Why didn't he want me to get close to John?

"It might sound harsh, yes, but I'd rather you know the truth. John may act like he's interested in you, but my nephew has a way with girls. And I feel connected to Michael, so I don't want to see you hurt. I hope you understand. Forgive me for being so forthcoming."

I nodded.

'Claudia? I'm here...'

"I mean, I'm sure he told you he already has a girlfriend, right?"

"Girlfriend?" I frowned at him, even though I knew he was lying.

"Her name is Rachel. They met the first day in class. You know her, right? The cheerleader. John has a thing for cheerleaders. It kind of comes with the territory of being a football player. Of course, he's decided not to try out this season, but that doesn't stop the girls from finding him." Joseph grinned, leaned forward, and put a hand on my shoulder. "I'm sorry, my dear. You didn't know?"

I shook my head, tears swimming in my eyes. I knew he was lying, but it didn't make the words any less hurtful. Joseph tapped his watch, I exhaled, and the cup of pens toppled over. He glanced beside him on the desk as pens and pencils rolled everywhere.

I got up and rushed toward the door. "I have to go to class."

"It was nice talking to you, Miss Belle." I glanced back long enough to nod at him, but before I could grab the handle, the door flung open.

"Claudia!" John gasped. "I've been looking—" The words died on his lips when he saw Joseph rising from the corner of his desk.

"Nephew! Look who came to pay me a visit. We were just having a little discussion—"

"What did he say to you?" John whispered. I gazed at him, and he reached up to wipe the tears from my cheek. I couldn't help but turn my face away. "Claudia, whatever he said, it's not true. You know me. I told you everything…"

Joseph walked toward us.

"Who's Rachel?" I asked. John just blinked in surprise, and now I saw in his eyes that everything Joseph had told me *was* true. Why hadn't I seen it before? Was I that blind to think that he actually wanted *me*? What else hadn't he told me? Maybe he was actually planning to take me to the people he said wanted me. Maybe it was a lot worse then I wanted to believe.

"I had to," he whispered. "It was part of the job."

"Am I part of the job too?"

"No. Never. You're different. You mean something to me."

I moved past him, and he grabbed my hand. My body reacted with a very real electric shock, but when he ground his teeth together through the pain, he wouldn't release his grip on me. "Let go," I whispered.

He shook his head. Only when Joseph stepped up behind him did he release me. I spun around and headed through the office door, but I didn't get far. Michael was standing right in front of me just outside Joseph's office, blocking my exit.

"Claudia, thank god. I've been looking all over for you. Mr. Thomas told me you were here." He looked up at Joseph. "I hope she hasn't been a problem." Michael wrapped his arms around me, and I fell into his embrace. His hands tightened around my back, and I knew he was suddenly concerned. "You scared me," he said, and when I looked up, I thought I saw tears in his eyes. "Are you okay?"

I nodded. "I'm sorry," I whispered, and he kissed the top of my head.

"Oh, not at all, Michael," Joseph replied.

'Claudia?' John was still trying to reach me, even now.

"Mr. Thomas said she was on the roof," the principal offered.

"What were you doing up there?" Michael asked.

I wanted to tell him, but first, I wanted to get out of here. "I'm sorry." He cupped my cheek.

"It's okay, Michael. We had a long discussion, didn't we, Miss Belle?"

I turned slowly around. John looked pained; I felt him wanting to comfort me, and I felt his rage toward Joseph. The last thing I wanted to do was to come between them. So I only nodded in response.

"I figured a few hours of detention in the cafeteria or working in the main office would help set her back on track."

Michael looked surprised, and I sensed that he thought it was a little harsh, given that I was the assistant principal's ward and the late principal's granddaughter. "Is that really necessary? It's her first time breaking the rules, and she's never been in trouble before..."

"I agree," John said. "Isn't that a little too much?"

"Now, now, nephew. We can't be too soft on kids. You know this. Michael. We do have to set an example, and rules are rules. If I give one student a pass just because I know her guardian, someone might consider that favoritism."

Michael glared at the man and forced himself to say, "Yes, of course. I apologize for the intrusion, Dr. Müller." He moved to leave.

"It's quite all right. Please call me Joseph. I had the impression we were on a first-name basis by now."

"Yes. Absolutely, Joseph."

'Claudia...' John tried to reach me again, but I spun away to avoid him.

Michael politely nodded and ushered me out. I felt John tugging at me again and I pushed back. *Leave me alone!*

I thought I heard him stumble in Joseph's office, but I didn't turn around to check.

In the hallway, Michael stepped quickly up beside me. "Maybe I was wrong about that man. A little. I think that's way too harsh a punishment."

"I'll survive," I muttered.

"Are you all right, sweetheart?"

I looked up at him and wanted to tell him everything. But I didn't. Maybe I wanted to protect Michael from all this strange information, and I definitely didn't want to make things worse than already were.

"Still," Michael added, "I can't just let this slide completely, Claudia. I have to ground you."

It was definitely a good call not to have told him what I was going through. I frowned. "Grounded? Why?"

"Why? You were cutting class, Claudia. On the *roof* of the school." I veered away from him, but he followed me, radiating disappointment. That was the last thing I wanted him to feel about me. "You *are* grounded..." he repeated. All I could do was offer him a scathing glance. "And I don't want you hanging out with Alex Burton anymore."

"*What?*" That was definitely going too far. "You can't tell me who to be friends with."

"I'm your guardian, and I'm responsible if anything happens to you. I don't want you talking to her again." It sounded so fake coming from Michael, like he was trying extra hard to make his voice sound strong and firm.

"But she's my friend, and we're going to a party on Saturday. I've already made plans with her." It rushed out of me, and then I wished I hadn't said anything.

"Well, then maybe you should have thought about that before you wandered off and skipped class." He didn't say it as firmly as the first time. I knew he wanted to take it all back, to un-ground me and apologize and just hold me. But he felt he had to say something, to be strict and firm so I didn't walk all over him.

"That's not fair," I snapped, pulling away from him. I felt him nearly give in as I turned and headed for the stairwell.

"Where are you going?"

"To class! Now leave me alone." Then I hurried away.

"Claudia, please understand," Michael called after me as I stormed up the stairs. "I'm only trying to keep you safe."

I ignored him.

26

DENIAL

AFTER MY EVENTFUL VISIT TO JOSEPH'S OFFICE AND MICHAEL'S lecture about skipping, I made it to my first class of the day. And after that, it was time for PE.

I wanted to talk to Alex about John but wondered if I should reveal what I knew about him—about what he was. She already knew what I could do, so I figured she wouldn't be as surprised to hear about John as most people would.

In the locker room, I got dressed in those awful, tacky shorts and gym shirt. Then I saw Rachel and her girlfriends looking in my direction, whispering. And I could hear them.

"She's so weird."

"Just like her grandpa."

"Why is she still here after what happened?"

The lights overhead flickered, followed by a moan from the old pipes. It sounded even to me like something was coming to live in the school. Rachel and her friends scattered.

"Freak!" one of them yelled. The girls giggled and headed into the gym. I buried my face in my hands. What I really wanted was to let myself cry, but I didn't want to give them the satisfaction of seeing—or hearing—me. The pipes groaned again.

'Claudia...'

I raised my head and glanced at the back of the locker room. A shadow moved up the wall, its arms extending and growing longer as its body followed. I stood from the bench and raced out to join my PE class.

Everyone was taking a seat on the cold gym floor, and the PE teacher watched us all before beginning.

Rachel and her friends were staring at me again. I took a deep breath, looked away, and slowly let it out. Control. I reminded myself to keep everything under control. I'd gotten plenty of lectures on that from my father.

'Claudia.'

I glanced back toward the door to the locker room again. Whoever called me—whatever called me—was there, a part of the shadows, climbing the walls like a spider and reaching out from inside the locker room. The lights flickered in the gym as we waited for the teacher to give us directions. She took a quick look up and motioned the girls out onto the basketball court one row at a time. I just wanted her to hurry. I took another breath, and the shadowy thing disappeared beneath the locker room door again.

My row was called, and I stepped up with the rest of the girls to follow the teacher outside to the track field. Our stretching routine consisted of stretching high and low, bending over to touch our toes. My hair kept falling in my face; I should have tied it back. The ridiculous shorts made me feel way too exposed, and I had to pull them down more than once. To say the least, this was not my favorite period.

Then an electrifying charge consumed me. I didn't have to look for more than a few seconds before I found John standing next to the water cooler, staring at me. Three other guys were with him, but I didn't care about them. He smiled at me, and I turned away.

His voice weaseled its way into my head again. *'Claudia.'* Why wouldn't he just leave me alone?

I bit my lip and shoved him away, and his laughter rang in my head, mocking me. What did I have to do to get him to stop?

'Talk to me. Please.'

I don't talk to people who lie to me. I pushed back again, but he seemed to think this was some kind of a game.

'I didn't lie to you. I should have mentioned everything, though. It just wasn't my plan to... I like you, Claudia. A lot. Please talk to me. I'm not going away...'

And I'm not buying any of it, I told him. He was either toying with me on purpose or thought I was a complete idiot. Rachel approached him and handed him a note. Then the teacher called the first group of girls back inside with her to grab and set up the volleyball net. The rest of us had to run. I stepped onto the track with five other girls and started jogging.

'Come on, Claudia...'

I ignored him and kept moving.

Claudia!

The boy's coach called for the guys' class to return inside, and I was instantly relieved. John didn't call me again as I ran, so I assumed he'd finally gotten the hint that I wanted nothing to do with him. Still, I couldn't help a little smile at the thought that a guy as good-looking as he still wanted to be around me.

A few of the other girls ran past me, and I slowed down a little. The next thing I knew, John was running around the track right next to me. I picked up the pace again, and he stayed right by my side.

"You know you can't outrun me, Miss Belle." He grinned.

I frowned at him before glancing back at the track again. "How do you not realize I don't want to talk to you?"

"Look, I don't know what my uncle said—"

I shot him a scathing look, hoping he really wasn't still trying to sell me that lie too.

"Joseph," he said, correcting himself. "But it's not how I feel, and it's not who I am. I like you…" His rush of emotions hit me hard, and I knew he was telling me the truth.

I stopped and turned to face him. I couldn't believe that after everything, I still felt something for him—connected, like John and I had been cut from the same cloth somehow. "Joseph made it very clear what you are."

"Do you believe that? Look at me and tell me you believe it. You know me, Claudia. You can see that in me. I can't hide any of it from you." I glanced at his watch as he dialed it back. Now he was completely open to me, just like that first time—fully exposed without a piece of machinery to keep him hidden.

"Now you can see it. Whatever Joseph told you, you *have* to know that none of it's real."

Complete honesty—that's what I felt. So why was I still so afraid?

"You know there's something between us. Something we can't deny…" A charge shuddered up my body, the same force radiating from him in waves. I was afraid to admit this between us, because something else was there. Something we hadn't seen, and I still couldn't see it. But I had no idea what would happen if something came to take it all away.

"Why are you scared?"

"I don't know if we should do anything, you and me."

He cupped my cheek, and the instant he touched me, his eyes pulsed a dull light with the energy running through us. It was a blissful charge, making us giddy and alive. The only thing I could think about was that when this was over, I'd wake up and realize it wasn't real at all. Or I'd wake up and find that John was something I actually did need to fear and to stay away from at all costs.

"Why do you want me when you can have someone like Rachel?" I muttered.

His pupils danced, that gold color returning and spreading into the bright green of his unnatural eyes. "I don't want her."

"What about Joseph? I don't want to come between you two or get you in trouble." His grin made me blush, my blood pulsing fiercely through my veins.

"Joseph does what I tell him."

"What?"

"I'm *his* boss."

That was definitely not what I had expected.

"He stepped completely out of line in saying anything to you." John caressed my face, both of us riding the current of this energy, and he let out a huge breath. "Claudia, give me a chance to prove how much I care about you. To prove that you can trust me." The PE teacher blew her whistle and called my group to come inside for the volleyball game. John slipped his hand around mine and held on. "Think about it. Please."

"I have to go," I said. Our fingers slowly slipped apart, and I left him to run back to my class.

After PE and dealing with the stares from Rachel and her minions, I headed to lunch, hoping to avoid anyone else for the entire day. I did want to see Alex, though, to explain what was going on. John's plea to give him a chance had left me feeling more alive than I could remember, which was odd. I couldn't keep denying whatever it was between us that wouldn't let us be.

I tried to imagine John—the boss—telling a big guy like Joseph what to do. It just didn't fit. Joseph had been especially menacing in his office. I wondered what he would say if he saw me with John again after that little meeting. At the very least, he had no idea what I could do. If he did, though, what would he do next? Would he take me to the people in the lab coats? Or would he have to follow John's orders?

Without John's touch distracting me now, I could go through all the things I'd seen in his mind when he'd dialed back his watch on the track field. John had been keeping Joseph away from me. I saw a portion of their conversation in his memory—of John defending me against Joseph's insults. He'd even slapped the man in the face. Then why was I so afraid of what would happen if John and I let ourselves grow even closer to each other? I didn't want to be afraid anymore, and I didn't want to deny myself what I wanted. The only problem was that I just didn't know exactly *what* I wanted.

I stepped into the cafeteria and looked around. The group of my so-called friends were sitting at their regular table, but Alex wasn't there. I stepped back out into the hall before any of the others saw me. The library was as good a place as any to eat my lunch. And I could be alone.

When I turned around in the hall, there was Joseph, heading right toward me. Shit. I ducked into the stairwell on the other side of the cafeteria and ran up to the second floor. It was quiet and empty up here, and it gave me an eerie feeling that the silence hid something else. A green light on the smoke detector above me blinked quickly over and over. The school really needed to get on changing those batteries.

When I reached the middle of the hallway, I planted myself on the ledge overlooking the library and thought about what I would do. Would I take John's offer? I hadn't thought so, but that choice didn't make sense when I couldn't help but smile whenever I thought about him.

'Claudia...'

I jumped and froze on that ledge. Below me, the library was completely empty, but the lights rising from it made the darkness up on the second floor less frightening.

'Claudia...'

"Who are you?" I whispered.

'Do you know what you are? Do you know what you can do? Why you're so important to me?'

"What do you want?"

There was a long pause, then I saw it. Within the darkness on the other end of the hallway lurked two bright, sparkling eyes, lighting up like stars or radiant diamonds lost in an ocean of endless black.

A part of the darkness stretched toward me, running along the walls in both directions and up across the ceiling. When it reached the blinking smoke detector, I realized the thing had now detached from its base and dangled there, alternately blinking in a red and green. That didn't feel right, either.

The dark arms reached toward me along the walls, the ceiling, the floor. *'He can't protect you. He can't protect what's not his. He can't protect what is mine to have. Come with me. Help me. Join me...'*

I screamed.

"Claudia, wake up!"

I gasped and bolted upright. John was looking down at me, his hands on my cheeks. I wrestled away from him and looked around, very likely looking and acting like I was completely deranged.

"Are you okay? Look at me, Claudia." He grabbed my shoulders, trying to snap me out of it. "Hey. Look at me."

Finally, I looked up into his beautiful, emerald-green eyes.

"Are you okay? What happened?" I didn't know what to say. He cupped my face again, and I finally stopped trembling.

"I saw something," I said. "Something dark and evil right here in the hall. It was coming for me."

"You're safe. It's okay. Tell me what you saw." John stroked my cheek.

"You've seen it before," I said. "That vision we shared in the hallway?" I wrapped my arms around him, wishing I could just forget all of it. The bell for second lunch period rang.

John held me tightly beside the ledge overlooking the library. Then he pulled me by the hand down the hallway to an empty classroom. He kicked open the door, then led me to a table and lifted me up onto it. "Wait here." He closed the door again, pulled the thick curtain down over the window, and walked across the room.

A few classrooms in Milton High had been empty for a while just because they needed repairs and hadn't gotten them yet. This room didn't have working lights. In the far corner of the room, John turned on one of the lamps, illuminating his face. Behind him was a door into an attached office, which made me think this used to be a science lab. I glanced to the other far end of the room and found sinks in the back tables.

"You okay?" John asked. I nodded. He stepped across the classroom and took my face in his hands again. "I'm not gonna let anything happen to you, Claudia."

"You believe me?" I asked, surprised that he hadn't questioned whether I'd just had a bad dream.

"Of course I believe you." He tucked a lock of hair behind my ear and grabbed my hand, placing it on his chest. "We're connected, you and I. You know that. Not only here." John pointed to his head, then his heart. "But in here, too."

I wrapped my arms around him. "Thank you. I'm so glad I found you," I whispered. He was the only one that could see the things I could see, and he was right. We *were* connected far more than mind and body. I dropped into his arms, feeling weak, my eyes struggled to remain open, but it felt like all the energy had been instantly drained from me. John's presence didn't make it any easier. Our energies connected, the current flowing between us, neither of us wanting to let go of the circuit. Things went dark fairly quickly, and I heard my name one last time.

'Claudia!'
'Alex? I have to talk to you. Where are you?'

I stood in the desert, hot air blowing dirt all around. I saw distinct forms around me—cacti, shrubs, rolling dunes. There was a town ahead, and as I drew closer, the sun set, turning day into night. I saw a figure in the distance, digging into the ground, a cloth pinned up around his nose and mouth beneath a cowboy hat. I approached him, wondering where I was. Behind the town rose a glow of dozens of streetlamps, the homes lining them all colorful blocks of various sizes.

Hello? The wind tossed my hair all over my face.

The stranger finally found what he was looking for and pulled out a large metal box. He fiddled with it, trying to get it open.

Hello? Excuse me...

The wind suddenly stopped, and the man looked up from what he was doing, finally realizing I was there. I caught sight of his clear blue eyes behind the folded fabric and beneath the tailored hat. They widened at the sight of me. The cloth dropped from around his face, and he lifted a gun at his hip to point it right at me.

Those blue eyes and the dark locks of hair falling beneath the hat, those lips parting as his jaw dropped...

A swirl of gold light danced from the center of his eyes. He dropped the gun, removed the kerchief from around his neck, and pulled off the hat. He looked just a little older than John, but maybe that came from the dirt and dust settled in layers on his tan skin.

'How did you...' He motioned for me to come closer, then glanced back at the town behind him. The gun went back into the holster at his hip. *'Who are you?'*

. . .

When I opened my eyes, John was looking at me, still stroking my cheek. We were on the floor, John's back against the wall and my head in his lap.

"Jack?" The name of the man in the cowboy hat just popped into my mind. What had I seen that time? The future—or maybe the present? I didn't know. My visions could be anything, but more often than not, they were a puzzle I had to solve.

"What did you say?" John asked.

"I saw a man digging in the desert. I was dreaming, I guess. That... couldn't have been real." He looked puzzled, but I still didn't quite understand why. "What happened?"

"You passed out."

Why would I do that again? Then I realized how overwhelmingly drained I still felt, though now I could actually keep my eyes open. What was happening to me? I immediately sat up, leaned away, and stared at him. "I'm sorry." My cheeks burned.

"I'm not," he said. "Who's Alex?"

I frowned. Did he mean Alex Burton?

"You were talking in your sleep. 'Alex, where are you? I need to talk to you.'" He smiled. "So, who is he? Should I be worried?"

"No," I whispered. "She's a friend."

"Ah. *She.*" He smiled and playfully wiped his brow in relief.

"I guess I was just thinking about her," I said. "I haven't talked to her lately."

"No need to explain," he said.

I nodded. "What time is it?"

He glanced at that magical watch of his. "Late."

"How late?"

"Bell rang two minutes ago."

"Why didn't you wake me up?" I stood, and he followed right behind me.

"You looked so peaceful just lying in my arms. And beautiful."

I blushed and moved to the door. Then I stopped, turned, and ran back to him before he embraced me again. He smiled as I rested my hands on his chest. "Sorry," I whispered.

He smirked. "No worries."

"Please don't tell Michael what happened. He'll freak. And I don't want to scare him any more with all this." I released John and stepped back.

"I'm not saying anything to anyone, Miss Belle."

"Thanks." When I opened the door, I paused again to look back at him. "Thank you. For keeping me safe."

"It was my pleasure."

For a minute, I knew I really didn't want to leave him. Finally, John joined me, took my hand, and led me out into the hall. It was crowded with students, all of them ready to escape from teachers and assignments and schedules.

He walked me to my locker, where I grabbed a few things, shoved them into my bookbag, and closed the door again. "I need to meet Michael in his office before he starts looking for me," I told him.

"I'll walk you there too, if you like."

"Really?" I whispered, clutching at my bookbag.

"Of course."

Michael's office as Assistant Principal was more personal and private up here on the second floor, just around the corner from the empty classroom. Mr. Claypool and Mr. Vasquez still shared theirs as the other two assistant principals, but Michael's office was now quite large. A few steps led up to the open office door.

I glanced inside and saw few students talking to him. Michael glanced up and saw me by the door, then held up a finger to tell me it would be just a few minutes longer. The students glanced at me as well, and I nodded before ducking back into the hall.

John still waited very quietly beside me. "Thank you for walking me," I said, unsure what else to say. I owed him a lot more than a simple thank you.

The warmth of his emotions soared, washing over me, though his thoughts were a little hazy. I guess it was better that way, and I really didn't want to pry into his mind. It was pretty rude, no matter whose thoughts I was reading.

"It was my pleasure," he said again and glanced back down at his watch. "Shit."

"Everything okay?"

"I hate to do this to you, but I have to go."

"Joseph?"

"Yeah." He stepped away from me down the hall, stopped, and turned immediately back around. That gorgeous smile resurfaced. "By the way." He stepped toward me again. "I wanted to ask you something." I swallowed my nerves, and he laughed. "I promise it's nothing... bad. I just wanted to ask if you..." He hesitated, smiling and frowning at me at the same time. "Sorry. This has never happened to me before."

I frowned, wondering why this was so hard for him, but he closed his thoughts to me again. However, I could feel his emotions radiating from him, loud and clear.

"There's a party this weekend," he said quickly. "Thought you might want to come with me."

If it was the same party Alex and I planned to go to, she was supposed to pick me up. I hadn't even talked to her about it since Michael had tried to ground me. I hadn't talked to her about any of this.

"I can pick you up," he offered.

The color returned to my face. Great. John was asking to take me to a party I couldn't even go to anymore, and of course I didn't want to tell him I couldn't go. I didn't want him to think I was saying it as an excuse because I actually *did* want to. I definitely did.

"Are you asking me out?"

He grinned. "Yeah, I guess I am. So? I promise to be on my best behavior..." I laughed a little, and he added, "Give me your phone." When I finally pulled it out of my bookbag and handed it over, he glanced at the picture on my home screen and just said, "Cute." Then he sent himself a text and returned my phone. "Now we're connected digitally, too." He winked.

"Is there a code or something I have to use when I call you?"

He chuckled. "No code, Miss Belle. Just call me."

"Is Joseph going to have an issue with this?"

"He's my guardian, not my father. He can't keep me from seeing you if that's what I want." I lowered my gaze, staring at his number on the screen. He glanced at his watch again. "I better go before he sends out a search party..." When I glanced up at him with wide eyes, he touched my shoulder and leaned forward. "I'm kidding. Maybe I'll call *you*." Then he walked down the hall, looking back a few times before he dashed down the stairwell.

After Michael was finished with the students and locked up his office, we walked down the stairs together. I didn't know what I was going to say to John, and I really didn't want to miss going with him to the party. Alex, being the way she was, would probably still try to come pick me up even if I'd told her I couldn't go. She was probably skipping class again today, too.

We turned the corner on the main floor, and I saw John down the hall. He smiled, and beside him, Joseph flashed me that eerie grin. I frowned and looked away. Did he seriously expect me to greet him with a pleasant smile after his little lecture in his office?

John's voice slithered into my head. *'Whatever you're doing, stop. Control your feelings.'*

I turned to my breathing practice, trying to regain control. Joseph was staring at me, making it worse when I thought about the possibility that he might know something.

'There she goes again with that heavy breathing.' The man's thoughts were so easy to pick up. *'I probably scare her.'*

"Hello, Michael," Joseph said as we approached. Then he turned to me.

Control, I thought, feeling John lend me his energy to help me. It made me think of what my grandfather had said about helping each other. Could John do the same for me? Help me control my gift in some way?

"Miss Belle..."

I said nothing. Michael didn't seem pleased by my silence, but I didn't care.

"How are those evaluations coming along?"

"Well, just about got them down," Michael replied.

"That's what I like to hear."

"Hi, Claudia," John said, trying to distract me from my anger toward Joseph. It was dangerous to provoke that anger—I already knew that—and he was determined to keep me from doing anything about it.

"Hi, John," I whispered.

A wave of displeasure radiated from Joseph when he saw John giving me so much attention. Why did it bother him so much?

"On your way?" Michael asked.

John turned away.

"Trying to get there," Joseph replied, still smiling at me.

I turned toward John instead. A tiny streak of energy shot out of me and reconnected with him. He smiled at me, the gold in his eyes still dancing but not nearly as brightly.

I reminded myself to maintain control; Joseph had a watch too.

"Plans this evening?" Michael asked.

I caught a vision in Joseph's mind of a woman's face, but more distortions from the watch shut me out again.

"As a matter of fact, I do." The man sounded way too proud.

I moved away, gazing back at John as he pulled away from them as well. He was busy watching me as I moved to the library window, just to remove myself from Joseph and to calm my nerves. Honestly, I wanted to be as far away from John right now as I could get so I didn't lose myself in front of both our guardians. He smiled at me, becoming a bigger part of me, the pull growing stronger. The tenderness, the devoted attraction, was still quickly growing between us.

Michael and Joseph finished their superficial conversation, and Michael waved me toward him. I lifted a hand to wave at John, then followed my guardian toward the school's front doors.

"Have a good night, Miss Belle," Joseph called behind me.

I spun away and hurried down the hall. Michael could barely keep up with me. When I stepped outside, all I wanted to do was scream. Then I felt Michael behind me; he wasn't happy with the way I'd acted, but he didn't know half of what I did. And I couldn't tell him any of it.

"You don't have to be rude because you're mad about not going to the party."

"I'm not—" I stopped myself and sighed. There was no point in arguing with Michael. We got into his car and drove in silence all the way home.

27

MEMORIES

ALEX SAT IN HER RUSTED CAR. THE PARKING LOT WAS QUIET. SHE waited patiently as the last bell rang; even now, the last of the buses were lining up one behind the other to shuttle students to their homes. Soon, it would be time for her to wander into hers as well.

She was afraid after everything that had happened and wondered why she had never noticed it before. It was always that way. Dr. Edwards had always given her a vibe, but she had never suspected anything else. Only after his death did it all make sense. She just hadn't made the connection before now; even visiting the grave was a hard thing to do.

The rusted gates of the old cemetery had greeted her the very same day the old woman had told her of Quinn's return. She'd decided it was time to see his gravesite, but she didn't know why it had taken her so long to do this. Alex had kept her distance, even after discovering who he really was.

It was for the best. Of course, she'd intended to one day reveal herself, but then death had come. And Quinn returned.

She swallowed now in the school parking lot, watching her peers climbing into the yellow buses and waiting patiently for

Claudia to come outside. Alex was about to get out of her car and wave until Michael descended the stairs behind Claudia. Alex immediately ducked down in her car. There was no way of reaching Claudia now, and Alex really needed to talk to her.

The crystal's light had warned her it was a bad idea, but Alex's conscience convinced her she needed to share it all with her new friend. If she didn't warn Claudia soon, it would be too late. She didn't want the same thing to happen to Claudia; the whole thing sounded crazy, even to her, and she had lived it.

Michael and Claudia climbed into his Honda SUV and drove out of the parking lot. When the coast was clear, Alex sat up and wondered what to do next. She could easily find Claudia later at night, or maybe she'd wait to drag her out of the house for the party. They had to talk.

She turned the key in the ignition, but the engine didn't turn over until she placed her palm gently on the dash. The engine roared to life, and she pushed down on the gas pedal, smiling at the memory of Claudia's confession.

Claudia was indeed naïve and such easy prey; she had no idea what was stalking her. It was time to tell her the truth about her grandfather, and that had to happen soon. First, Alex had to make one more stop. She'd go to see him again, maybe for the last time, and do what she should have done a long time ago. She sped out of the parking lot, startling a couple on the sidewalk.

When she arrived and turned off the car, she felt like fleeing; she hated cemeteries, always had. That was all thanks to the shadow man. He was called many things, even Death, at one point. The well-dressed blond man in the black suit; Quinn had frightened her with all his stories, and normally, she couldn't bear to step a foot into a cemetery. But today, she had to. There was no turning back.

She stepped out of her car, carrying a rose. Her hands trembled. Alex stepped through the open gates and saw the funeral service on the other side of the cemetery. So many black cars and people dressed in black. She'd fit right in. Most people just assumed she'd be into spending her time at a place like this. She wasn't.

This was where the shadow man lurked. He was always looking for them, the beings and their counterparts—those like her. And Alex still didn't know what he wanted.

She hurried on and found the grave easily enough. Standing in front of it, she was already crying as she knelt in front of the tombstone. She pulled out the black pouch she had taken from her locker, wiped her eyes, and set the rose in a vase sitting near the stone.

"I met her," she began. "She's so beautiful and so much stronger than I expected." Alex opened the pouch and pulled out a long, cylindrical crystal. "She's in danger. But I think you probably already knew that."

Alex held the crystal; it had stopped glowing. "Why didn't you give her this? I'm sure you meant to. Don't worry. I'm not going to let anything happen to her. She won't suffer like we have." She took a breath. "I'm going to stop him." Running her fingers over the words on the stone, Alex sighed, then put the crystal back into the pouch.

"I miss you so much... I never stopped hoping that one day, we'd find each other again. I should have come sooner. Forgive me..." A sob escaped her, the mascara smearing beneath her dark eyes. All her white makeup felt so hard on her face.

"Okay. I have to go now." She leaned forward and placed a kiss on the hard stone, one more time running her fingers over the words engraved there.

Neil Edwards
Beloved Grandfather and Devoted Educator
"I'm sorry I wasn't there, my son."

She turned away and rushed through the cemetery toward

the gates. Something caught her eye a few yards beside her, and she spun around.

From behind a tree among the headstones, bony fingers curved around the bark, followed by a darkened head peering out in greeting.

"Maya, come here!" the blond man hissed. He couldn't touch her; certain laws bound him against it. But he loved to toy with her.

Alex hurried away as his laughter filled the cemetery. She stumbled out into the parking lot as the funeralgoers lowered their deceased loved one into the ground. She climbed into the car and closed the door. The bracelet on her wrist was still a pale white, and she sighed in relief.

The car started at the first turn of the key, and she sped away. Night was falling now, and it was dark by the time she reached the old woman's house. She would have to leave soon, always running. Quinn was never far behind. She knew she was running out of time.

When she got home, she made sandwiches, served the old woman her tea, and joined her in watching *The Bachelor*. It was the old woman's favorite show. Alex's host talked on and on about the different women on the show, once mentioning that Alex herself should apply to be on the next season.

By 9:00 p.m, the old woman was falling asleep on the couch. It was time to take her to bed.

Alex helped her up the stairs and into the first bedroom. After tucking her into the large bed, she closed the door behind her and moved across the hallway. The floor creaked under her steps, and she stopped to hear the wind outside. The house almost sounded like a living thing.

She'd picked her bedroom in this house because it was the only one not painted in a nauseating pastel color or cluttered with things. But anything was better than sleeping in an abandon building.

A shadow moved across the floor, and she froze just in front of the stairs. She wanted to run, but she couldn't leave the old woman alone. Instead, she stood at her bedroom doorway; the moonlight spilling through the open window cut a little of the darkness. She pushed the door farther open with a creak.

"Maya, Maya, Maya. What am I going to do with you?"

Alex moved her hand over the light switch, but it didn't work. She reached for the lamp next, and when the light came on, she found him sitting on the window ledge, looking back at her. There was an eerie grimace on his pale, youthful face.

"Quinn!"

"The one and only. Who else would travel the regions of the universe to come find you, my love? I missed you. Your touch and your smell. You intoxicate me. Why do you do this? Why do you run from me?"

His hair was dark as the night, his skin the color of milk. He was beautiful, especially his purple eyes. A scaly leather uniform covered his frame—the same military attire he had worn when they'd fled the frozen wastelands of Antarctica.

"Would you rather live in squalor here than return with me as my queen?" He leaped off the ledge but didn't approach. The crystal on her wrist made sure of that. "You think any amount of makeup will hide your beautiful face from me? We are bound together."

"Stop it," Alex shouted.

"I will never stop, my love. I've tasted you, and I want nothing else but you. You're mine..."

"No, you took me. Just like you've taken everything else *from* me."

"I long for you, Maya. I miss you. I need you, and I can't be without you any longer. Please don't make me... I can't bear it anymore. I want to be with you. I love you."

"Stop!"

"Don't make me do something horrible. You know I will."

She frowned at him.

He moved forward, the hunger running through in his veins, the energy pulsing through both of them. She turned away.

"I need you, Maya. Please. You're all I think of every moment of my existence. You're in my blood now, coursing through my veins, coursing through my soul. You're a part of me. Nothing can change that."

"You don't have a soul," she whispered.

He laughed. "That's the fire I desire, my Maya!" He stepped closer.

"Stop!" She lifted the crystal on her wrist, and he darted back. "Don't come any closer. I am *not* yours."

"It's time to stop this foolish game. I've allowed it, even tolerated it, but enough is enough. Your place is with me. What is it you seek? What is it that pulls you away from me?"

She shook her head, trying to fight his stare.

A slow smile spread across his lips, and he laughed. "You don't think I know why you've come all this way?"

She couldn't hide the truth from him, no matter what she did. "Don't you dare hurt her." Alex rushed at him, holding the crystal in front of her like a shield.

Quinn leaped through the window, laughter fading behind him. When Alex reached the window, she leaned forward out of it to find him, but he was gone.

Dear reader,

We hope you enjoyed reading *The Source*. Please take a moment to leave a review, even if it's a short one. Your opinion is important to us.

Discover more books by C.S. Luis at https://www.nextchapter.pub/authors/cs-luis

Want to know when one of our books is free or discounted for? Join the newsletter at http://eepurl.com/bqqB3H.

Best regards,
C.S. Luis and the Next Chapter Team

You might also like:

Heir of Ashes by Jina S. Bazzar

To read the first chapter for free, please head to:

https://www.nextchapter.pub/books/heir-of-ashes

The Source
ISBN: 978-4-86750-911-1

Published by
Next Chapter
1-60-20 Minami-Otsuka
170-0005 Toshima-Ku, Tokyo
+818035793528

24th June 2021

CPSIA information can be obtained
at www.ICGtesting.com
Printed in the USA
LVHW112321120721
692545LV00001B/44

9 784867 509111